CHIEF

THE KINGS OF GUARDIAN BOOK SEVEN

KRIS MICHAELS

WWW.KRISMICHAELSAUTHOR.COM

CHAPTER 1

*O*ne *year ago—an undisclosed, secure facility near Washington D.C.*

"You don't have to do this, Mike." Gabriel, his boss and mentor, leaned forward grasping his drink in his hand. The man was ageless, but Mike White Cloud could tell the constant worry about when the Bratva would strike next was wearing on him. Gabriel took care of his people, and since the Russians had targeted his immediate family and several members of the King family, Gabriel was on guard. The man had practically adopted the Kings into his family. The Bratva made a huge tactical error by targeting the key players at Guardian. The Kings were the lifeblood of the organization, and more than friends to both of them.

"I understand the dangers, but someone has to infiltrate at the highest level, and the cover is a good one. It has to work." He pulled down the French cuff of his handmade shirt and ran his hand nervously over his freshly cut hair. He'd spent five months prepping for this assignment. There was no way he would stop now.

"The lack of time to prepare you for such a deep cover has me the most concerned."

Mike nodded. It was a valid point. He'd made great strides, but there was no way he'd be able to impersonate David Xavier without making mistakes. Only a handful of people knew that the billionaire, David Xavier, and Gabriel were, in fact, the same person. He leveled his stare at Gabriel. "I'll do my best."

"I know you will, but I've pulled in a favor. When my father died, I inherited his assistant, who is a Harvard-trained lawyer and, in my opinion, a certified genius. He retired about three years ago when I started diversifying and giving more control to the CEOs of the companies that I oversee. He is one of the very few who know me. He has agreed to come back and stay with you until you no longer need him. Joel can't be bought, and his loyalty is without question." Gabriel took a sip of cognac.

"I won't say no to some assistance." He knew the obstacles he faced. Hell, they were the size of mountains, and he had very little climbing gear in his undercover pack.

"I will oversee my holdings and the CEOs I have in place manage the majority of the day to day business activities. I will give you enough so people see you working the events, but not so much to over-whelm you. Hell, I've been doing this my entire life and it still swamps me. But remember, you are here to set the trap. You are not to engage the bastards. Period. You are the bait, not the trap. You will not engage."

"I understand. I'm portraying a businessman, and that is the way I'll act. But, thank you for bringing someone in to help, I appreciate it." Gabriel's comments instilled relief. When they'd developed the idea of his assuming David Xavier's persona, the business end had always been a concern.

"Don't thank me. You will still be swamped, but we want that appearance. Nothing sells a cover more than being immersed in the world. Believe me; you are going to be baptized by fire. But, all we can do is prepare you for the worst case scenario." Gabriel sighed and swirled the liquid in his glass.

"And you have. I leave tomorrow and become you…or rather David Xavier. I won't let you down, sir."

"Mike, you could walk away this second and you wouldn't let me down. Walking out that door tomorrow morning sets a host of events into action. You will be on your own except for Joel. I can't reach out to help you without compromising your cover. You will be David Xavier."

He nodded and found an interesting spot on the floor as he thought. He knew the score, and he was willing to take the risk if it meant his friends, hell—

the Kings were his family—he'd risk it all if they'd be safe from the Russian threat. He shook his head and expanded his focus to the thousands of young lives that he'd be able to help. No, he didn't have a choice, not really. He was going to do what it took to get to the top of the Bratva while Guardian worked to take out the bottom. With a two-pronged attack from Guardian and the help of the foreign agencies working in concert with them, there was a chance they could decimate the Russian Mafia's human trafficking organization. His undercover operation wouldn't be shared with the other agencies. They couldn't take the risk of a leak, but if it worked... He leaned back and gazed out the window. His words were almost a whisper, but they needed to be said, "The worst case scenario is I die. I'm expendable."

"Bullshit!" Mikes's head whipped around at the shouted response. "You are part of my family, and I'll be damned if you are going into this plan without an exit strategy. We are asking you to become someone you are not, to buy human beings for Christ's sake! You'll be dealing with the scum of the earth who will kill you rather than look at you if they think for a moment you are not who you say you are." Gabriel stood up and strode over to the window that overlooked the New York City skyline. "You are not expendable, Mike. Not to me. Not ever."

He swallowed hard. Outside of his team, he'd never been told he was important. Gabriel's words pointed to a place in him that he'd thought was long dead. "I am willing to do what it takes to make sure we get to the top of the organization. Are you sure the introductions I need will be available?"

"After the groundwork is laid, yes. The old money at that club is well connected. However, if my source is correct, you are looking for one man in particular."

Present day—Bern, Switzerland

Mike glanced out the tinted window of the brand new Rolls-Royce Wraith he now 'owned.' His phone beeped, and his glance flicked over the emails highlighted as urgent. The Rolls-Royce slowed, and he glanced at the completely unremarkable limestone building his car approached. The car slowed drastically and entered the underground parking area that allowed the occupants of the facility to come and go without notice. An immaculately uniformed doorman ran out of the plain entrance, the only indication the building was anything other than another in a series of office buildings. The man stopped immediately when his bodyguard pushed open the passenger door and blocked the man's attempt to do his job. A second guard dismounted from the front of the sedan. The protective detail, while excellent, had no connection to Guardian. There could be no tie between Mike White Cloud and David Xavier. He waited until his men motioned for him to exit and then strode into the building "he" owned and handed his gloves, coat, and scarf to the butler waiting for him inside the door. He'd seen numerous pictures of the interior and had the blueprints memorized.

He paused, gathered his thoughts, and focused on the assignment he had undertaken. He nodded to his security detail and entered the main room of the most prestigious, private club in Europe. The wait list to join this establishment was longer than his arm, which was impressive considering the membership dues to join tallied no less than seven figures. He glanced at the $4,000,000 Louis XV Savonnerie carpet flanked by the original Henredon furniture. Designed exclusively for David Xavier, the furniture for the entire building cost over $25,000,000. He turned right, striding through the main lounge. Several people did a double-take, and two older gentlemen lifted fingers, summoning their assigned servant. How long would it be before he was identified and approached? He glanced at his Cartier watch. Fifteen minutes? He headed straight for his reserved seating area. He had no more lowered himself into the chair than a snifter of cognac appeared.

"1858 Cuvee Léonie?" He carefully modulated his words in the speech pattern and inflection he'd adopted over the last year. His listeners heard upper-class, eastern seaboard United States with a slightly British warp to the vowels.

"But of course, sir. Your private reserve." The man who served him wore the dark maroon vest of the club's premier staff. The owner rated only the best.

He took the proffered drink and cradled it in his hand as he swirled the caramel-colored liquor to warm it gently. His security detail took up position, standing discreetly behind him. His gaze took in the men and women in attendance at the club today. He'd arrived with less than three minutes notice, so the members present weren't staged unless they'd been camping out for the last five months in hopes of meeting him. There was a total of fourteen members in the lounge. Wait staff floated around the periphery filling glasses and replenishing small delicacies that were casually assessed and consumed by the ultra-rich in attendance. He wondered how many were upstairs in the sound-proofed, secluded quarters constructed to ensure total privacy?

Mike raised the crystal balloon snifter to his nose, closed his eyes and enjoyed the fragrant bouquet of the cognac. Over the course of the last year, he'd learned to appreciate the nuances of David's life. This spectacular cognac, in particular, had become his favorite. If he made it out of this assignment alive, he was going to hit up Gabriel for a bottle. A bonus for surviving. His lips lifted in appreciation of the graveside humor. He had every intention of surviving. If he was very careful, he could make a bottle last for years. Hell, with a price tag of over $150,000 a bottle, he would be very, very careful.

He lifted the lip of the glass and drew in a small amount, allowing enough air in his mouth to properly "feel" the decadence against his tongue. *Perfection.*

He felt rather than saw his bodyguards tense and glanced to his right. Hans Schneider, one of the original members of the club, approached. Mike stood, extended his hand, and in impeccable German, greeted the man. "Mr. Schneider. A pleasure to meet you in person. I appreciate your membership."

The man's red cheeks turned even ruddier while he blinked back his surprise. "Mr. Xavier?"

"David. Please, sit." He kept his expression blank, a talent he'd perfected long before this assignment.

"Thank you...David, this is a unique and, may I say, startling surprise."

"Really? How so?"

"Well, to be honest, I thought you'd be..." The man accepted a glass of the reserve cognac as he spoke.

"I assure you, Mr. Schneider..."

"Hans, please."

He dipped his head in acknowledgment. "Hans. I assure you that my parents, despite all their idiosyncrasies, had a valid reason for concealing my identity. I am, after all, *not* my mother's son."

He took a small sip of his cognac and watched as Schneider put two and two together. Anyone who had met David Xavier's father and mother would know he wasn't their biological child. His Native American characteristics could be attributed to a myriad of cultures but not to the Anglo-Saxon couple captured in numerous photographs. The Xaviers' actual son had never been photographed or seen. Raised under another name and never publicly acknowledged, David Xavier was a ghost. Dealing with his ethnicity was simple. He outed himself as a bastard as they had planned.

"I've noticed you take after your father, not your mother."

What a load of horseshit. He lifted an eyebrow and nodded before he took another sip from his crystal snifter.

"Is there a reason we are enjoying your presence in Switzerland?"

Mike glanced down at his glass and swirled the remaining liquid. Hans Schneider was a bastard with a capital B. He'd followed in his father's footsteps and sold weapons to the highest bidder. He would lay odds he'd been shot at with weapons the fucker had sold illegally.

Schneider's paltry billion, however, was comprised of new money, and that was an advantage Mike leveraged. Old money, like David's, had connections that new money would never be able to understand or utilize. He glanced at the others in the room. He could identify their weaknesses immediately. He'd memorized minutiae about many people connected to the Russian syndicate or Bratva—the Russian word for brotherhood.

"Business. I'm in search of a...discreet vendor ... for a very specific item." He leaned back in his chair.

The cushion wrapped him in comfort as he continued to scan the people gathered. Three more had entered since he had. They were either upstairs or had been summoned when he'd arrived. Three of the richest members were currently working their way through the lounge area. Schneider was a poor, unkempt urchin compared to the wealth that now circled the waters. Sharks smelling fresh blood, no doubt.

Schneider followed his gaze. The man's eyes narrowed almost imperceptibly. He leaned forward, and Mike returned his attention to the conversation and sighed as if bored by the entire exchange.

"I happen to be well connected to several such vendors who provide specialty items and guarantee anonymity to their clients. What type of product are you trying to obtain?" Schneider eyed the current Crown Prince of Historia as the man's robes flowed around him when he stopped abruptly to speak to several other members.

He stared at Schneider. It took all of fifteen seconds before the man's gaze fell. Schneider lacked the spine he needed in a go-between. He wouldn't trust the ogre with any information he didn't want to be bartered or sold.

"I'm sure you are well connected; however, I don't believe I need any assistance. I appreciate the offer. If you will excuse me?"

He rose, summarily dismissing the German. He'd

been taught the subtleties about snubbing the ultra-rich and had no problem using them. He strode forward, stopping to introduce himself and speak at length with each member. The early afternoon slipped by coated in thinly disguised curiosity and veiled innuendo. The constant twists and turns of old money versus new, power versus prestige and self-important posturing became a dance, and Mike led his partners across the club lounge like a champion ballroom dancer. Finally, his dance led to Prince Khalid Tawfeek. The man Mike had hoped to find here tonight.

"Prince Tawfeek. A privilege to meet you." He kept his eye contact direct, as not doing so would offend the prince.

"Mr. Xavier, I presume?"

"You would be correct." He motioned for the prince to sit and waited as the staff provided the prince a glass of the royal's favorite vintage.

"What brings you to Switzerland, Mr. Xavier?"

Mike let out a carefree laugh. "That's the question of the evening it would seem."

"You are rarely, if ever, seen in public. I'm intrigued by your sudden appearance." The prince's hand opened in a broad gesture that indicated the surrounding room. "As are the rest of the members of your social club."

"Ah, well, let me disabuse you of any intrigue. I am here for business and only business. More's the pity. I rarely stay in any of my homes for an extended period." He sighed and shrugged. "Unfortunately, the contacts I seek may not be available."

The crown prince leaned forward. "What do you require? I would be personally offended if I could not provide...introductions."

Ahh...the shark circled him, excited by the chum he'd thrown into the water. Unlike Schneider, who would have swallowed what he was selling hook, line, and sinker, he knew he needed to set the hook for the prince. He waved his hand at his protective detail who stepped back to an even greater distance, affording him complete privacy. "I wouldn't dream of offending you, Prince Tawfeek. I'm in search of a certain Russian. This one can obtain specific...toys."

Recognition immediately formed on the prince's face, as easy to read as an open large-print book. Careful to keep his expression impenetrable, Mike lifted a finger toward his butler who stood across the room. The man refilled both his and Prince Twafeek's glasses. The prince considered the bubbles in his champagne for a few moments. "The brother you are looking for does not meet anyone. Representatives, however, can be approached."

He laughed, drawing the eyes of all those in the room. The prince glanced around with a fake smile plastered on his face. "You do amuse me, Prince Tawfeek. Please, by all means, approach a representative for me." Mike lowered his voice and let the burning hatred he felt show in his eyes. "Be warned Your Highness, those who have leaked knowledge of my dealings don't live long enough to regret their actions."

The prince lifted an eyebrow at the threat, and a genuine smile appeared. "It is good to surround oneself with like-minded people. I will reach out to you when a representative is available."

"Inform the brother that I have discerning tastes in femininity. If he wants an extremely lucrative association, it will behoove him to keep that in mind and not to delay. There *are* alternative vendors; although I am told, the product is not of the same quality."

Khalid smiled. "I have made several purchases from this vendor. The product is exquisite, and if the merchandise becomes defective, the brother will assist in repair or replacement."

He cocked his head. That was information he hadn't known. Replacement? The Russian was killing the slaves his clients no longer wanted? Or perhaps recycling them into the herds of drug addled prostitutes he sold across the globe. As if the information was welcomed, He covered his disgust and smiled. It was time to spend some of David's money and schmooze the prince along with the rest of the ultra-rich that had gathered. This was his coming-out party, after all—one he needed to ensure was perfect.

He tipped back his snifter for a small sip before he turned on the charm he'd cultivated over the last year. "Excellent. May I interest you in dinner? I'm told the chef is amazing and has been working with the staff all day for a special welcome celebration."

Jason King handed his brother, Joseph, a tumbler of forty-year-old scotch. His glass held ginger ale, his comfort drink of late.

Joseph swirled the amber liquid gently before he took a sip. He sat the glass down before he looked at Jason and broached the subject of the Russian mission. "Jacob and Jared briefed me on the locations, operations, and timing of the assault against the Bratva."

"And?" Jason knew his brother didn't talk to hear himself speak.

"The way they have the operations set up makes sense, to a point. But, if you'd use Jacob's seek and destroy methodology and temper it with Jared's procedural point of view, I believe the results would be better."

Jason turned in the chair. "You mean put an investigator on each team?"

"Exactly. With this mission, we have to guarantee we have the criminal aspect managed. We can't lose a case because our teams don't follow proper evidence collection or chain of custody procedures. I'd say assign one or two depending on the operation. We have to be able to remove the legs of the beast if our man doesn't succeed. At a minimum, we can snow-

ball the efforts and maybe get a lucky break somewhere. Sooner or later, we *will* find someone who
can identify the people above them. This veil of
secrecy the Bratva is weaving has to have a loose
thread somewhere."

"That is a good point and one that Gabriel and I
have already discussed. In addition to Guardian's law
enforcement specialists, I was considering putting
local police on the teams. I'll have them corralled
until our people have secured the scene, but having
the cooperation of locals can't hurt. They get credit
for helping us. Additionally, we are coordinating
with our counterparts in all the major agencies, both
foreign and domestic. All evidence will be compiled
so all interested parties can pursue legal remedies in
their countries."

Joseph took a drink of his scotch and cracked his
neck, first one side and then the other. Jason waited.

"What happens if we identify the target and the
legal remedy isn't…satisfactory?"

Jason eyed his brother. He'd addressed that exact
possibility with Gabriel. What happened if the heads
of the Bratva were beyond the reach of the law? A
coded and sanctioned hit on the bastards at the top
of the Bratva was on the table, but every current
operation would have to go to hell in a handbasket
before such unilateral measures would be considered. All the planning in the world wouldn't matter if
they couldn't ID the fuckers pulling the strings.
There were over fifty missions planned, half of which

were in foreign countries, in addition to the under-cover mission that Mike was currently working—too many variables to make that call at this point. What did he know for sure? He'd never ask his brother to come out of retirement to make the hits, no matter how personal the mission got.

"Considered. Our options have been weighed." Jason finished his drink and leveled his gaze at his oldest brother. Jason knew Joseph would kill to protect his family. "You will not be activated." The statement held a finality he dared his brother to address.

Joseph's low, evil laugh filled the office. "Who the fuck told you you'd have a choice in the matter?"

CHAPTER 2

Tatyana Petrov finished trimming the fingernails of her latest shipment. She examined the toys closely. They were lightly drugged, but still restrained and tied to the bulkhead of the van they were sitting in. Her cell rang, startling her and the toys. One started to cry silently.

"What the fuck do you want?" She wasn't known for her patience. Her no-nonsense attitude was one of the many things that had endeared her to her superiors in the Bratva.

"Always such a bitch, Anya. One of these days you will respect me." Evgeniy Kuznetsov's disgusting voice penetrated the confines of the van. Even through the drugged haze, the toys started to whimper. Evgeniy was sadistic in ways she'd never imagined a person could be. He didn't violate the toys, but there were worse fates for those who misbehaved. As

17

long as there were no *permanent* marks, or the merchandise wasn't sexually defiled, the bosses didn't seem to care what sadistic games Evgeniy played. She'd overheard the bosses felt his abuses made the toys compliant.

She took the phone off speaker and spoke in a calm tone, trying to settle the mildly drugged cargo. "You scare my deliveries, and they will arrive with tearstained faces. Not a good impression. The boss will be upset, and I won't take the fall for it, asshole." She purred the response in Russian and smiled at the deliveries who were still agitated at the sound of Evgeniy's voice. She'd probably fear the bastard too... if she didn't hate him so much.

"Ha, like you haven't benefited from the training I put the toys through. Makes your job easier. Besides, what does it matter to you?" Evgeniy arrogantly taunted her.

"What the fuck do you want?"

The disgusting bastard laughed, "You have an appointment. Be at the Old Lady for afternoon tea service tomorrow. And for the record, I told them they were making a mistake." The line went dead.

The Old Lady referred to the majestic five-star hotel in the city center. Tatyana's heart raced. Could she finally be getting an introduction to the bosses? A squeal of tires at the entrance to the parking garage drew her attention away from the future and back to her duties.

Tatyana took a deep breath and reclined against

the wall of the van as she glanced at her watch. Fifteen more minutes before the client was left high and dry and the toys were returned to the store. Not one second more. That policy was written in stone, and customers obeyed the rules because the purchase price was non-refundable.

A flash of headlights through the tinted back windows confirmed the arrival of the client. She refused to allow the toys to travel alone in the rear of the van. Tatyana felt the van rock as Thing One and Thing Two clambered out of the front. She'd never cared to learn the names of the Bratva muscle who always accompanied her.

She looked at the three unfortunate souls across from her. They dressed in the exact costumes specified in the order. Tears fell down the male's face, his body carried a sheen of perspiration, and his face was pale. The leather harness, bondage cuffs and G-string he wore were his only clothes. The girls? One was dressed as a baby doll; a see-through silk wrap draped the other. This particular client, an Italian billionaire, had an extensive collection of toys. Carefully she inserted a ball gag and strapped it around the male's head. His eyes teared up.

"Do not cry. All of you. Be strong." The only words she'd spoken in English were also her last to the trio. The door opened, and she exited, leaving the toys secured in the back of the van.

Without her approval, the transaction wouldn't occur. She walked to the limousine and waited. The window rolled down, and a document was shoved in her direction. Tatyana did not reach for the paper that would have the offshore routing number for the payment. She crossed her arms and waited. The rules and instructions were explicit. They would not transfer the toys until the buyer's vehicle was emptied, the occupants were swept for tracking or listening devices, and the car was cleared. No words were ever exchanged. If the rules were violated, Things One and Two and Tatyana would object— with prejudice. They'd killed a buyer's guards before. The ones who felt they could bend the rules. Taty had no patience for the scum. She couldn't kill the Brat-va's clients, but the paid security? They were fair game. The product the Bratva sold was perfect. The cost was astronomical, and the clientele knew the consequences of failing to abide by the rules.

The doors opened. Four, large, armed men exited before the buyer. A slender man, five foot ten or so. His hair was combed back and kept there with a shiny product. The bastard had the audacity to smile at her as if they were old friends.

Tatyana watched the doors open, and the trunk was popped along with the engine compartment. The Things did their job, quietly and effectively inspecting the vehicle and the occupants. They nodded to Tatyana who returned to the van. She removed the restraints tying the male to the van and led him out. His feet faltered. Taty gave him a moment to find his balance. Between the drugs and the bonds that held him in the van, he needed a few seconds to gain his stability. One of the men moved toward them. Taty held up her hand, and Thing One stepped in front of them. Taty leaned into the young one and whispered, "You must survive this."

She wiped the boy's face and guided him to the car where she turned over his lead to the buyer. He accepted it, performed a complete, invasive inspection before he nodded and allowed the boy into the vehicle. The process continued until the girls were inside the car. The paper originally offered was proffered again. Tatyana snatched it and whirled on her heel. The Bratva hired muscle stepped aside as she went to a second vehicle prepositioned for her before the meeting. The hounds of hell couldn't have stopped her from leaving after she called in the routing information. Upon receiving confirmation of payment, she honked once. The Things allowed the Italian to leave, and she hit the gas.

Taty drove uncaring of the speed limit. Her car sliced through traffic. Inside the confines of the car, she drew a deep breath and screamed. Her throat burned as she filled her lungs again and shattered the cabin with another ear-piercing shriek of bitter frustration.

"What do you mean?" Keelee Cassidy lay down her daughter, careful not to wake the sleeping toddler.

She'd been fussy all day, and they both needed a good night's rest. She glanced over her shoulder at Adam, her husband.

He waited until she tiptoed out of the room and closed the door behind her. The baby monitor would let them know if Elizabeth so much as squeaked. "I can't get into the details, but it looks like the Wonder Twins and I could be called in to do some work for Jacob and Jason."

Keelee's stomach dropped. She grabbed her husband's solid bicep and stopped him in the middle of the hall. "Do you mean consulting or what you used to do?"

Adam's eyes closed. He only wore the eyepatch when he worked now. The white film that covered his injured eye didn't bother her at all, and the patch was damn uncomfortable, or so Adam said. He folded her into his chest and kissed her forehead. "Babe, I don't have any idea what is going to be needed. Jacob and Jason wouldn't put us in danger unnecessarily, and if they are calling us in, it is personal."

"Does this have anything to do with why Mike left?" Keelee missed the hell out of him. His quiet friendship was a strength that was immediately missed when he left...well, shit, it was a year ago now.

"Babe, again, I don't know and even if I did, you know I probably couldn't tell you." His arms squeezed her closer to him.

"Adam, I can't lose you. You promised no more

missions." She pushed away from him so she could see his face. "You have a daughter, now. How can they ask you to go back?"

"Babe, they didn't ask. I volunteered." Their gazes locked as Keelee tried to understand the rationale behind his completely asinine decision.

"You—volunteered." Keelee shook her head and turned on her heel. She headed toward the kitchen and her coat. She needed to think, needed space… needed to go to the barn. Adam would take care of Elizabeth. She couldn't stay in the house, or she'd say something she might regret. *Like, oh say, what the fuck are you thinking you stupid, stupid man!*

She kicked rocks and muttered to herself on the walk to the barn. *What was wrong with him?* Uggg! She needed the familiar smells of horses, hay, and well-oiled leather. The ranch dogs raised their heads when she walked in. Several danced around her seeking attention. She dropped onto the straw covered floor and hugged on each one of them. Once the animals were satisfied, she closed her eyes and listened to the rustle of the animals in their stalls. The familiar sounds and smells soothed the storm of thoughts that twisted through her mind.

The dogs lifted their heads and growled quietly. Keelee heard the latch to the side door lift. She hushed the animals and waited. Her father appeared, dropped to the hay with her and was immediately covered in collie. Her dad's dog waited patiently for her ears to be rubbed.

"Can't ask him not to do this." Frank Marshall was never one to beat around the bush.

"I don't know what *this* is." Maybe that was what was bothering her. She didn't know what was going to happen. Memories from the darkest part of her life were far too sharp tonight.

"My point."

"What the hell does that mean, Daddy?"

"Don't cuss. You sound like a ranch hand. You don't know, and I don't know. He doesn't know…but he knows his family, those boys, need him. If you ask him to choose between you and them, you'll drive a wedge. It may not happen in the short term, but sooner or later, that wedge will cause a crack."

"So I'm supposed to be the good little wifey and smile as he goes off and leaves Lizzy and me?" A tear slipped over her eyelid, and she swiped it away in irritation.

"Nope. Didn't say that."

"Well, what exactly did you say?"

"When did you become selfish, girl?"

"Excuse me?" Keelee felt like she'd been hit by a right hook! How in the hell was she selfish?

"I won't excuse you. You think you are the only one this will affect? That man had a hard life before you. These people are the folks to whom he owes his very existence. He loves you as much as any man can love a woman, but he needs to be there for them. He's not stupid. He'll be careful. Trust him to do what he needs to do and for God's sake stop sulking in the barn. What would happen if he got called away right now? You've been there and done that. Stop this shit now, and go back and talk it out with your man."

"That's what I'm afraid of Dad. I'm afraid something will happen again." The tears she'd held at bay broke, and she crumbled against her father. He hugged her and waited. Her father was her rock growing up. He was solid, strong and her hero. She wiped her tears away and drew a stuttering breath.

"Girl, you can't stop living in the hopes of not being hurt again." Her dad's collie flopped over both of their laps. She stroked the animal's fur.

"I'm scared."

"Tell him, not me."

"When did you get so smart?"

"Had two strong-willed fillies that I raised alone. Made my share of mistakes."

"I love you, Daddy." She moved up and gave him a quick kiss on the cheek.

"I know. Get your ass out of here."

Keelee lifted off the straw and brushed a few stray pieces off her jeans. "Thank you."

"You're welcome. Now, git."

She laughed as the dogs scattered at his command.

He clicked his tongue and drew an exaggerated breath. "Well hell, at least the animals listen to me."

Keelee reached a hand down to help her dad up. "They are better behaved than I am."

"Lord, ain't that the truth."

CHAPTER 3

The intense burn of the muscles in his back and arms felt damn good. Exercising was the only thing Mike had left from his previous life. He focused on the pull-ups and his form. His trainer matched his up and down rhythm. He loved the competition, even if he won every challenge his trainer gave him. The physical exertion provided an outlet for the stress he was under. The trainer was damn good, but for most of his life, he'd honed and survived on his physical stamina. He *knew* when others stopped, he and his brothers at Guardian would continue. Physical sacrifice was ingrained in his psyche. He zoned out and let his muscles do what he'd trained them to do. Richard Garrett, his trainer, slowed and then finally dropped. He continued. After all, his trainer said to go to exhaustion, and he wasn't close to that limit. He closed his eyes and moved. *Up, breathe, down, up,*

breathe, down, up, breathe, down. The pattern, the mantra and the burn of his muscles, melded into a place for escape and he took it, losing himself in the physical routine.

"If you are doing this to make me feel worthless, it's working." Richard's unrepentant whine brought him out of his head. He muscled up again and held, looking down at his trainer. The man was all right. Not the type he'd usually find himself around, but then again, he rarely associated with anyone outside of Guardian.

"What? Did you get tired already?" Mike taunted.

"Hell, man, a robot would be tired by now. I don't know that I've seen anyone do that many pull-ups before."

"Then you don't know the right people." He relaxed his arms and allowed a full stretch of his biceps, triceps, and back before he dropped to the ground.

"Obviously. The question I keep coming back to is why do you keep me around when you could do this on your own?" Richard handed him a bottle of water.

"I know myself. If I don't have someone keeping me accountable, I'd forget to work out."

"Bullshit." Richard dropped to the padded workout floor.

He tipped his head back and laughed. The comment reminded him of Dixon and Drake. "No bullshit. With all this," He gestured to the mansion they were currently residing in, "...and the business demands that fill my day I *would* forgo working out. And I'm sure you've figured out this is my relief valve. I'd explode, implode or hell, maybe even cease to exist without my two hours a day down here with you."

The cover he'd assumed demanded he become a business savant. Thank God for his master's degree in organizational management. The work that was being sent to David wasn't quite over his head, but it was damn close. The appearance that he was who he claimed had to be maintained. God only knew how long it would take to work his way to the head of the fucking organization while Guardian, Mossad, MI6, the CIA and SISMI, the Italian Secret Service, gathered evidence to decimate the worldwide organization.

Richard dropped back on his elbows and crossed his legs at the ankle. He leveled his gaze at Mike and squinted his eyes. "Well, at least I don't feel like a loser anymore, but dammit, man, would you please quit emasculating me with my own workout program?"

He walked over to the treadmill. He powered it up and straddled the belt. "Sure, as soon as you beat me on a 10k run."

Richard groaned and rolled onto his side before popping up and walking over to the adjacent treadmill. "So we've been working out together every day in some form or fashion for what...the last seven months?"

He bumped up the speed on his treadmill to an eight-minute mile. He'd go faster after Richard stopped being a Chatty Cathy. After years of enduring the Wonder Twins' nonstop talking, the small amount of banter Richard engaged in wasn't too much of an annoyance. The thought of the brainiacs squared made him smile. He'd never admit it, but he missed those two. He extracted himself from his reminiscence.

"I believe you are correct. Seven months on the third. Why?"

"Well, I was just wondering if there was a significant other or if you were single?"

Mike glanced over at his trainer. The unusual topic piqued his curiosity. "There is no one. Not for a long time, just the job." Desiree was the last woman he'd cared about, but she had moved on liked he'd asked. Last he'd heard, she'd relocated to the eastern part of South Dakota and married the owner of a huge farming co-op near Aberdeen. She was a sweetheart, but deep down he knew that she wasn't strong enough to deal with the life he led. He wasn't averse to settling down, but he needed someone with the capacity to deal with his life. All of his life, both the good and the bad.

"Oh. So, you know this place has some awesome nightlife."

He laughed and asked, "You've been sampling it?"

"Well, yeah. I mean, I am single! Look, I know you'd have to take a cast of thousands, but maybe you should try to get out and have some fun. Come with me to a club."

He slowed his treadmill to a walk and then stopped it before he turned toward Richard. "I appreciate the thought, but that will never happen. If I need companionship it is purchased, private and devoid of public scrutiny."

"Man, it must suck staying hidden all the time." Richard hit the stop button on his machine.

"I've never known anything else." He wiped at the sweat rolling down his neck.

"You shouldn't bury yourself under a mountain of responsibilities. Life is so much more than work."

"Your life, perhaps. Yet, here you are, every day. Should you practice what you preach?"

"No, sir. I have a year contract with you. I get paid an insane amount of money to have you humiliate me at every workout. So far I've been to seven countries, cruised with you on two epic yacht voyages around the Caribbean *and* Mediterranean and watched you lock yourself behind very solid closed doors with advisors and business associates. *You* are never alone, but you're always isolated and, hell, I don't know…kind of removed from the world, I guess?" He motioned toward the armed guards that followed him everywhere. They currently standing at the doors to the gymnasium watching one of the maids gather towels. "One thing I've learned for sure, being David Xavier sucks. You don't have much of a life, even though everyone would think you do. No, after this gig I'm going home. I'm using the generous salary you've given me to open my own gym. Then I plan on finding someone to settle down with."

The kid was perceptive. The "business meetings" started just as Garrett had been hired. That was after Mike had endured five months of etiquette, diction, foreign language classes, and tutelage on all things David Xavier. The tour around the world cemented his cover, and the few people who his handlers selectively let into his world could confirm his identity if anyone asked. The last year had been nothing but a pressure cooker of events that would hopefully culminate with the bastards that ran the human trafficking ring dead or behind bars. Dead would be his preference, although that wasn't the mission. He brought himself out of his dark thoughts, glanced at his trainer and popped back into the conversation. "Where's home?"

"A little town called Atwater. The place is in the armpit of California. Hell, even the Air Force pulled their people out of the area when they started closing bases. But, it's home. I love the people, the community festivals and the small town feel. What about you? Where's home?"

He cocked his head looking at his after-a-fashion friend. "I was raised in the States, but my secondary education was primarily overseas. I don't have any roots. I own eighteen homes, three yachts, and several railroad cars that I use to tour when I'm in

Europe, but as far as a home? That would be hard to say." Except his heart knew exactly where home was. A huge ranch settled just south of Hollister, South Dakota. Highway 85 North out of the Black Hills was his road home. If this assignment went well, he'd go back.

Richard accompanied him over to the mats, where he led Mike through some intense stretching. Post workout stretching was the one thing he never really did when he was training at the ranch, and he was damn sure going to incorporate it when, or if, he got back home.

"Seriously, though, I know it is a stupid saying, but maybe you should take the time to stop and smell the roses. Find someone special, otherwise, when you're old and used up, the only memories you'll have are of the people after your money."

He lowered into a hamstring stretch and closed his eyes. With the exception of his time with Guardian, money had been *the* driving factor of his life...too little of it, not too much. He lifted, switched legs and dipped again, feeling the strain work its way through his muscles.

A distinct clearing of a throat brought Mike's head up. He glanced over at his personal assistant, Joel. The man was a godsend. Just as Gabriel had predicted, Joel had faultlessly led him through a myriad of meetings, business transactions and day to day minutiae that could have sunk his fledgling cover. The man was a mild-mannered, spry, sixty-seven years young. Joel's never ending energy proved the man was a machine and he kept everyone on schedule. He glanced at his watch again and frowned. He had twenty-five more minutes according to the schedule he memorized this morning.

"Sir, forgive the interruption, but Prince Tawfeek called on your private line. He expressed a desire to speak with you about a venture you'd discussed."

"Thank you, Joel. I appreciate you letting me know. Please clear the next hour. I'll be up."

The little man bowed and turned on his heel. Mike threw a glance at Garrett and shrugged before he half laughed, "I'll keep those roses in mind. But until then, work calls." He stood and gave a two finger salute and a half-hearted smile.

He spun on his heel and headed out the door, followed closely by his security detail. He glanced at his watch. Joel, Gabriel's faithful and trusted assistant, now turned business puppet master, had set up a dinner meeting tonight. A smallish merger of seventy-five million dollars he needed to work through with a trigger shy CEO. The merger was the first in a line of four deals that must go through. Joel explained that David Xavier wouldn't normally deal with such a small scale acquisition, but based on the size of the remaining three dominos; he needed to prompt the CEO into a Rube Goldberg launch that would trigger a series of events culminating in a cool billion dollars profit.

He'd delay before he called the prince. He couldn't

seem too anxious to set his plan into motion. The reality was it could take months to get through to the person at the top of the Bratva organization. But he would get to the filth at the top. He'd take the bastard out.

Mike shed his clothes as he entered his private quarters and headed for the shower. If anyone would have told him a year and a half ago that he'd be impersonating David Xavier, putting out feelers to purchase sex slaves and returning the phone calls of crown princes, he'd have told them they were insane. Well, hello insanity.

"I love this compound. South Dakota is a hidden treasure."

Frank Marshall watched Gabriel closely. They'd ended up on his front porch after a long day. The weather held brisk, damn near cold, but Amanda had bought outdoor heaters and installed them. The porch was his haunt, and now it was comfortable when the temperatures dipped. The peace and quiet out here allowed him to wind down from the physical demands the ranch placed on him. He wasn't a yearling anymore, but he still spent the day dealing with two thousand pound beasts that had more attitude than his daughters, which said something. Gabriel, well hell, who knew what he was doing here. As a matter of fact…"Figured you cottoned to it. You spend enough time here. Thought you were retired."

"Yep."

"Still here. Don't look retired." He didn't. The man still wore the office even if he didn't go into it on a daily basis.

"Got one more thing to do." Gabriel pushed his swing into an easy back and forth.

Frank toed the wood under him and let the gentle noise of the chains swinging the seat ease his soul. "What's that?"

"Got to get my boy Mike home and the kids off the Russians' scope."

"That's two things."

Gabriel shrugged. "Same thing, actually."

"Going to get messy?"

"Oh, yeah." The finality of his statement left little doubt.

"For them or us?"

"Both."

"Shit."

"Yep."

Well, that was the way of life. Frank would be ready to deal with the fallout. He drew a long breath. Amanda didn't need any more pain in her life. He'd put his knees on the floor and say some words with the Lord, and then he'd wait.

CHAPTER 4

"Anya, you look marvelous." The sleazy smile that peeked out of the civilized shell Dima Orlov wrapped around his sinister aura was enough to make her skin crawl. The bastard had tried for years to tempt her into his bed. The last time he told her if she slept with him he could advance her position in the organization. She'd turned him down immediately. *"I'm very happy doing what I do now and what I won't do...is you, for any reason."*

His leathery face had reddened, and the veins in his forehead and neck bulged under his well-known temper. That had been a year and two deliveries ago. Working her way to the top of the Bratva would prove she was the leader they needed. She'd never bend over for a pig like Orlov.

"Dima, to what do I owe this revolting meeting? Another attempt to fuck me?" Taty settled into the chair across from him and watched as his eyes traveled over her body. She suppressed a shiver of disgust.

"Not this time. You've been selected to meet with a customer." His lip lifted in a sneer.

"Another delivery? So soon?" The Bratva were very cautious with the wealthy clients. The time span between order and delivery could be up to a year. She wasn't aware of any toys currently being held by Evgeniy.

"No. This is a new client. A very important man. He has expressed the desire to meet with a representative of the Bratva. A female. You are the only woman the boss trusts to convey his messages to the client." Dima reached into his pocket and retrieved a phone. He placed it on the table and slid it across the pristine white linen keeping his middle finger on the screen. "You will answer it when it rings. You will listen, and you will respond only when asked a question. Do not fuck this up, Anya."

"Or what?" Taty asked with her signature strain of pure cockiness perfected over the years.

Dima lifted an eyebrow at her. The look spoke volumes. She'd be dead. "Who is on the other end?"

"The boss. Do well, and you will be rewarded. Fail, and you will be dead." A shrug of fatalistic indifference accompanied the bored response.

"I do not fail, Dima." Taty moved the phone out from under the man's finger. "When will he call?"

"When the time is right. Enjoy the tea." Dima

lifted from the small table and strode across the resplendent dining area. Tatyana nodded when the waiter approached with a tray of small pastries. She hadn't enjoyed anything in years, but finally, *he* was on the other end of the line. She'd do anything to impress *him*.

Mike strode into his office. He nodded to his security team, and they headed out the door. Briefings for today's meetings on the merger talks would wait. He felt pleasantly relaxed from his workout. He undid the button of his suit jacket and hit the intercom. "Joel, get Prince Tawfeek on the line, please."

"Right away, sir." The man's calm tones floated back at him.

Mike removed his jacket and sat down just as his phone buzzed. He hit a small divot beneath the phone and waited for the green light to flash, indicating the conversation would be recorded, before he lifted the handle. "Prince Tawfeek, thank you for taking my call."

"It is I who is honored, Mr. Xavier. I have some information for you concerning the business we discussed earlier."

"Indeed?" Mike left the conversation to the prince. The less he said, the more others spoke.

"There is a representative of the business that can meet with you tonight."

Ah...they were eager. "No, I'm sorry, that won't work for me. I'm booked. If you would be so kind, please relay to the representative that they may come to my residence the day after tomorrow. Promptly at three in the afternoon. While I am interested in the product they are selling, this foray isn't my only current endeavor, and several very advantageous propositions are on the table. Hopefully, the business owner understands I cannot limit my schedule to accommodate a single source."

"Are the other sources for the same merchandise?"

"One can't be too careful."

"I fear you would be putting fresh wine into used wineskins by using the other vendors. Simply a waste of effort, but I do understand the requirement to be sure of the product. I will relay your directions and concerns, and then I will remove myself from this process. Good day to you, Mr. Xavier."

"And to you, Your Highness." Mike ended the call and hit the button on his phone. Three different servers had saved the entire conversation. The prince could remove himself...for now.

"So you have two on this op. We made sure they briefed my guys on what they can and can't touch this time." Jacob King handed a headset to Jared. His brother put on the equipment while continuing to stare at the screen. Getting the teams to work with the investigators had been a challenge, but as long as the cops didn't go all cowboy and let the teams do their job entering and securing the scene, Jacob's men would play lackey and gather evidence. Obviously, learning not to contaminate the crime scene was a big sticking point, but hell, they'd figured it out.

"This is what the…tenth raid?" Jared watched the team breach the warehouse doors.

Jacob nodded and pointed at the far left monitor hitting his mic. "We have movement at the rear."

"Affirmative, Alpha One." Two large men exited the building and held to the shadows.

Jared leaned forward as if the act would bring the images into better focus. "Fuck, they have one of the women."

Jacob did a double take. "Kilo One, two perps with one hostage."

"Affirm. We have them. Standby."

Jacob made a survey of the helmet cams and hit Jared's arm. Two members of Kilo team approached what he assumed was the back door. The infrared cameras allowed them to see far better than the surveillance camera installed outside the warehouse. Three fingers appeared in the view of the camera at the same time as Kilo One counted down the move. Jacob's knuckles turned white as he gripped the tabletop. He knew what was coming and fuck him if it didn't send a shot of adrenaline straight through him.

Close your eyes. He mentally reminded the team members. He lived each of these missions whether he was on the ground or not. Jacob saw the flash-bang launch and the next second the infrared cameras blanked.

"What the fuck just happened?"

"Flash-bang." They stared at the grainy image of the small surveillance camera in the alleyway because it was the only image not blanked by the intense blast of light. There were several smaller flashes. Gunfire, probably not from his guys, they had flash suppressors on their weapons. Fuck, this was the hardest part of the op. Trusting his team leaders to do what they needed to do and waiting for the report. It fucking sucked.

The infrared cameras started to flicker back on. Jacob knew from experience not to bother trying to see a damn thing until the camera was fully functional. The momentary glimpses as the lens recalibrated were frustrating as hell.

"There." Jared pointed toward the end of the alleyway. Three team members walked forward. One had a small person in his arms. They sprinted toward the recovery point. The other two dropped a man in a suit to his knees. Two local cops came into the picture. They assumed control of the perp and the team members headed back into the alleyway.

"Alpha One, this is Kilo One."

"Go ahead." Jacob flicked his eyes to the images now coming in on the infrared camera.

"One in custody. One dead. They opened fire on us, sir. The hostage, she wasn't hit sir, but she's in a bad way."

"And the rest?"

"Standby."

Jared ran his hands through his hair. Getting evidence on these fuckers was driving them all insane. The compartmentalized way the Bratva ran their business was a maze of brick walls, dead ends and leads that fizzled more times than not. They'd been lucky several times, but the information they were able to retrieve was usually because of pure unadulterated luck, that was something everyone involved in these operations acknowledged. The Bratva had fucking mastered the ability to hide in plain sight.

"Alpha One we have two perps inside. Twenty-seven hostages and, sir, we have paperwork."

Jacob fist bumped his brother. "Roger that, Kilo One. The paperwork comes to me. No copies, no local law enforcement involvement."

"Affirm sir, we have the documents and will upload."

"Negative! No electronic copies. Standby for a courier. They will have the operation's sign-countersign."

There was confusion in the team leader's voice when he acknowledged the strange order. Jared took off his headset and ran his hand through his hair. "We are losing valuable time by using couriers."

"True, but I'd rather lose time than information. That hacker has proven he can infiltrate our systems. Jewell is running a counter broadcast now, rerouting the audio and using encryption she knows the hacker can violate to bait him away from this mission. We have to play the smoke and mirrors game to protect Mike."

"Yeah, I get that, but I don't like the Stone Age techniques."

"But it has been working." Jacob glanced at the camera feeds. Hopefully, they'd catch a break, and their luck would hold. The alternative wasn't something he'd care to think about.

CHAPTER 5

Taty jumped when her phone vibrated against the countertop. She put down the knife and the vegetables she was chopping to answer it.

"Yes?"

"You will drive to the address I will text you. This client owns businesses that have become inconvenient to our endeavors, yet he has reached out to us for a supply of toys. We are more than a little suspicious. Gather what information you can without revealing your position within the organization. Ascertain the extent of inventory he's requesting. You have impressed us with your ability to know when something is off. Use that talent. You must be available to the client promptly at three tomorrow afternoon. Do you understand?"

"Yes, I understand," Taty answered the direct question as instructed.

"And Anya?"

"Sir?"

"This man is a skittish recluse. Only a few people in this world have met him face-to-face. This may be our only opportunity to impress upon him our ability to provide the service he is requesting. We will provide whatever he requires to secure him as a client. *Whatever he requires*. Is that understood?"

"It is understood."

"We will contact you after your meeting." The face of the phone went dark as she stared at it. They would provide whatever he wanted. Should she suggest a face-to-face meeting with *her* boss? She was the exclusive go-between. One side would not know what the other required without her. If she played this right, it could be the means to finally identifying her boss.

Tatyana reflected on the conversation. The man spoke fluent Russian, but he had an accent. Obviously raised somewhere besides Europe. If she was forced to guess, the man's accent seemed...American? She shook her head and returned to the mission at hand. She had a recluse to seduce.

Mike glanced at the wall mounted digital clock again. The third time in as many minutes. His training session had actually been challenging this morning. He felt amazing, and Garrett was going to get a bonus if he kept coming up with innovative workouts.

He took a deep breath and released it slowly. He'd invested a year of his life to get to this point. Everything hinged on this meeting. He'd run every conceivable scenario through his head. Each move he made gave his opponent several options. He'd worked through the primary, secondary and tertiary responses and prepared himself for every tactic the enemy could throw at him. His head snapped up at the knock on his office door.

"Come in."

Joel stepped in and shut the door behind him. "Sir, the three o'clock appointment is here. Where would you like to receive?"

"Take them to the Grand Library and offer refreshments. I'll be there after a fashion." Joel's eyebrows lifted slightly, the only indication that he was surprised at Mike's actions. He'd never made an effort to impress another person or stall a meeting before, so having both happen simultaneously would be unusual.

"I have my reasons, Joel. Oh, and please make sure the guards complete a thorough search and scan before they allow the representative into my home. I'd hate to find any listening devices during our daily sweep. I'd rather not deal with the inconvenience."

"Of course, sir." Joel executed a perfect bow before he departed the room. Mike passed his hand over the computer screen embedded in his desk. He dragged his finger across several drop down menus and activated a screen split into six squares. The camera feeds displayed the lower quadrant of the palatial chalet. With his elbows on the desk and his hands clasped together, he framed the screen with his massive forearms.

The image on the screen surprised him. A woman. He thought back to the conversation he'd had with the prince. He'd told the prince to inform the brotherhood that he had discerning tastes. Mike assumed the prince would know he was talking about the orders, not the representative.

The image on the screen was feminine. Her light brown hair was cut short. Natural curls framed her face and flattered her delicate features and huge eyes. The woman reminded him of a wild doe in the woods. Her gaze moved, constantly surveying her surroundings, as if looking for potential threats. As she walked through the security checkpoints, he noted the white leather pantsuit and matching spike-heeled boots. Even though the leather covered every inch of her skin, from just under her chin to her toes, it revealed every detail of her small athletic body, from the dimple resting above her pert ass to the firm rise of her breasts.

Mike suppressed a chuckle. She was miffed at the guards. He could read her indignant attitude from three floors away. One of his guards gestured to the grand library and opened the door for her. He switched monitors and watched the awe displayed on her face at the enormity of the room. Her head snapped back toward the guard who motioned toward the tray a butler was currently depositing at one of the numerous conversation groups arranged throughout the cavernous library. The woman spun around when the door closed behind the guard and butler. Mike wondered what she would do when left alone in the huge room. She walked to the middle of the library and did a three-sixty, put her hands on her hips and shook her head. Mike allowed a small smile. The woman's reactions had been nearly identical to his. He studied her. She was a looker, and she knew it. The way the leather molded to her lithe body left little doubt she was very proud of herself. Not that Mike didn't appreciate the view because he did. He adjusted in his seat and gave himself a bit more room. It had been a long time since he'd thought about a woman in the way he was thinking about the one downstairs. The vision currently inspecting the tomes lining the impressive room wasn't the type of woman that held his attention —usually.

He blew out a long breath of air. It would be an even longer wait until he acted on any spark of desire he felt. *She* was part of an organization that bought and sold people. *She* wasn't a romantic option. *She* was the enemy, and he was going to take her down, along with every other sleazy bastard involved.

Taty slowly walked around the library. She paused at an imposing glass case. The UV filter and air circulation system were almost undetectable, but she knew what she was looking at from her years at university. Inside the case sat what she assumed was a Gutenberg Bible. The geek in her longed to examine the pages, to sit with pen and paper and translate the language into Russian, to feel the parchment and smell the distinct odor of a priceless original work from the Gutenberg press.

"That is one of the twenty-one complete versions of the Gutenberg Bible."

She turned at the voice. For a moment she lost all thought of anything other than the man standing in front of her. His sharp cheekbones, tan skin, black hair and almost black eyes could be from Mediterranean or Eastern Indian paternity, but his stature was far too tall and broad to be anything other than of American Indian descent. There were no lines on his face or gray in his hair. His lips were full and curved in a slight smile. His age could be anything from 35 to 50, but he was a splendid specimen of man no matter how many years he'd lived. His American accent, however modulated, reverberated around her senses. A high paid puppet for the master of the realm perhaps?

"I assumed. Your employer has good taste."

A smile tugged at the corner of the man's mouth for a split second. There appeared to be a sense of humor buried beneath the veneer.

"I was told there are over fifty thousand volumes in this room. Most are first editions and all are exceedingly rare." He gazed at the floor to ceiling shelving directly in front of him.

"Many people wish to obtain that which is unique. One-of-a-kind things are priceless. Few have the financial wherewithal to be able to do so." Taty's words were well considered. She wanted to know how much the recluse's people knew about what he was after.

The man turned to face her. His eyes narrowed, and Tatyana felt the intensity of his stare. "Your name?" The question seemed more of a demand. Tatyana felt a slither of discomfort crawl across her skin. *This* man exuded menace. Far more so than she had originally thought. No, he wasn't a lackey for the boss. This man wouldn't bow down to many. The muscles under his hand-tailored suit were taut, poised for action, yet she detected no weapons. Not that he'd need them; she could tell by the way he carried himself. His demeanor screamed danger. The polished exterior he presented barely concealed the aggression she sensed.

"Anya Krupin." She gave her Bratva-devised cover name, the one she'd been given when she started working with the toys. "And you are?"

"David Xavier. This..." He removed his hand from his pocket and cast it around indicating the massive library and the chalet in general, "...is mine, and yes I do enjoy rare, one-of-a-kind treasures."

Tatyana's gut dropped at the introduction. This magnificent man could have any man or woman he chose. Why would he need the perversion of toys? Not that it mattered to her. She had a goal, and he was the means to the introduction she'd been working for years to achieve.

She glanced over her shoulder and turned away from him under the pretense of looking at the volumes contained within the next shelving unit. "I understand you are looking for someone who can provide you another treasure."

The man walked up behind her. She could feel his body heat and smell the rich aroma of spice in his cologne. "Do you speak with authority or are you a messenger?"

Taty glanced over her shoulder and up into his dark eyes. The intensity of his stare forced her to drop contact almost immediately. "I'm only a messenger. I go; I talk; and when they call, I relay information." She glanced back up at him and shrugged. "I have no authority. I am…how do you say it…a buffer?"

Mr. Xavier's left eyebrow rose a millimeter. It was the only indication he'd heard her. His eyes were cold, and his expression revealed nothing. Taty had never dealt with a man who emanated such absolute power before.

He turned on his heel and walked toward the silver service tray the butler had left only minutes before. Taty followed him and nodded when he indicated a delicate china cup. He filled it with tea.

"Milk? Sugar?" He wielded the service like he'd done it a thousand times.

"No, thank you."

He handed her the hot drink and settled back into the chair. "I have numerous orders. The order would be substantial and recurring. However, I will not do business until the quality of the product is inspected; and I never do business with… buffers."

"I understand." She sipped the tea and took a calculated risk of revealing her knowledge of the business. "Their terms are set in stone. You will pay only after your inspection. You provide bank routing, and after you confirm the merchandise is acceptable the money will be moved." Tatyana searched the tea she was drinking and prayed she didn't telegraph her desperation that this man proceed with his purchase.

"So you are not a buffer. Very well, however, I will not do business without meeting the head of the organization I am associating myself with."

Shock lifted Tatyana's eyes to meet the obsidian gaze across from her. "They may not agree."

"Then they will lose access to a vast stream of unequaled income. I have people who will pay what your organization charges and a…" He nodded to her, "…buffer fee to ensure they are not directly asso-ciated with your employers. I have no such reserva-tions and will act as their agent. Let them know they would be cutting off a lucrative source of revenue."

Tatyana set the cup down on the table and swallowed as she digested the information. "You do not purchase the treasure for yourself?"

"That is not your concern."

The reprimand stung. It was true, and he nailed her to the wall with her slip up. She lowered her eyes and tried to determine what a billionaire would get out of such an arrangement. The question whirled through her mind.

When she glanced up again, he'd cocked his head and was staring at her. "Leverage."

She blinked before she asked, "Excuse me?"

"You were wondering what I would receive from being an intermediate."

"I was. Is this leverage worth the personal risk of the association you seek?" She could have bitten her tongue off at the abrupt question.

He reared back and laughed as he stood. "Go. Do your job, Anya." He handed her a thick metallic gold card with only a telephone number engraved in black print. "Text me, so I have your telephone number. Have a good evening, Ms. Krupin. You were an unexpected...buffer." He started to leave but then turned. His voice floated across the expansive distance between them. "You believe your employers are dangerous people." The statement sent shivers down her spine because obviously, this man did not make such an assumption.

Anya lifted off the chair and nodded. "I do."

"Interesting."

She watched as he left the library. The soles of his shoes made little sound against the marble flooring. Trepidation broke through her like a crashing wave pounding the shoreline. She had lived in the primordial ooze of the Bratva and had dealt with the rich bastards who purchased the merchandise, but never had she met a man that scared her as much as this David Xavier. The man wholeheartedly believed the Bratva would bend to his will. That either made him insane or the most dangerous man she'd ever met.

"Ma'am?" Taty's gaze snapped to the guard who had escorted her in. She drew a deep breath and headed his way. Regardless of her concerns, she had a job to accomplish.

"Archangel, we have a positive contact on Eagle's Nano RFID trackers. They activated thirty-four minutes ago. Our system has confirmed the signature."

Jason King acknowledged the message and hit the doors to his office heading to Guardian's Operational Command Center. Jacob and his wife Tori stood in front of the massive video screens.

"Mike has activated the trackers. That means he's made contact and the mission is moving forward." Tori handed Jason a red folder which flagged it as Top Secret. "His schedule for the next two months. He's going to be in New York. If I were a betting woman, I'd bet he'll have the first transfer done there."

"I trust your instincts, babe. I'm on it." Jacob pulled out a binder and started thumbing through the tabbed documents.

Jason flipped through the contents of the folder and spoke over his shoulder. "He'll need someplace that is vacant. Close enough to drive to but far enough not to attract suspicion."

Tori's fingers flew over the keyboard as Jacob picked up a secure line. "This is Alpha One. We need Tango Team deployed to the New York City safe house. Call the ranch and have Alpha team members Three, Four and Five put on standby for imminent deployment."

The large screen to the right suddenly held maps and Tori used a laser pointer to pinpoint locations and draw the men's attention. "There are three places that I'd look at first. There is a building under renovation in New Jersey. The project is on hold pending inspection by the city, and that's bogged down. There is a factory in Queens that was just purchased. It's going to be demolished, and low-cost housing will replace it. The area is highly populated. And then there is a warehouse in the Bronx. This is the one I'd choose. The area has limited traffic at night. Hell, the warehouse doesn't even have power, but it is guarded. No homeless people in the building and security would be easy to remove or manipulate for the meet." Tori spoke as she dropped the pointer and started typing again.

Jason thanked God for the duo in front of him. They worked together seamlessly, each anticipating the other's actions and feeding off it as they researched the anticipated mission. Granted, it wasn't strictly an overseas operation, but there was no way any King would be left out of this one. He and Gabriel had nearly been blown out of the sky by a Russian bomb. Gabriel's wife Anna was targeted that same night, as were his own wife and son. They were damn near incinerated in an explosion that leveled Faith's home in Savannah. Hell for that matter, Jared, Christian, Jasmine and Chad had all been targeted. It was personal on so many levels.

"That's a good start. Let's make sure we haven't overlooked anything. Alert Jewell and let her know we are starting our offensive tonight. Remind everyone, all contact with anyone in this operation is face-to-face or handwritten. No phones, no texts, no electronic communication of any kind is to be made, that fucking uber hacker they have will be fed what we want him to know via Jewell's mirror system.

"Jacob send word to Jared and Joseph. We have some payback to dish out. Those bastards will never know what hit them. Shit, don't forget to tell Jasmine. I'd be in a world of shit if she's left out."

Jacob glanced over his shoulder. "Time to kick some Russian ass, old school style."

"We've got it down to a science now. Let's get this

shit shifted into high gear. I want my man home safely and the Bratva leaders in jail or in hell. My preference is dead, but I'll work within the confines of the law." He mentally added *'for now'*. Jason glanced one more time at his brother and sister-in-law, who worked and danced around each other with precision and ease. Yeah, they'd get the bastards and bring him home. There was no other alternative.

CHAPTER 6

"The merchandise would be resold?"

"He stated he would be the 'buffer' so the buyers and the product would not be associated with our organization. The exact words were that you would lose access to a vast stream of unequaled income. He wants to meet you." Taty's voice cracked. She knew it sounded like fear and, in a way, it was. She feared the boss would never allow the introduction.

"That is unacceptable."

"Then you will lose him. He will not bend. He is unlike any man I have ever met." *Powerful, dynamic, sexy.*

"How much business?"

"He didn't say. It was an initial contact to make his demands known."

"Demands." The contempt rolled through the connection. "Go back. Get specifics. If the order is big enough, we will discuss his *demands*." Her boss' accent grew stronger when it was tinged with emotion. The accent was definitely American.

"Yes, sir."

"And Anya, do whatever it takes to get the information we need. Understood?"

Taty closed her eyes and swallowed her fury. She'd been ordered to prostitute herself for information.

"Yes, sir. I understand."

Mike settled behind his massive desk. He grabbed a pen and started carding it through his fingers. The rhythmic action was a habit he'd developed in his childhood. Once, when he was about thirteen, he witnessed a magician on television tumbling a coin through his fingers. That summer, he worked relentlessly until the motion became second nature. He did it now more out of habit than anything else.

His mind turned over the information he'd gathered from his brief meeting with the Bratva's representative. The woman wasn't only a messenger. He didn't know how deep her connections to the Bratva were, but they were strong enough that she would be trusted to contact him and relay information to her superiors.

Did she know what the merchandise was? Of course. She wasn't an innocent, no matter how much he wanted her to be, and for some reason, he wanted her to be. She was an oddity he hadn't anticipated. The woman wore inner strength like a halo. Mike saw it in an instant. She'd tried to hide the emotions that churned in her expressive brown eyes. What prompted such unrest? He'd bet money she hadn't been raised in wealth. Her teeth were slightly crooked. One front tooth overlapped the other and accented her slight overbite. The flaws didn't detract from her appearance but were obviously never corrected by braces. Her awe of the library's enormity and grandeur had been genuine. Yes, the beautiful sprite in white leather intrigued him.

He sat forward and dropped the pen onto the desk. If he could entice her away from the Bratva, if she thought she was working for David Xavier, she might give up information on the people who ran it. Of course, there were other ways to get information. He could get close to her. That thought split into two distinct issues. The first, and most powerful, was the fact he would do anything to put away the bastards she worked for. Second was the physical desire that filled him when he stood next to her in the library. Would he ever act on that need? No. He was a master of denying his desires. He'd been celibate for years. His spirit longed for the connection, but his mind and heart had yet to find the woman who could complete him. Desiree had been the closest he'd come to finding his life partner, but she was destined for another, as was he. Or so he thought. At this point in his life, he doubted he would find the one to fill his empty soul.

He pushed the image of Anya's over the shoulder glance and smile out of his mind. He'd use her if he must. It was a reprehensible thought on many levels, but she'd allied herself with the darkness of this world. A knock at the door interrupted his musings. A welcome interruption.

"Sir, do you have time to go through the travel arrangements for next week?" Joel stood at the door with his tablet in hand.

"Of course. Come in." He waited for his personal assistant to sit before he asked, "Meetings on the merger in New York, a conference with the Chinese ambassador, and....?" Mike leaned forward and brought up his calendar.

"Several meetings with your law firm, sir. An annual review of holdings, liabilities, acquisitions and contractual requirements for the upcoming year."

Mike groaned, resulting in a smothered laugh from Joel. "Dry to be sure, sir, but necessary."

"I'll suffer through it. You know the drill, only the people necessary to accomplish the meeting."

"Yes sir, as a policy, your privacy is protected for every meeting. Before you travel to San Diego, there is an opportunity to attend a function in Washington D.C. A white-tie dinner for the charities run by your benevolent association. The invitation arrived today from the coordinator." Joel pulled up the email and scanned it before he spoke, "Ten thousand dollars a plate. The usual suspects on the invitation list. Politicians, actors, possible benefactors. I would recommend you not attend. There are several who have RSVP'd with whom Mr. Xavier had significant business dealings. The possibility for mistakes would be more than marginal"

Mike glanced at the organization and felt a wellspring of affection for Christian and Anna's new shelter in D.C, but Joel was right. He didn't need anything to bring his cover under suspicion. "Decline the invitation, but buy two tables and send the tickets to the organizers to give away or resell as they see fit. Also, leak to the press that I may be attending. That will sell out the rest of the tickets."

"Very good, sir."

"Three weeks in New York and a month in San Diego, correct?"

"Yes, sir. Your yacht will be moored and at your disposal once you arrive in California."

"That works. I'll let you know when to make arrangements."

"Excellent. Also, the documentation you requested earlier is on the private server."

"Thank you, Joel."

"You are most welcome, sir."

Mike extracted the documents from the server and settled in to grind through the information when he felt his cell vibrate. He pulled it out of his breast pocket and read the text.

Vendor is interested.

No shit. He tapped out a response and hit send before he keyed his intercom. "Joel, inform the chef dinner will be for two tonight and inform the guards, Ms. Krupin will be returning."

"Daddy! I got an invitation to Marcus' birthday party today!" Jason bent down to catch his son Reece as he catapulted across the living room. "You did? That's great! What are you going to get him for his birthday?"

"He likes *Transformers*, too!"

"He does? Well, then we need to go buy him some *Transformers*."

"Uh huh! His party is Saturday. Can you come? The invitation says bring your parents." Reece grabbed a crumpled piece of paper from his pocket.

"I don't know, buddy. I'll try. Did your mommy see that?" He took the proffered invitation and grimaced at the tattered mess.

"Yep! She put it on the chalkboard in the kitchen." Reece wiggled to get down. As soon as his feet hit the hardwood floor, he started running down the hall. Tippy launched from the couch and danced around the little boy, barking with delight. Jason took off his suit jacket and hung it on the hall rack. "Faith! I'm home!" He'd never make the mistake of not announcing himself again. The last time he snuck up on her he'd almost died of pepper poisoning.

His beautiful wife popped her head out of the kitchen and smiled. "I'm not packing pepper tonight." It had become a running joke, but damn his bride was a klutz and, when she struck, he usually paid the price.

He pulled her into his arms and got the kiss he so desperately needed. It had been one hell of a day. The meeting with Gabriel, Jacob, Tori and Jared had examined every detail of what they believed would transpire next. There was no way of knowing exactly what cards Mike would play, but the extensive pre-planning they'd done gave everyone a good idea of where Mike would try to lead the Bratva.

Reece and Tippy raced by, this time Reece had his Superman cape on and held a model of an F-15 in his hand making jet noises.

"He's happy." Jason loved that little man with all his heart.

"He got invited to Marcus' birthday party."

"I heard."

"We were invited too. Saturday at two." Faith walked with him into the kitchen and handed him a plastic tumbler full of soda.

"Yeah, about that."

"Don't worry. I've already told Sullivan. Lima team has the address, and I've asked Marcus' mom for the invitation list so I can 'make personalized cupcakes.'" Faith air quoted the words. She smiled up at him and popped a pecan into her mouth. "I'll give Sullivan the list as soon as I get it. We'll be fine."

Guardian would be able to run the guest list to make sure there was no threat to Faith or Reece. Lima team had adopted his family as their own. He trusted them to ensure nobody came near Faith or Reece. "How did I get so lucky to find you?" Jason sat down on one of the bar stools and tugged her between his legs.

"You had the good sense to listen to Gabriel. Besides, we are the lucky ones." Faith picked up another pecan half and popped it into his mouth.

"I beg to differ."

Faith's eyes lit up, and she moved close enough to lean forward and whisper, "I'd rather be the one begging."

Well, shit. How the hell was he supposed to think now?

CHAPTER 7

Tatyana followed the huge armed security detail through the labyrinth-like halls of the chalet. The text she'd received left little doubt her presence at dinner was a requirement and not a request. She shivered at the chill in the air. The palatial opulence notwithstanding, the place had the feel of a mausoleum. Cold, lifeless and empty. Her simple, black, silk dress gave little warmth as they made their way through the massive residence. Her coat and purse were waiting for her at the guard station. She'd been scanned prior to entering this morning and scanned just as thoroughly this evening.

She'd tried to keep track of where the guard was leading her, but it was hopeless with all the twist and turns. Finally, he paused at a door and knocked. A muted response from inside beckoned them in.

The guard opened the door and stepped inside. Taty followed him in. Warm air immediately wrapped her. A huge fire blazed in an enormous fireplace. Its golden hue flickered over the small table set for two in the center of the room. David Xavier stood from one of the high wingback chairs facing the fireplace.

The intimacy of the setting wasn't what she'd expected. The thought of discussing the purchase of the merchandise over a meal disgusted her, but not enough to stop what she was doing. She would get to the man at the top of the Bratva, and she'd use David Xavier to do it. Turn around was fair play, after all. He'd sought out the Bratva. He was purchasing the product that the Bratva harvested from under the noses of countless law enforcement agencies. She had no problem using *him* to get what *she* wanted.

"Anya, please come in and warm yourself. This chalet is beautiful but cold and drafty."

"Thank you." She walked across the room taking in the lavishness of the appointments. Flickers of flame danced inside golden sconces around the room and accented Monet paintings on the wall. Original, no doubt. Everywhere her eyes darted, wood surfaces gleamed in the firelight. Vivid arrangements of red, white and yellow roses softened the dark wood side tables. As she approached him, she noticed a slender silver vase, a work of beauty, sat as the only adornment on the table between the two chairs. It held a single red rose. The simple beauty of the flower muted the sensory overload and allowed her to focus on her reason for being here. She took the seat he gestured at and crossed her legs. His eyes traveled the length of her exposed calf and thigh before he moved his eyes up to her face.

"May I offer you a drink? Dinner will be served in about twenty minutes."

"I'll have whatever you're drinking." She noted the warm amber liquid in his crystal balloon goblet. He nodded toward the side of the room, and a uniformed butler moved from his location against the wall. The man poured her drink and topped off David's.

"That will be all until dinner is served."

The man bowed slightly and exited like a ghost.

She took a small sip and hummed in appreciation. "This is very good."

"My guilty pleasure. Cognac of this caliber is a treat for the soul." His warm, inviting smile and the innocent joy of his comment surprised her. He swirled the liquid in his glass before he sampled it.

"I assume you can afford any treat you desire," Tatyana said it more to remind herself the man was the Bratva's client more than anything else.

His expression closed off immediately. Gone was the openness and the tactical businessman from this morning reappeared.

"What did your contacts instruct you to say to me?"

"That they were interested."

"Indeed." He focused his attention on the fire that blazed in front of them. Taty swirled the liquor like she'd seen him do and caught a delicious aroma wafting toward her. She sipped the drink again and closed her eyes. The flavor was unlike anything she'd ever had before. Devine.

"What else did they instruct you to do?"

Taty's eyes popped open, her boss' instructions to do whatever was necessary to get the information from him was alarmingly fresh in her memory. "I'm supposed to get the information they desire by any means necessary."

"Ah… well, your *means* are quite enticing, Anya. Exactly what information had you planned to pump out of me?"

The double entendre pushed up a small smile. "I'm to find out the number you require and what the follow-on orders will be. They will consider a meeting should your business be of sufficient size to benefit them."

"Then let's get the business out of the way so we can focus on the enticement portion of the evening, shall we?"

Tatyana put her crystal glass down and folded her hands in her lap. "That works for me." She moistened her lips deliberately and watched his eyes track her tongue's movement. She wouldn't mind a night with the man in front of her.

"I want fifteen units delivered to me in New York in ten days. The particulars will be given to you, and you will relay the request. Additionally, from this point forward, you will remain in my company until the first shipment is received and inspected. You will then be given the second order. I believe the number required at this point is thirty-two, but that number may increase. I anticipate semi-annual orders after that. I will guarantee the price of ten units each order, and whether or not I place those orders is a moot point. I will consider it a retainer."

Taty's brain did a rough calculation. The man was willing to spend close to a hundred million dollars to acquire the leverage he spoke of this morning.

"Why would I need to stay?" Her mind raced. How could she work these requirements to her advantage?

He leaned forward and pinned her with his obsidian eyes. "You will be the single point of contact with the vendor until we meet. There will be no electronic trail, no emails, no documentation and no final payment until I am satisfied. You will give them the account number for the down payment, verbally, after you have memorized it. There will be no written, electronic or video evidence. The money will be deposited in shell corporations with no connection to me or my holdings. The Bratva will receive the final account numbers only when the merchandise is received and inspected. The first time I will inspect. The second, you will do the inspection while I have a face-to-face with your bosses. You have quite the reputation, my little concierge." He swirled his cognac and smirked at her before he took a drink.

His statement stopped every thought except one.

He *knew* who she was and what she did for the Bratva. His intelligence on her employer was more than impressive. His demands would mean there would be no way to track his involvement. The simple genius of the plan earned him a level of respect she'd never given anyone else. Additionally, he would be taking her to his meeting. She'd work out a way to be present for that conversation. There was no way the Bratva would ignore this type of money. They would meet, and she would be there.

"I will be needed here by the Bratva to assist in the endeavor; the order is quite large." The idea of being held without the freedom to do what she needed concerned her.

"If you leave, the offer is canceled. Consider me... enticed." He leaned back, and his eyes lingered on her with impenetrable intensity. Goosebumps rippled across the surface of her skin in response. Even the warmth of the roaring fire couldn't diminish the cold ,sinking feeling in her soul. This was it. The culmination of years of work led to this. She'd been sent to dance with the devil, and the music was playing.

"All right. Someone will need to retrieve my cell phone from my apartment. It is the only means of communication I have with them. They call me. I don't call them."

"Consider it done. Of course, the phone will not be allowed within the confines of my residence. Security reasons. We will go outside the chalet after dinner and await their call. I'll have my men collect your personal belongings. No computer, telephone or electronic devices. I will supply needed electronics to you for any activity you require. They will, of course, be monitored."

Taty nodded. "Of course."

"Do you have a passport?"

"Yes. It is in a small lock box at the back of my closet."

"Good. Please excuse me for a moment. I will make the arrangements, and then we'll have dinner."

Taty nodded and watched him walk out of the room. She clutched the cognac and downed the rest of the liquid in one huge gulp. The fire burned down her throat and brought tears to her eyes. She was so close. She took several deep breaths and calmed her nerves. *So damn close*.

"Bring me up to speed on Mousetrap." Gabriel had worked with Jason on putting together several other missions before he asked about Mike's operation. Gabriel was happy to lend his knowledge to his successor. Jason's management of Guardian had been spot on. When the man didn't have the answer, he researched solutions and collected information. Gabriel scheduled routine stops in D.C. to keep his fingers in the pie. He didn't run the place any longer, but Guardian was *his* baby, even though Jason wore the mantle. Besides, his wife would murder him if he tried to take the reins back. She'd shared him long enough. Her words, not his.

"Well, as you know, we've started taking out the foot soldiers. Right now I'd say we are disrupting significant cash flow in the States. Our contacts in Germany, England, Italy and France have indicated roughly the same success."

"Irritating the tiger. We distract the beast so Mike can sneak up on it." Gabriel nodded his understanding.

"Two days ago, I would have said yes. But we found some documents in a warehouse raid. We were able to round up several Bratva. One of the two stupid shits that fought us died. However, his partner has a beautiful singing voice. We've verified most all of the information he gave us. We now have intelligence on several mid-level personnel within the Bratva's hierarchy.

"Do we have a plan on acquiring these representatives?" Gabriel should be impressed with the efforts of his company, but he expected this caliber of professionalism, and so did Jason. That was why the company was the absolute best at what they did.

Jason leaned over and thumbed through several large folders. "Of course. I have them... here." He dropped the paperwork in front of Gabriel. He was tempted to pull out the ops sheets and read the synopsis, but he didn't. He slid the folder back toward Jason. "No, I don't need to know the information. If you need my assistance, then I'll look. If not, I trust you to make the right decisions."

Jason blinked at him as if taken by surprise.

"The only thing I need to know is that you have a plan in place to make sure our family will be safe."

Jason nodded. "Jacob, Joseph, Jared and I have worked through the potential scenarios. Jasmine, Jewell and Alpha team will be in play. Justin will be a conduit only at this point."

Gabriel laughed. Hell, the entire damn family was involved in removing this threat. Well, all except Jade. That woman had enough shit on her plate, and quite honestly, Gabriel was glad that wild card wasn't in the mix. He never really knew what that woman would do.

"All right. You know how to get ahold of me if you need me."

Jason stopped him as he was standing. "Do you want in when we take these bastards down?"

Gabriel tapped the folder and considered the question for several seconds. "No, I trust you, Jason. You'll take this company to the next level. I know you'll grow it for my sons to take over... one day. My time being involved in active operations is in the past. I'm here if you need me, but I'm tapping out."

Jason stood and offered his hand. Gabriel grabbed it and hauled the mountain of a man into a hug. "You're the right man to lead this company. I'm proud of you."

CHAPTER 8

Mike stood at the door to the parlor outside his quarters where he'd left the Russian. He'd sent one of his security teams to the residence where they'd tracked her. They'd empty the apartment and search it. The team had no idea what they were searching for, but that was irrelevant. They would bring anything odd or unusual to his attention.

When he'd formulated his course of action, he hadn't planned on keeping her with him. She was a distraction, admittedly one he didn't need, but there was something about the woman that spoke to him in a way he didn't understand. His gut told him not to let her go. Not to let her out of his control. Something dark and deep within him needed her to be here. Before she'd arrived, he'd spent an hour in deep, prayerful meditation searching for the reason for the intensity of his reaction to her. He'd come away just as confused as he'd started.

He'd lived his adult life based on two principles. Protect those who cannot protect themselves and honor all things with the respect they deserve. This woman violated both of his tenants, and yet the small voice in his mind demanded that he keep her close and protect her. His inner-self had placed him on a tenuous precipice, but he'd learned to trust that small, quiet voice.

He strode into the room to find her where he'd left her. He noticed only one change—not only was her drink gone, but his glass was also empty. Liquid courage? He diverted to the sidebar and brought the decanter back with him. He refilled both of their snifters and sat down while observing her. A rose-colored hue flushed her cheeks. Whether the blush was from the fire or the alcohol, he couldn't tell. Her riot of brown curls framed her face. Under the simple, modest black dress, her body was even more enchanting than when wrapped in leather. Her long, sexy legs crossed at the ankle were a visual feast of feminine beauty.

They sat in silence. She stared at the fire apparently lost in thought. He stared at her and interrogated his inner voice. It steadfastly refused to answer. They moved to the table when dinner was served. Classical music floated in the background. "Tell me about Anya Krupin."

"Is that a request or an order?"

Mike glanced up at her question. The little spitfire had finally adjusted to the curveball he'd thrown her earlier. Good. She had spunk. He liked the fact she'd rebounded. Mike raised his eyebrow and said nothing. He'd let her be the judge.

She wrinkled her nose at him and took another forkful of salad before she responded, "Why don't you tell me what you know about me, and I'll fill in the blanks."

"Ah, well that would be interesting, wouldn't it?" Mike wiped his mouth and leaned away from the table while the butler removed his salad plate and placed a small dish in front of him. He watched Anya's puzzled expression at the amuse-bouche that sat in front of her. "It is a palate cleanser. To ensure you enjoy the subtleties of the next dish without the lingering tastes of the last offering."

"You're joking." Her eyes rounded in surprise.

"I'm not." He spooned the small offering into his mouth and watched as she did the same. Inside he was laughing because that was almost verbatim what he'd said when his coaches had pushed him through charm school. Fuck him sideways; it had been one hell of a surprise that there were so many rules and regulations to eating a proper meal. After the main course was served, he flicked his eyes to the butler and gave a nod toward the door. The man discreetly left the room.

Mike waited for her to sample the lobster dish before he spoke. "The real Anya Krupin died thirty-five years ago. Three days after she was born." Her fork paused halfway to her lips, and her eyes popped up to his.

"What?" Her voice squeaked and broke. It would have been adorable on someone who wasn't involved in selling humans to the highest bidder.

"I assume you have a real name."

She wiped her mouth and sat back. Her gaze told him she was considering how to answer him.

"It would be much better for you, my dear, if you leveled with me. Believe me. I will eventually have all the answers."

She diverted her attention to the fireplace, which had burned down to a large assortment of red coals and smaller dying flames. The pink tip of her tongue slid over her bottom lip before she sucked it into her mouth and worried it with her teeth for a moment.

"The Bratva gave that name to me when I joined this particular arm of their operation."

"And why did you join?" Mike probed.

"Why does anyone sell their soul?" She stared at the fire and shook her head against whatever ghost was haunting her. "At first, it was to eat. The Bratva had several small errands that I ran for them. I understand people and speak several languages. I was useful, and they paid me. I ate regularly, kept warm and had good clothes. My errands became progressively more detailed. I had no idea what I was taking to whom, but I did it to the best of my ability because I enjoyed eating and yes... I enjoyed the praise I received. Then one day I was given an opportunity." She rested her head back against the chair and sighed. "I thought I'd be delivering packages. They said I would ensure the merchandise met the exact specification of the client. I would deliver the packages to the new owner, receive a document that stipulated payment of the cargo and... poof... mission over."

Tears welled in her eyes and spilled down her cheek. She didn't lift a hand to wipe them away, apparently lost in her memories. "When I found out what the merchandise was, I tried to get out, but the Bratva have a unique way of ensuring you continue to work for them." She lifted a shoulder in a shrug. "I was beaten as a warning and told of my excruciating rape and death should I not follow orders." She turned and glared into his eyes. "I would have gladly died, but they threatened my aunt. She is innocent and all I have left."

She turned away again and peered into the fire. Mike digested the information. He wasn't going to buy it until he could validate it, but damned if it didn't seem that her emotions were real.

"What is your real name?" His question was low, but she heard him.

"Tatyana Petrov."

Mike stood and nodded. It appeared neither of them felt like finishing dinner. "You need to tell me about your aunt. I will provide for her safety, and then we will go for a stroll and allow your employers to call." He extended his hand and waited. She placed her hand in his and lifted from the table.

He would relay the information to Casey, his head of security. They would be instructed to provide security for Tatyana's purported aunt but to confirm they did not make contact. He'd have to investigate before he did more.

Mike escorted Tatyana to her new quarters. Her belongings had been transferred, examined, x-rayed and swept before his staff unpacked the items. The only thing they did not bring was her perfume. The perfume selection Mike would provide her was... unique.

He watched as she wandered through the rooms and stopped to examine the display of antique bottles and atomizers. She lifted several, smelling them before she selected one to spray on her wrists. He leaned against the doorframe and allowed himself a sad smile. His first move in the chess match had been made.

The crunch of the hardened snow under their feet was the only sound disturbing the cloak of silence that surrounded the chalet. Tatyana slipped on a patch of ice. Mike reached out and grabbed her elbow steadying her.

"Careful." He slid his arm around her, guiding her around another icy patch. Her smaller body tucked perfectly under his arm. She carefully maneuvered around the ice. Her designer snow boots had no traction, and her toes had to be frozen.

"What do you want me to tell them when they call?" She shivered against the cold.

"Exactly what I told you. No more, no less. The terms are nonnegotiable." He motioned toward a small gazebo that sat off the path. The roof and walls would break the wind that had to be cutting through her thin jacket.

As they approached the small structure her phone rang. Mike activated the recording device he wore as she removed the telephone from her pocket. "Yes."

"What have you discovered?" the voice on the other end of the phone demanded. Mike hesitated at the sound of the man's voice. He was speaking Russian, but the tenor was familiar. He immediately dismissed the thought. He didn't know any Russians, so any familiarity he perceived was his mind playing tricks on him. Tatyana glanced up at him, took a deep breath and began, "He wants me as the single point of contact. Full stop. No others. There will be no electronic documentation and no final payment until he is satisfied. You will receive the account number for payment after he has inspected the first shipment of fifteen toys. The descriptions will be forthcoming. After the initial fifteen, a minimum of thirty-two more will be delivered at his instruction. He will meet you at the second delivery, or you will not receive payment for the thirty-two or the annual order for ten more, twice a year. He will pay for the semi-annual requirement of toys regardless if he orders or not."

"Fifteen the first shipment and thirty-two the second."

"Correct, as a minimum, with a standing order for twenty a year following the second order."

"You told him the premium?"

"I have not, although I do not believe the price will be an issue."

There was a long stretch of silence. Tatyana shivered so hard her teeth chattered. Mike moved behind her, blocking the wind that raced through the trellis walls of the gazebo. She continued through her shivers. "There is one other thing."

"What?"

"I am not to leave. He will not allow this phone inside his residence. He is here now listening. If you wish to contact me, you need to give me a time and a date so this phone can be activated again."

"I will call you back in five minutes."

Tatyana slipped the phone back in her pocket. "He's calling me back, shortly."

Mike nodded as if he hadn't heard her boss' words. "You did well."

He moved closer before he unbuttoned his long wool coat and draped it around her, bringing her body next to his. "You're freezing. You'd never make it where I lived."

~

"Where do you come from? America, yes?" Tatyana felt him tighten for the briefest of moments.

"Yes." The comment may have answered her question, but it also ended the conversation. There was no invitation to talk in the clipped response.

They stood in silence with her tucked close to him until the phone rang. "Yes?"

"What is the timeline for the first fifteen?"

David was so close that he could hear the question. In her other ear, he whispered, "They will be delivered in exactly ten days to a warehouse in Brooklyn. You will activate the phone at noon New York time on the tenth day to tell them where the meet will be. If there is anything amiss, they will not receive payment." She parroted the words as he spoke.

"Unacceptable. We receive full payment beforehand."

She glanced up at him and shivered. Not from the cold, but from the fury in his eyes. "No. If you want his money, you will play by his rules."

The silence stretched for a moment before the voice asked, "When will we receive a shopping list?"

He whispered in her ear, and she repeated, "You will call the day after tomorrow, three p.m."

"You know what will happen if you are leading us astray." The threat was wielded like a sharp blade.

"I know."

"We accept." The line went dead.

"You did well." He extended his hand, and she placed the phone into his palm. He turned and headed back to the pathway, leaving her with a stray thought. *Who was more evil? The man buying the toys or the Russians selling them?* He waited for her at the path and took her hand, helping her across the slick surface.

"I promise, your aunt will be safe."

His words halted her ruminations. Seriously? She'd always wondered about the mind of the people who bought the Bratva's merchandise. How could he care so much about her aunt and still purchase humans as if they were no more than numbers on an invoice?

As if he read her mind, he stopped and blew out a breath of air that floated into the cold air in a swirling white puff. "I am not unaffected by your poorly hidden scorn. I'm not a good person by any stretch of the imagination. I'm not pretending to be one. You, my dear concierge, are not in a place to judge me or my actions. I believe you are stuck in a web of your own design, as am I. I'll try not to judge you. I would appreciate the same consideration."

Tatyana broke away from his gaze. The sincerity in it struck her hard. She nodded, and they continued to the warmth inside. He turned over her phone at the security checkpoint and escorted her to her room after they were both scanned. Obviously, he didn't trust her not to try to slip a device onto his person.

"Sleep well, Tatyana. Hannah will be here in the morning to assist you with whatever you need. I expect you to take your meals with me. I exercise every morning from six until eight. If you'd care to accompany me, have Hannah bring you to the gymnasium. Good night." He dropped a soft kiss onto her forehead and turned down the cold dark passageway. She watched until he opened the set of doors at the end of the hall. He turned and winked before he shut the doors to his bedroom.

She stared at his closed doors for several long seconds before she pivoted on her heel and entered her room. Their conversation, no, make that this entire situation, disturbed her on a basic level. She'd been living and working with the Bratva for years. She understood the deviants that dealt with the criminal element she represented. There was a common lust for the forbidden, a desire for the unattainable and a need to be perceived as ultimately powerful. What was his impetus for dealing with the Bratva? True, David struck her as extremely dangerous, but he lacked that... Tatyana considered what it was he lacked. She couldn't put her finger on what was missing, or perhaps present, to make her question his involvement. She'd learned how to read people and what her gut was telling her wasn't what her mind perceived. There were too many unknowns to formulate an opinion.

Taty broke out of her swirling thoughts and gawked at the room she'd been given. A fire crackled in the fireplace, and her king-sized canopied bed had been turned down. The affluence and excess in her suite alone were astonishing. The man could be a tyrant, but he wasn't. David Xavier was a consummate gentleman, which acted as more fuel for her suspicion and concern.

Jewell drew a deep breath and squinted at the computer screen. She pushed up her glasses and rubbed her eyes. *What freaking time was it anyway?* She glanced down at the time and date icon and suddenly felt tired. It was 2:14... but morning or afternoon? She looked around at her bodyguard. Zane's face lit up from the glow of his tablet. He was a very attractive man, but a royal pain in her ass. It didn't help that her brothers had given him carte blanche to stick his nose into her business. She squinted at him before she turned back to the computer screen. His voice carried across the room. "You have two more hours before we are leaving for an early dinner."

Jewell spun and lifted her bare feet into her over-sized ergo-something leather chair. "What in the hell did you do to get assigned as my wet nurse?" She hadn't been able to find anything but laudatory comments in the man's files. He'd seen a shit-ton of action overseas, but had cross-trained into PSO duties. She'd never admit it to anyone, but the man was growing on her.

"Just lucky I guess. Have you finished the search?" He set his tablet down.

"Yeah, I'm waiting on a secondary validation before I go talk to Jason." She leaned back in her chair and closed her eyes.

"I'll call Sonya and make an appointment." Zane lifted his huge form out of the straight-backed chair. Damn, that thing looked uncomfortable. Jewell swept her office. There were no other chairs available. She swung back to her computers and ordered something more comfortable. Hell, she wasn't a bitch... well, not that much of one anyway. The man had never complained about the chair in the time that he'd been tagging after her. She had closed the screen before he turned back from talking to Sonya. Her notification box popped up at the same time. Jewell opened several windows and compared the numbers. Seven. Only seven. Atlanta, Houston, Las Vegas, Los Angeles, San Francisco, Boston, and Miami. Bingo. She needed to get the information to Jason... like, now.

She hit the print button and grabbed the sheets as they spit out. She headed toward the door. "Come on Starsky; this isn't going to wait for an appointment."

She didn't wait to see if he was following her. They had a way to close down the intake portion of the Bratva in the United States. Halle-fucking-lujah all those hours had paid off. Finally!

CHAPTER 9

A feeling of mild annoyance had followed Mike out of the gymnasium this morning and continued to grow as he approached the empty breakfast table. Garrett had been relentless and talked way too much. His endless chatter and questions grated on Mike's nerves. Tatyana's no-show at the gym or at breakfast was what was really pissed him off, but Garrett's overt friendliness of late blurred the lines Mike had drawn.

He turned on his heel and strode toward Tatyana's suite. Her absence for breakfast nudged the irritation into anger. Granted, he was tired. He'd worked every possible scenario of the altered mission parameters last night before he retired for three hours of sleep. While he didn't like the fact that he was going to use a physical relationship to get this job done, he would follow through with his planned seduction. She might not have been a participant in all the crimes that had been committed by the Bratva, but she was the singular key he had to affirm the meeting took place. Mike would do everything in his power to link her to him and only him. The fate of thousands depended on the success of this mission.

He strode down the hall and opened her chamber doors without knocking. The room was shrouded in total darkness. He allowed his eyes to adjust and moved quietly toward the bed. She was curled up into a tiny ball in the middle of the massive mattress. Her brown curls fell over her cheek, exposing only the tip of her nose and her full rose colored lips. In her slumber, she looked small and vulnerable. Opposite of the ice-cold Bratva concierge his reports described. The head of his security detail had repeatedly warned him of the peril of keeping a member of the Bratva under his roof, but his lead security specialist had no way of knowing what was going on under his nose.

He sat down on the side of the bed and leaned over. He threaded his fingers through her silky brown hair and pushed it away from her face. Her eyes twitched in her sleep moving her long lashes. A sprinkle of freckles fell over her nose. Her makeup had concealed that beauty from him. He preferred her without makeup. He placed his hand over hers. "Are you going to sleep the entire day away?"

She stirred and buried herself deeper into the covers. A faint hum was her only reply. He allowed a small laugh at her response. She stiffened and pushed to the other side of the bed. She was up on her knees and immediately ready to defend herself. Mike raised his hands in a symbolic gesture. "You failed to show for breakfast. I came to see if you were being obstinate."

He watched as his words sunk in. She relaxed for a moment before she grabbed at the sheet covering her silk camisole and thong. He'd be lying if he didn't admit he'd noticed her small, hard-peaked breasts, tight abs, and perfect ass. The woman's body flipped every switch he had.

"You scared me. What time is it?" Her accent was thick first thing in the morning and held a different sound, more rustic than the usual. Her w pronounced with a sharp v sound.

"A few minutes after nine."

"I'm sorry. I rarely oversleep." She swiped her curls away from her face and blinked owlishly, as if she was trying to orient herself.

"I won't deny I enjoyed finding you snuggled in bed." Mike let his eyes travel over the skin not covered by the silk sheets. "Although I think I would have preferred it if you were waiting in my bed."

He studied her, waiting for a response. Her expressive hazel eyes traveled to his. There was shock and confusion before understanding settled. He had a front row seat as her mask fell into place. The undiluted version of the woman he was dealing with was hidden once again. Tatyana cocked her head and dropped the silk sheet. There was nothing he could do to prevent his body's reaction. His cock filled at her willing offering. He stood and put his hands in his pockets as if he could camouflage his desire. "If that is an offer, Tatyana, I will accept. However, I must refrain until tonight. Business before pleasure. I'll send Hannah in shortly. She should have awakened you earlier. I'll make certain the staff knows to attend to your needs. Lunch will be served promptly at one. Don't be late." He turned to walk away but changed his mind. No, he needed to set the tone for the relationship. He stalked around the bed to her. She turned as he approached. He reached out and tenderly pulled her against him. His erection pushed against her abdomen. Mike cupped her chin and studied her face before he lowered his lips slowly. He ghosted a kiss across them and felt a shiver run through her. He lowered again and let the union linger. Her lips opened under his, but he moved away. Her eyes opened and locked with his. Her breaths came shallow and fast, and her pupils were wide, blown to the edge of her irises. The desire in her eyes cemented the fact he *could* use her. He released her and walked out of the room before his lust overran his mission. He *would* seduce her, use her to finish the mission, and then he would walk away.

Taty sank onto the bed as he stalked out the door. Her hand rose to touch her tingling lips. Her hand shook because he'd startled her. It wasn't about the kiss. She flopped down onto the bed. That was a lie, but it wasn't just the kiss, it was the way he held her. His absolute possessive certainty that she would allow it. The sweetness of the kiss when he could have been ruthless. She ran both hands through her hair and groaned. If only things were different, but they weren't. She jolted at the soft knock on her door. *My assigned keeper no doubt.*

"Enter." She glanced over at the door and smiled at the older woman who balanced a breakfast tray in one hand as she came in.

"Ech, sorry lass. Had a wee bit of an emergency this morning. I was late, and dinna see we had a guest or your schedule until just couple minutes past. I hope my tardiness dinna cause you any troubles. The master of the castle was a wee bit huffy and puffy just now."

Tatyana smiled despite her emotional turmoil. Hearing David described as huffy and puffy was too funny to deny. "There was a problem. He was upset I didn't join him for breakfast. I slept through it." Taty allowed the woman to fluff a pillow behind her back and then settle the tray on her lap.

"Och, well if you slept through it, obviously you needed the rest, then. I dinna know if you wanted tea or coffee. I settled on coffee. If you'll be needing tea, I can pop out and fetch it."

"No, coffee is perfect, thank you." She poured out the strong brew and inhaled the wonderful aroma.

"I'll go run your bath. Oh, I'm Hannah, by the way. I'll be tending to you while you are with the master. I travel with his household." She went into the bathroom.

Tatyana called after her, "Do you know him well?"

Hannah peeked around the door. "What was that, lass?"

"My name is Tatyana. My friends call me Taty. Do you know David well?"

Hannah smiled. "As well as anyone can, I'm sure. The master is very private but polite and a gentleman. I've only worked for him for the past year. There were a core of us brought on after he fired the last lot. Rumors are they were not as discreet as necessary. I dinna know if that is the truth. From what I have seen he is a wonderful man. He is kind, generous to a fault and works far too hard. If it isn't business, he's working for any number of his charities. He'll drive himself into the ground with the schedule he keeps. My husband is his gentleman's gentleman. The hours the master keeps make that job trying for sure."

Taty let the conversation go as Hannah popped back into the bathroom. The sound of water played in the background as she drank her coffee and picked at a delicately fruited pastry. Hannah's description of David was counterintuitive to what she'd witnessed firsthand. The man she'd dealt with was cold, calculating and a criminal. Granted, he had a civil veneer, but that was an act. Up until the kiss this morning, she would have bet her life savings on that. But now...

"Your bath is ready, lass. Would you like me to wait to assist you with your wardrobe?"

Taty blinked. Repeatedly. *Help her with her wardrobe?* It was already unpacked. What? "Ummm... I'm not sure I know what that means?"

Hannah threw back her head and laughed. "Aw lass, it will be fun having you stay with us, that's for certain. Will ya be needing help into the bath or getting dressed afterward?"

Taty felt the blush of embarrassment creep up her face. "Oh. No, thank you. I won't need any help."

"Fine. I'll leave you to it then. The water will stay heated, no need to rush your breakfast. I'll pop back and give you the grand tour before lunch. The master said you'd be taking your meals with him from now on."

Taty nodded and tracked the older woman as she headed toward the door.

"It's good to finally see Mr. Xavier taking a shine to someone. Such a wonderful soul he is. There's a button on your dressing table. If you need anything, push it, and I'll be here in short order. Enjoy your coffee and your bath, lass."

Taty finished her coffee and wandered into the bathroom. The gentle aroma of the bath oils tickled her senses. She slipped out of her camisole and thong and slid under the perfectly warmed water. She closed her eyes as she relaxed back against the padded neck rest. The disconnected data points she'd just learned about David Xavier conflicted with her first-hand knowledge. Why would someone worth billions be willing to take part in human trafficking? She'd Googled him. Seriously, who wouldn't? He was reportedly the fourth richest man in the world. There was no reason for him to get involved at such an intimate level with the Bratva.

Taty turned on the bath jets and adjusted the pressure. The one thing she'd always relied on was her gut instinct. It had served her well, and she'd developed a sixth sense that kept her out of trouble during her years with the Bratva. That sixth sense was telling her David Xavier *wasn't* a criminal even though he *was* dangerous. He had no motive for doing what he was doing. Leverage? No, while plausible, it didn't pan out past a cursory level. The Bratva hierarchy was blinded by money. They wouldn't look at motive farther than to ascertain they were not being set up. The only reason she could determine they hadn't asked why the man was dangling an obscene amount of money in front of them was she was present and would warn them of any impending danger.

Taty pulled her knees up and rested her chin on them as the jets swirled the perfumed water around her. Without a doubt, all the information, conflicting and firsthand, boiled down into a very basic equation. She had a decision to make. Did she trust her instinct and look for the *real* reason David Xavier was playing such a dangerous game, or did she accept that the man who held her so tenderly this morning was an uncaring criminal?

"Are we set?" Jason's voice cut through the din of murmured comments in the operations center. Jared glanced over his shoulder and nodded. He was running point for this operation. With the information the tech team had been able to work, they were about to cut the Bratva's concierge service in the United States off at the knees. The operation was complicated and being done in one coordinated event. They couldn't alert the Bratva or the people involved at one site without sending the other six sites underground. So they were coordinating a simultaneous strike at all the sites. And now that Jewell had a way of locating the bastards that were identifying vulnerable people, they'd be able to monitor for the fuckers if they tried to set up business in another city.

He reviewed his team's positions. They'd mitigated as many circumstances as they could. Yeah, they were fucking ready. Seven cities, seven perps and seven teams of his investigators—all being monitored live. The kaleidoscope of screens showed all seven teams were set and waiting. Jacob and Tori entered the ops center and waited out of the way, but were there if needed. Jared acknowledged them both and turned to Jason, anticipating the command to proceed.

"Let's get it done." At Jason's words, Jared keyed his microphone. "All teams, we have a go." The echo of acknowledgment rang out. Jared's eyes raced from screen to screen. Jewell's technicians were damn good and the action being fed through the helmet cams was as clear as last evening's news on the local broadcast. Five of the perps were so stunned they froze when the teams approached, but two fled. Jared swiped the two screens that showcased the chases and threw them to the larger debriefing monitor so they could focus on the pursuit. The movement of the helmet cam would have made him sick to his stomach had he not been so focused. One perp was caught almost immediately. The other was fleeing through a congested building that he obviously knew far better than Jared's team. "Find out who had perimeter. I want to know why that asshole got out of the area." Jared threw that comment over his shoulder toward one of the three the IT gurus who were running the operation.

The foot race through the building shouldn't be happening. Someone blew it or was compromised. Neither was a good situation.

"We've lost him!" The shout rang over the comms.

"You have coverage of the building?" Jared spun, talking to the console operators. They all nodded but didn't say a word. Eyes glued to their screens, their hands flew over the keyboards. "There." One of the techs pointed toward the screen.

"Houston Leader we have a visual at the rear of the facility. Suspect is getting into a late model, red Chevy pickup." Jared released the mic key and directed his next comment to the computer operator. "Get me a plate."

"When he exits."

Jared watched his team spill out of the huge office building, now on the exterior cameras. The truck launched from its parking space. Instead of turning to exit the facility the truck turned right. "Holy fuck!" Jared keyed the mic, "Houston, watch out! Incoming!" The truck accelerated and headed straight for his team.

"Holy fuck, he's going to…" Jason's voice stilled as the truck slammed into the side of the building. The bird's eye view of shattering glass, crumpling metal and flying debris from the building froze everyone in the operation center for two heartbeats.

"Status, Houston!" Jared called the demand over the radio. He could see two of the team moving toward what remained of the cab of the truck, but there were three others unaccounted for. The seconds stretched before his lead answered, "We need an ambulance. Suspect is still alive. Two officers down."

"Houston PD has been notified sir, and two ambulances have been dispatched." Jared nodded before he relayed the information and asked, "Status of downed officers?"

"One is mobile, minor injuries, but sir... Harrison couldn't get out of the way. He was hit by the truck. Sir, you need to tell that ambulance driver to expedite."

CHAPTER 10

ike's fingers beat a rapid, staccato against his desk. The four video screens held David Xavier's personal net worth and charted to show the exponential growth over the last year. He nodded, glad that *his* investments while acting as David hadn't cost the man anything. The next screen held offshore accounts, shell companies and money tucked away in tax havens such as Grand Cayman. His tax lawyers and personal accounting firm were briefing him on the projections for the next two quarters. As was the norm, they couldn't see him, but they could hear a slightly modulated version of his voice. The few people he'd interacted with in the last year were an anomaly, as David Xavier had never allowed anyone to see him outside of his tightly held reality. The real David Xavier had decided to control his vast empire through masked video conferences, telephone calls, and anonymous, faceless contact. Which made Mike's cover perfect.

Mike stifled a yawn and scrolled through his email, pausing to read one marked urgent. The meeting had run through lunch, which irritated him more than it should have. He penned a quick note for Tatyana and had Joel give it to Hannah to deliver. The empty carafe of coffee on his desk had washed down a delicious meal that he'd mindlessly eaten as he waded through the tidal wave of information his lawyers and accountants detailed. He shook his head. He was going to need more caffeine. He'd gone days without sleep under the worst possible conditions, and here he was sitting in a chair that cost more than his truck, wearing a bespoke suit while sequestered in a warm, secure environment and he was tired. Fuck, he was getting soft. All the exercise programs in the world couldn't condition you for the extremes that had become the normality of his life. After the last mission with Alpha team, he'd settled into a routine. One that had obviously made him soft. He chuckled to himself at that thought. If Jacob, the Wonder Twins or Doc ever heard him admit that, he'd never live it down. He missed his brothers. And they were brothers, if not in blood, in spirit.

The screen flashed and drew Mike's attention. Oh, thank God, the summary. He leaned back in his chair and concentrated on the presentation. An hour and a half later, he killed the connection and rubbed his eyes.

Mike retrieved a folder from the corner of his desk. His security team was impressing him. Not to Guardian's caliber, but effective and efficient. The background information on Anya or Tatyana that he'd been given had some holes, but it was enough to confirm his suspicions. The aunt she spoke of did in fact exist, but she wasn't related to either Tatyana or her cover identity. The old woman's husband was Bratva, and so were her sons. There wasn't a threat to the woman. There was nothing forcing that little viper to stay in the Bratva's employment other than greed. The threats to her personal security could be mitigated enough to allow her to escape. No, if the Bratva wanted to find her, they would. He cracked his neck and reminded himself there was no smoking gun here. She worked for the Bratva, end of story.

He tossed the folder onto his desk and rubbed his eyes. He was disappointed that she'd lied. Admittedly, the woman intrigued him. Her beauty captured his imagination, and her sexuality drew his desire like a flame draws oxygen. But, she was spoiled, deadly fruit from a poisonous tree—a fruit he would devour in order to make sure no one else was harmed.

He needed to stretch his legs. A glance at his calendar confirmed his meetings were over for the day. Rightfully, he should be going through his correspondence, but he'd had enough. It was time to find the pretty doe-eyed woman who was evil to the core. The big brown eyes, curls, freckles and this morning's kiss floated through his mind. He pushed the warm thoughts away. He had a job to do. She was a means to an end and nothing more.

The fireplace in the master suite flickered, sending a warm light over the intimate dinner table. Mike sat holding his nightly cognac while he waited for Tatyana to arrive. He'd changed the location of their dinner so there would be no pretense as to his intentions. He swirled the amber liquid and gazed at the fire. He was in foreign territory. If she refused his advances, he'd have to figure out another means of tying her to him. He needed her stripped bare of pretenses, and an intimate relationship was the quickest way to reach that goal.

The door to his suite opened slowly. Tatyana stepped inside and took in the setting. She searched the room. When her eyes fell on him, he could sense her hesitation. He watched as she straightened her shoulders and slipped into the persona she wanted him to see. The tiny slivers of who she once was were hidden.

She walked across the floor toward him. Her pink skirt floated demurely away from her long legs. The matching top dipped enticingly between her breasts, exposing the delicate column of her neck to his eyes. She wore the same scent she'd chosen last night. The Nano RFID trackers that were mixed with the perfume when it was pushed through the antique atomizers not only activated the mission but would track his lovely distraction should she slip out of his control. He thanked the brilliant minds that were able to work the size of the trackers into picograms, which allowed trillions of the trackers to be produced from three grams of product. Now that the transmitter distance issue had been solved, the trackers were monitored from satellites. Guardian was the only agency using the new technology and the only ones who had the frequency to track them.

He rose and extended his hand to her. "You look beautiful." He noted the subtle blush to her cheeks and applauded her acting skills. If he didn't know what he did about her, he might have fallen for her demure act.

"Thank you. I'm sorry about this morning. Did Hannah explain that it wasn't my fault?"

He threw back his head and laughed hard. "Oh, Hannah explained in detail that it, and I quote, 'wasn't the lass' fault' and then reprimanded me about the expectation that you should join me in the gymnasium. Evidently, it isn't seemly for a young lass to sweat in front of her paramour."

He offered her a glass of cognac. She took it and swirled it in her hand. "Seems it is a foregone conclusion that you and I will be sleeping together."

He took a drink. He purposefully raked his gaze down her body and back up again. He needed to sell this bag of goods, and she needed to pony up and buy every bit of it. "I won't deny the fact that I want you.

We are together for the foreseeable future. You are free of the Bratva while under my care. Your aunt is being monitored to ensure her safety. Once the business necessities are over, you will be free to leave, or if the situation between us is mutually acceptable, you may stay as long as you want."

She glanced over at him and then down at her drink. "Would this be an exclusive situation?"

"By exclusive you mean?" He knew exactly what she meant, but he wanted to hear it anyway.

"There would be no others in your bed?"

"Do you think you're not enough to hold my attention?"

She sat the drink down and lifted off the chair to stand in front of him. She slowly lowered to her knees in between his legs. Her fingernails trailed up his thighs toward his swelling cock. "I'm more than enough to keep your attention."

Her fingers deftly unfastened his belt and released his filling shaft from his slacks. She traced the swelling bulge in his boxers through the silk and then palmed his length. "I'm impressed, Mr. Xavier." She maneuvered his hard cock out of the opening and fondled his balls as she extracted them. Her small hand circled his shaft and stroked up to the top. Mike drew shallow breaths. The sensation of Tatyana's soft, warm hand brought his orgasm raging forward. It had been years since he'd been with a woman. His self-enforced celibacy crumbled under her feather light touches. She held his stare as she lowered and sucked the head of his cock into her mouth. Mike closed his eyes and dropped his head back onto the cushion of the chair. His gut clenched when her tongue circled his foreskin, dipping in repeatedly to circle his head before she drifted lower and trailed along the vein under his cock. The magnitude of what he'd personally surrendered to ensure this mission succeeded slipped away, along with the reasons he needed to keep an emotional distance from the woman. His hands found their way to her hair. He gently cupped her head and followed the motion, not stopping or encouraging… just grounding himself. Tatyana lifted and drew a deep breath before she lowered onto his slick shaft. He could feel his cockhead at the back of her throat. She swallowed him down further. He fisted her hair and pushed deeper as he lost his load. His first orgasm brought on by anyone other than him in years. He released her, but she continued to swirl around his over-sensitive dick. He grabbed her under the arms and lifted her into his lap. Her lips covered his. He dipped his tongue into her mouth and tasted his release.

He leaned back and pushed her curls away from her face. "You are dangerous. I want what I shouldn't with you."

She leaned back in and kissed him softly but not before she murmured, "Take what you want."

CHAPTER 11

Taty grabbed at David's massive shoulders. He stood without any hesitation after she'd invited him to take what he wanted. His arms cradled her against his body, effortlessly carrying her toward the bed. He carefully set her down on the feather soft linens. He removed her shoes and traced the arch of each foot with his fingertips before he kissed each toe. She shivered at the erotic feel of his tongue against the sensitive flesh. Transfixed, she watched as he mapped her skin with tactile precision before he trailed a line of kisses up her calves. His fingers and lips left a trail of heat along the outside of her thighs. His hands pushed the material of her skirt up around her waist as his tongue traced the thin lace of the pink thong she wore. His large hands cupped her ass, and he pressed a kiss above her panties.

He captured her eyes with his, released her and then rose to his full height. His gaze held her prisoner as he unbuttoned his shirt. The crisp white linen contrasted vividly against his bronze skin as her eyes bounced from his hands to his exposed skin and then back to the dark, sensual heat of his eyes. The shirt fell away. My God, no wonder he could carry her as if she were nothing. The man's sculpted body was beyond beautiful. Even the darker lines of scars that tattooed his bulging arms and defined chest seemed to enhance his features. Everything about this man surprised her by being more. His chest and abdomen were hairless except for a small happy trail that formed just above his uncut cock, which was once again hardening. She'd never been with a larger man, either in physical build or... her eyes drifted down to his impressive shaft. Taty licked her lips in memory of his delicious taste. Michelangelo could have chiseled him in marble; he was that perfect. He turned, giving her a view of a scar on his thigh. The size and shape resembled a large caliber bullet hole.

All thoughts of his scars ceased when his hands danced up her legs and tugged at the material at her waist. She lifted her hips, allowing him to remove her skirt. Her shirt lasted only a few seconds longer as his fingers nimbly removed the cloth. He lifted onto the bed and straddled her. His fingers once again started their relentless pursuit of awakening every nerve ending in her body. He lightly traced her collarbone with his fingertips. His hands and eyes traveled over her throat around her jaw and then over her lips. He leaned down and kissed her softly before he began a slow, tortuous trail of touches, kisses, and licks to her breasts. He mouthed her nipples through the thin lace of her bra. Hot breath dampened the sheer lace fabric and cooled as he moved to worship her other breast. She panted in anticipation, her body's need overtaking any higher cognitive abilities. Her only thoughts were of him. His touch, his kiss, his scent and oh… God… his tongue.

An unbidden moan fell from her lips as his teeth found purchase and teased her through the lace. He lifted his head and smirked before wrapping his arms under her, moving up to take her mouth. He lifted her enough to unfasten her bra. His sensual assault once again stoking her need as his mouth and hands traveled down her body. He nipped the skin at her hip and licked the sting away. Her body bucked, trying to find anything to provide the friction she desperately needed. Her hands skated over the planes of muscle in his back and gripped the ropes of sinew that formed his shoulders and neck. She slid her hands into his hair and gasped when he snapped the material of her panties and sent the thong flying. A low rumble of laughter preceded his large hands cupping her hips and pressing her into the bed. He continued his assault, relentlessly adding layers and layers of sensation.

Tatyana grabbed his shoulders and tried to push him with absolutely no effect. Her overstimulated body wept in anticipation as he trailed his tongue along the apex of her sex.

"Please." She ran her hands through his hair and tugged, lifting his head. His dark eyes were hooded with lust when he drew them up her body. "Take what you need, David."

He blinked as if coming out of a trance. The desire in his eyes muted before he nodded. Taty felt she had said the wrong thing, but she had no idea. He stretched, reaching for the drawer of the bedside table.

Mike grabbed a condom, took a deep breath and rolled on the latex, using the time to ground himself. He'd lost his mind. Tatyana had bewitched him in ways he'd never experienced. He'd worshiped her body until she'd called him David. David, not Mike. He grabbed her thigh and twisted her over onto her stomach and then pulled her onto her knees. He couldn't look into her eyes knowing this wasn't real. He centered himself at her core. His hand tracked up her spine. He pushed her shoulders into the bed, gripped her hip with his free hand and entered her. The heat of her tight body branded him. Her soft whimper before she pushed her hips back asking for more seared through his mind. He hated himself. He hated the situation that brought him to this point, and he hated that he couldn't bring himself to stop.

"More, please."

"You want this?" He pulled out and slowly pushed back into her, giving her body time to accept his size.

"Oh… God… yes." She grabbed the sheets in her fists and moaned when he finally seated his cock deep inside her. "Take me hard."

Mike wrapped a handful of her brown curls around his fingers. He lifted her up and positioned her against his chest. She gasped, and then her soft, sexy laugh filled the air. He pulled back and drove into her. His eyes rolled to the back of his head from the sensation. It had been years since he'd enjoyed the pleasures of a woman. She pushed back as he thrust forward. He gritted his teeth against the flood of white-hot pleasure pooling in his balls. God forgive him, he didn't want to want this woman… but he did.

He pulled out and spun her onto her back. Mike scooped the tiny woman up and moved her onto his lap, holding her with her legs draped over his arms. His cock found her center, and he lowered her onto his shaft. She wrapped her arms around his neck and held on. Their eyes clashed as he lifted her. He slammed his cock into her as he dropped her body. She clenched her eyes closed, let her head loll back and gasped, "Fuck, yes!"

Mike set a punishing pace. Her body jolted with each thrust, and God help him; he loved the feel of her around his cock. Her fingernails scored his skin as he consumed her moans and gasps. Right now, the evil in this woman didn't matter. The only thing that did was that she was in his arms and that she desperately wanted what he was giving her. God knew he wanted it too.

He cradled her closer and took a nipple into his mouth, lurching forward and pushing her onto the bed at the same time. He nipped her taut skin before he lifted her leg over his hip and ground deep into her. He could feel sweat pooling between them as he worked to bring them to release. She ran her hands through his hair and pulled him down. Her huge brown eyes open and staring at him. "Don't stop. I'm... don't..."

Mike groaned when she came. Her entire body tightened, and then her heat clutched him in a rippling, sucking sensation that enticed him over the edge. His shout as his orgasm blazed up his cock was instinctual and unbidden. He dropped onto her momentarily to gain his breath and some semblance of vision. His mind worked well enough to remember to grip the top of the condom. He slid out of her before he moved to her side and disposed of the filled latex.

She rolled into his chest, and he draped his arm over her. There were no words exchanged. There was nothing he could say. Sex with Tatyana was as phenomenal as it was horrible. Horrible, because putting this woman behind bars would be one of the hardest things he'd ever be required to do. She leaned forward and kissed his chest softly. He froze for a moment and then leaned down to kiss her forehead. Perhaps *the* hardest thing he'd ever done.

CHAPTER 12

Taty clung to the warmth of his hard body when he rolled off her. She wasn't a virgin, hell she was thirty-five-years-old. She'd had sex, but she'd never had sex like that. The exotic, gorgeous man that held her made love to her like no one else ever had. *Made love?* Taty trailed her finger over his chest, watching his muscles jump in response to the sensation. *Did he make love to her?* No, they were most assuredly not making love. They fucked, but the way he treated her... the tenderness... it was the closest thing to making love she'd ever experienced.

His arm lay over her back, giving her the illusion that he was holding her, protecting her. She leaned forward and kissed his chest. He tensed momentarily before he dropped a warm kiss on her forehead. The dichotomy the man presented continued to baffle her. She'd wracked her brain looking for a sensible rationale for his business dealings with the Bratva. There was no reason that she could conceive of that would bring this man to the Russian mafia. Everything she'd discovered about him screamed that his association with criminals was off... somehow suspicious. If Taty didn't know for certain using him would lead her to an introduction to her boss, she'd have walked away and told the Bratva it was a trap.

Her finger stopped her mindless wandering across his chest. It did feel like a trap for the Bratva. *Virgin Mary, could it be?* Was this man trying to lure the Bratva? Was he using the insane amount of money to blind them to his intentions? But he was American. Was he CIA? No... the staff, the house, the opulence... even the best-funded intelligence operations couldn't put up this smoke screen, and David Xavier was real. He was a billionaire, many times over.

She leaned away from him and met his eyes. For a split second, she saw sadness and then his feelings shuttered. How could she ascertain the truth? Was there a way without compromising everything she'd worked so damn hard to acquire?

"What has you so concerned, little one?" His words ghosted across her skin, bringing the hair of her arms up in an instant reaction.

She searched his face for any indication that her extrapolations could be true. It was the only thing that made sense. The only piece that fit into the puzzle David Xavier had presented her. She sat up, taking the sheet with her. Her hair flopped into her eyes. He lifted his hand and swept her curls aside. "Tell me." He lifted onto his elbow.

She opened her mouth to speak and then stopped. She narrowed her eyes and thinned her lips before she blurted, "I think you're building a trap for the Bratva."

He stared at her blankly for a few seconds before he rolled off the bed and walked into his massive closet. "I'm a businessman, not a police agency." His voice carried from behind the wall. He walked out with a robe in his hand, wearing only a pair of exercise pants.

That wasn't a denial.

He handed her the robe that she slid over her shoulders. The sleeves of the robe hung a good six to ten inches past her fingertips and the silk material pooled at her feet. The giggle that escaped merged with a deep chuckle from David. He made quick work of rolling up her sleeves. She hoisted the belt, which had draped around her ass, to her actual waist where she tied it and folded the lower fabric over the top making a small balloon drape. It wasn't sexy, but it allowed her to walk without tripping.

She trailed behind him as he opened the door to his rooms. She sighed. He was escorting her back to her room. When he kept walking past her door, she ran a few steps to catch up with his long strides. "Where are we going?"

"To the kitchen. Our dinner is long past cold, and I've released the staff for the night."

"Oh." Taty's feet were cold, but she kept up with him as he made his way through the twists and turns of the rambling mansion. They pushed through a door, and he flipped on the light. The fluorescent bulbs illuminated a massive commercial kitchen with four, eight-burner stoves. A wall with six ovens, three broiling stations, huge stainless steel sinks and countertops caught her attention. Copper pots and silver pans hung from the massive center island. David strode over to the wall-sized refrigeration and freezer units. He started opening random doors.

"What are you doing?" She pulled some of the material out of the fold at her waist and stood on it. Her toes were going to freeze. The chalet needed better heating.

"Looking for something quick and easy." He glanced over his bare shoulder and winked. "You made me work up an appetite."

She shook her head and marched over to where he stood looking into the freezer. "Men. Go, find two baguettes." She shooed him toward the pantry before she marched over to the oven and turned it on. A quick wash of her hands and a two-minute search later, she had eggs, three types of cheese, chives and flat leaf parsley on one of the islands.

David returned with two foot long loaves of French bread. She laughed and split one in half. "Here, dig out the center, but leave enough to form a boat." She peeled most of the soft interior of her half out and waited for him to finish. "Now on both sides put down slices of cheese. You do this one."

He took the shredded cheese and watched her for a second before he scattered it carefully over the bread. Her fingers quickly layered the other cheeses on both boats as he finished. She nodded toward the open shelving. "Now we need a small bowl, a cutting board and a knife." Taty smiled at the soft whistling she heard as he gathered the needed supplies. When he returned, she had him break six eggs into the bowl while she minced the chives and parsley together. The herbs were sprinkled on top of the cheese.

"Now we pour the eggs. Three in this half, three in that one." She grabbed a baking sheet and carefully placed the stuffed boats on the sheet and then into the oven under the broiler.

"What did we just make?" David grabbed her waist and sat her on top of the counter. The cold stainless steel brought an undignified squeal from her. He laughed and cupped her ass, lifting her off the counter. She wrapped her arms around his neck and snuggled closer to his warmth. "That is a poor man's quick version of a Khachapuri."

He hoisted her higher, so their eyes met. His eyebrow lifted, and a smirk spread across his face. "And I repeat, what did we make?"

She scrunched her nose at him making him laugh. "Basically, this is a cheese sandwich with egg. When I was growing up, my mother would make the bread and form them into little boats. The cheese was usually the last bits and pieces that she'd keep in a bag. Many different flavors. The egg, sometimes yes, sometimes no... but it is always good. Food for the heart."

"Russian home cooking?"

"No. Georgian. My mother would not be happy if I didn't correct you. She was proud of her heritage." The childhood memories of better times tugged at her heart. She dropped her head to his shoulder and melted into him as one arm rubbed her back and the other literally held all her weight. The sense of security his presence evoked pulled at her.

"If you are trying to stop them, I may be able to help you." The momentary hesitation of his hand against her back was the only indication that he'd heard her.

"Once again, I'm a businessman. I didn't say I was trying to stop them." His words rumbled through his chest under her ear.

"You didn't deny it, either." She leaned back, and he lowered her to the floor. Without heels, he towered over a foot taller than her. His muscled frame stepped back allowing her to talk without straining her neck back to see him. She peered straight into his dark eyes and stated, "The people I work for should not be trifled with, David. You have no reason to associate with these men. This leverage you talk of? It is *dzalian t'kheli*. Too thin. You throw all this money at their greed. It blinds them." She leaned against the counter and watched him closely. He walked around the stainless steel island in what appeared to be an aimless meandering. The fluorescent lighting highlighted the darker scars on his shirtless back.

"I'm just a businessman." He put his hands in his pockets and rocked onto the heels of his bare feet a couple of times

"A businessman with a large bore rifle wound to his thigh?" She shook her head while keeping him pinned with her stare.

"A hunting accident."

"Someone shot you while you were hunting?"

"While *they* were hunting."

"I have a hard time believing that. You do what you must, but I've offered you good advice. Walk away."

"Why would you want to cross the people who could cause harm to your aunt?"

Taty caught a whiff of aroma from the oven. She walked across the expanse of the kitchen and glanced at the golden-brown crispy bread, melted cheese, and perfectly poached eggs under the broiler. "The woman isn't my aunt. She is part of the cover the Bratva gave me."

She removed the baking sheet from the oven, and put the food on top of the burners to let it cool. His silence prompted her more directly than a question would have. His neutral expression hid the mental gymnastics her admission *had* to have caused. His reactions, or rather the lack thereof, tugged at her gut bringing her up short. *Finally!* His neutral expression and silence were the anomalies that confirmed he wasn't the typical buyer. Her instinct had been honed working with the Bratva. She was right. This man's motivation and desire made him different from every other client that had crossed her path. If somehow she'd misread him and he told the Bratva of this conversation, she'd die. *Chemu byt', togo ne minovat'.* What will be, will be. She'd made peace with that possibility years ago. Exhaustion, frustration and lack of communication with her superiors had beaten her. Her mind made up, she turned, crossed her arms over her stomach, and waited.

He walked to the cabinet and retrieved two plates before he asked, "Then why, if there is no threat to you or your family, are you working with the Bratva?"

She examined the end of the silk belt in her hand before she lifted her shoulders and held her head high. She'd play this chess game. Somewhere between the lies and the deceit that lay thick between them was the reason someone as powerful as David Xavier was trying to enter the Bratva's world. She contemplated him for several long seconds before she spoke. "Vengeance."

CHAPTER 13

"Vengeance?" He couldn't hide the disbelief in his question. *Vengeance?* Mike's thoughts swirled around the foreign concept. His shocked question should never have been uttered. His absolute incredulity shattered any trust building between them.

"Yes, I want to stop selling people. I told you they tricked me into this." Tatyana's voice echoed around the vast kitchen area. Her face flushed red and a vein in her neck pulsed. The emotion appeared real, but he sure as hell wasn't going to be drawn into any of her half-truths. There was too much at stake.

"Unfortunately, what you want and what I need are at opposite ends of the spectrum. You'll place my order tomorrow. I'll give you a verbal list of my requirements in the morning. You'll memorize it. I will escort you out of my residence at the prearranged time so your superiors can make contact."

He watched her closely. Her eyes roamed the room, and she pulled her hand through her curls. The silk robe slipped down, baring her shoulder. With a frustrated tug, she righted the fabric. She paced back and forth on the other side of the stainless steel counter. "You don't understand them. You will never have leverage on these men you fill the orders for. The Bratva will have leverage on you! They will expose you if you do not do their bidding." She stopped and braced both hands on her hips. "They will own *you*."

"No," Mike spoke with certainty. He had faith the operation he currently worked was the best Guardian could provide.

"No? Just No? You have a problem with your ears, yes?" Tatyana stared at him, her eyes wide and her chest heaving. Her accent became more pronounced the madder the conniving, frustrating, manipulative woman grew.

"No, I heard every word you said. Are the sandwiches done?" He glanced over her shoulder, purposefully shifting the conversation. He needed the distance of time to evaluate *this* version of Tatyana. The layers of lies she'd told solidified his belief he would never be able to trust a word that came out of her mouth. She still lied. He'd bet a sizeable amount of David Xavier's fortune on that fact. The question was—what was her endgame?

"Sandwiches?" Her eyes narrowed, and her voice rose an octave. "You want to eat when I'm telling you this is a disaster waiting to happen?"

Mike picked up the plates and walked to the stove where the food sat cooling. "I do. Sex makes me hungry." He winced when he said the words. It wasn't his nature to purposefully toy with a woman, but he needed to resume control of this situation. She was siding with him now. That is what he wanted and what he'd work to strengthen. He'd never trust her. She was Bratva. Period. He considered her tangent about wanting vengeance another carefully constructed lie. He would use her to help end the human trafficking ring and then go back to South Dakota while she rotted in a prison cell.

He plated both of the sandwiches and grabbed forks and knives on the way to a small break room for the kitchen staff, off the main work area. He deposited the food and headed back out to the kitchen to grab a couple of beers. She trailed him to the table and sat down. She didn't eat, but he did. He wasn't lying. He was hungry, and the woman's Khachapuri thingy was damn good. The yolk was soft enough to run over the crisp bread, and the melted cheese made the entire thing fantastic. He demolished his half of the sandwich while she stewed on the other side of the table.

"You are not facing facts." She pushed her plate away.

"Are you going to eat that?" Mike pointed his knife toward her food.

"No."

He moved her plate toward him and cut into the bread. "I ignore very little, Tatyana. I have business to transact. You are the broker I need to work with to achieve my goal. Your desire for vengeance does not necessitate action on my part." He took a bite of the bread, egg and cheese mixture. What he wanted to say was 'you fucking made your bed, lady. Now lie in it'.

"I'm a pawn in your game." Her soft voice floated across the table to him. He had no idea what realization hit her, but he could tell she'd come to some conclusion.

"I never play games. You are a beautiful woman, Tatyana. I enjoy our intimate time together. You are not in my confidence. I don't trust you. I don't trust the Bratva. I have faith in my abilities, alone. I'm sorry if you thought I'd assist you in some epic scheme to avenge past wrongs." He finished her meal in silence, and wiped his mouth and leaned back in his chair.

"I'm more pragmatic than you give me credit for, David. I will have my vengeance. If not with your assistance, then so be it." She lifted her beer bottle to her lips and drank the entire thing in one go. If there was bravado involved in her statement, he couldn't detect it.

"Good to know." He stood, leaving the dishes and

empty beer bottles. "Shall we?" She rose from the table and walked with him through the cool corridors toward his wing of the mansion. He stopped outside her suite of rooms and opened her door.

She glanced inside and then at him. "I take it my services are no longer required?"

Mike forced himself to smile and pushed her curls out of her face. The silky hair wrapped around his finger. He tugged it lightly before he whispered, "I don't recall forcing you."

"You didn't." She pushed her cheek into his hand.

"We part here for the night." He shrugged before adding, "I sleep alone."

She untied the belt to his robe and slid it off her shoulders, revealing the expanse of her naked skin. Her nipples were hard and peaked. The soft glow of a dying fire cast a golden hue around her body. Tatyana glared at him as she held out the robe. He took it as she shut the door.

Mike rolled his shoulders and cracked his neck. The tension of his unnatural actions, words, and mannerisms rode hard on his conscience. God knew how much it cost him to treat a woman like a piece of meat. He'd seen his mother endure that shame from too many men. He'd sworn he'd never treat a woman like that, and yet here he stood. The ghosts of his past bore witness to his pain because, during this mission, no one else could.

Knowing he wouldn't be able to sleep; Mike pulled a folder out of his bedroom's wall mounted safe. A picture of his mother and the man he was told was his father lay on top. He'd turned the photo over and picked up his mother's last letter to him. He'd received it two months before he'd been accepted into Guardian. Her handwriting scrawled across the sheet of paper that had been torn out of a spiral notebook. She'd asked for more money. He sent every dime he didn't use to exist to her each month, but her rant scribbled in a gush of misspelled words accused him of forsaking her and his heritage. She called him worthless, told him he was a mistake and he was the reason she'd never found a good man. He would never be loved; he was cursed. He'd heard it all before. Each time she'd fall into the bottle the words would lance his heart. He flipped the photograph over and traced his mom's smiling face. He loved her with a fierce devotion only a child could manifest. Each time she belittled him, he built a stronger wall against her hurtful words and the pain he felt at neither being fully Sioux or fully white. He was stuck in the middle, rejected by both worlds, and wanted by no one. Yet, he'd accepted his life with a utilitarianism that allowed him to function until he joined Alpha team. The sense of purpose, fellowship and belonging he found with his brothers fed his soul and allowed him to flourish.

He shut the folder and closed his eyes. Visions of Jacob, Doc, Dixon, and Drake filled his mind. He would spill his blood to protect those men, as they would for him. He thought of the poor ones bought and sold by the Bratva. They had no champion. He felt their pain. It was with that singular thought in mind that he developed the list of requirements for the sex slaves he was purchasing. He'd give the requirements to his little Bratva representative tomorrow. The list in itself was benign. Females. Five with brown hair, five with light hair, five with red hair. Sixteen youngest, nineteen oldest. There would be no other requirements. The people the Bratva had already kidnapped could fill this order, and he'd be ensuring fifteen young women would be returned to their lives. The team he'd worked with for the first five months of his undercover operation had thought the preorder through. The amount of money that would be transferred for the minimal work the Brotherhood would have to perform would either entice them or caution them. It was the massive second order that would set a trap for the bastards.

Mike stood and rubbed his face as he dropped the folder into the safe, securing it. He turned and focused on the bed where he'd ended his self-imposed celibacy. Tatyana's scent taunted him. The echoes of the acts they'd performed replayed in his mind. He shook his head and massaged the back of his neck. Whatever game the woman was playing, he absolutely could not get entwined. The operation was too important. The woman was only a single piece of the massive puzzle, a tool he'd use to get his job done. He cringed at the reality of it, but it could be no other way. He slid into the sheets and pulled a pillow into his arms. Small crackles from the fire-place broke the quiet darkness. His mind raced through the details the events of tomorrow would require from him. With Tatyana's declaration tonight, a wild card had been thrust into the mix of possibilities. Vengeance was a volatile emotion, a feeling that could force smart people to make stupid mistakes. He'd have to keep her close. He already monitored her every move, but he would need to inform David Xavier's security team of their upcoming responsibilities outside the chalet, plus the requirement to surveil her in New York and San Diego. Mike groaned at the thought. He'd make sure the transaction was completed. There was no alternative.

CHAPTER 14

Tatyana sat in her gilded cage while Hannah bustled around the room cleaning imaginary dust from the immaculately maintained quarters. The book she held in her hand was a prop to allow her to escape the matronly woman's cheery banter. It had taken all of thirty seconds to memorize the list David had recited to her at breakfast this morning. He'd explained he wouldn't be able to stay or have lunch or dinner with her today. More than once the thought that she'd screwed up by opening up to him raced through her mind. Death while working for the Bratva was a constant threat, but the reality that she may have misstepped escalated her fear level.

"I'll make time to escort you tonight so the Bratva may make contact." His words this morning gave her a serious reason to pause. Although his charming veneer didn't slip, she wondered if last night was

some type of conquest for him. Perhaps she'd be relegated to a convenient fuck, or maybe he was done with her? A shiver ghosted across her skin. Maybe he was contacting the Bratva and informing them of her admission. But how? She was his point of contact. No, he'd known how to reach out to them when she was tapped on the shoulder to meet with him, didn't he?

The constant back and forth of her mind's deliberations forced her out of the room earlier. He'd given her leave to ramble about the chalet, which she did at length this morning, ending up back at the massive library on the ground floor. She'd brought several books back to her rooms to fill the long, drawn-out minutes of the day.

"It is a shame about the explosions isn't it?" Hannah trudged through the sitting area with her hands full of new towels.

"Explosions? I'm sorry, what?" Taty put the book down and followed Hannah into the ensuite.

"Have you seen the news?"

Taty shook her head.

"Well, I dinna know that. Those radicals in the Middle East, they blew up a whole town in retaliation for something. Who knows what this time? But the pictures coming out of the region? They break my heart. Little ones hurt and the parents unable to help. Young lives being torn apart. The master is working hard to send humanitarian aid. He was up at three this morning, right after it happened. The master said he missed his gym time and has been working nonstop, except for the quick breakfast he had with you this morning.

"He's sending humanitarian aid?" Why would missing his gym time be so damn important?

"What? Of course. Omega International is his. He has so many companies, and most of them have the la-de-da big wigs running them, and they report to him, you understand? Omega is more... I dinna know, personal, I guess. The man has a heart for service the size of which I've never seen."

"He has a big heart?"

"Absolutely. The man wouldn't be rude to a cockroach if it ate his last sandwich. I've never worked for such a selfless person." Hannah glanced over her shoulder. "Do you want me to run you a bath? The master might not be down for dinner, but I've been instructed to have it served in his quarters again."

Tatyana smiled and nodded. "Thank you, Hannah."

The woman beamed from ear to ear. "Och, 'tis my pleasure, Miss Taty. You give me something to do!"

Tatyana wandered back to the sitting area. Her gut *was* right. She knew it was. There was nothing about David Xavier that added up to his buying innocent lives. She'd find a way through the armor he'd surrounded himself with and ensure she was included at that meeting with the Bratva. She'd hate to use him to get to the head of the serpent, but there was no other way.

Taty closed her eyes while she listened to Hannah moving around the bathroom and wondered what her handlers back in London were thinking. She'd never gone more than two days without dropping a line in the shadow email account set up to communicate. Regardless, MI6 would have to deal with the ramifications of David Xavier finding his way into her undercover operation. To stop the scum she worked with, she'd sold her soul. A black hole had been carved deep in the center of her chest by her actions while employed by Bratva organization. That hole could only be filled by one thing. Revenge. She was the Bratva's exclusive concierge for the ultimate illicit fantasy for the fanatically wealthy. The Bratva trusted her—to a point.

She'd been undercover for eight years and worked for the Bratva for five. She'd worked her way up the ranks. Tatyana knew everyone in the organization *except* the key players. Her handler at MI6 wanted the bastard at the top. *The* boss. She'd yet to meet him, but the day she did, she was going to take him down. She'd fantasized about killing him. It didn't matter if she'd die or spend the rest of her life in jail. The scum who did this to people? He didn't deserve to breathe, and Tatyana wished it was her destiny to make sure he went straight to the special place in hell reserved just for him. She'd sworn on her sister's life that she'd make them pay. *Every. Last. One.*

Taty recalled the young ones of her last delivery. Was the cost of bringing the entire system down worth the cost these vulnerable young men and women paid on a daily basis? She tried hard not to cry behind her closed eyelids. *Now was not the time to show weakness.*

She focused on remembering the smallest details about the people she'd helped sell. Tatyana documented every person she delivered, down to birthmarks, both for the Bratva and for MI6. For MI6, she also provided DNA samples for most of the merchandise. Simply gathering samples of hair or fingernails risked her life. Getting the information to her handlers was even more dangerous. She had no idea if MI6 retrieved the information. The communication back to her had always been sparse.

Regardless, she continued to make the drops. She delivered the DNA samples weeks after the transactions to avoid any attention to her actions. She left the evidence at different, prearranged locations, the list of drops meticulously adhered to so her handler knew exactly where to retrieve the information and evidence she'd planted.

She monitored the ghost email account they established for communication religiously. Simple and effective, they both logged in under the same username and password, wrote draft emails and left them for the other to read and delete. They constructed messages in practically untraceable code.

Tatyana was close. So damn close. Soon, she'd sever the snake's head and blow open the operation. She didn't know if her agency had rescued any of the people she delivered, but she hoped so. *Hope.* What a joke. Unless she succeeded, the "cargo" she delivered had none. Regardless, she would stay the course, and she would reach the top of the organization.

She'd been working for eight lonely, miserable years to get to this point. Originally, she'd approached MI6 with the information she'd gleaned from the massive kidnapping that almost decimated her small country village. She'd returned there from university when her baby sister and at least ten other girls had been abducted. Her advanced degree in linguistics and fluid accent made it easy for her to blend in and follow the kidnappers' trail. She couldn't approach the FSB, the Federal Security Service of the Russian Federation. It was fraught with corruption. MI6 was her only hope. Initially, they'd refused to listen or to look at her information, but she'd persisted. After an extensive background check and training, MI6 assigned her as an under-cover operative.

Her mission was to integrate into the organiza-tion and make herself indispensable. Her only objec-tive was to reach the head of the organization and have enough evidence to convict the son of a bitch in international court. She *was* the singular tool to take the head off the snake. She'd documented the countless underlings, the arms of the beast which included methods, covers, money laundering, acqui-sitions, holding and training of the merchandise. While she worked, the serpent grew in reach and strength. The operation was now global and vastly lucrative.

David Xavier was an unknown. She needed to ensure the man had reason to keep her around and if that meant using sex as a lure, then she'd bait the hook. She must be included in the meeting, and David Xavier was the key. With a course of action solidified, she found a new resolve to do what needed to be done—seduce David Xavier into trusting her, and finish her mission.

Taty carried the dinner she'd whipped up precariously in one hand and knocked on the door to David's office with the other. A muffled response called her in. The guard who had escorted her from the well-guarded entrance of this private wing opened the door for her. She waited for David to look up. His suit jacket was off, his tie loosened and his crisp white shirt was wrinkled. His sleeves were folded haphazardly up his forearms. It looked as if he'd been carding his fingers through his hair. He gave her a sideways glance and did a double take.

"What are you doing here?" His brow creased as he looked past her to the outer offices. The guard stood behind her. David motioned for him to leave. Thankfully.

"It is almost eleven. Your staff has gone for the night. You didn't come down for dinner. I found the kitchen again and made you something to eat." She entered his office and set the tray at a conversation group near the door. She didn't want to give him any reason to think she was there to spy on him.

When he hadn't come down for dinner or shown up after, she'd groused around in the chalet's massive refrigerator and mixed together another of her mother's favorite recipes, mashed potato pancakes stuffed with meat and cheese and fried. She also brought two of the beers he'd chosen last night. Glancing up from the small table she caught his questioning gaze. "What?"

"Why?" His one-word reply held no indication of irritation, so she answered honestly.

"Because you've spent your day making sure people got the help they so desperately needed. I thought it was only fair someone took care of you." She popped the top off both beers and settled back into the chair.

"I employ people to cook for me. You are not required to do so." He swiveled in his chair and gave her his full attention.

She shrugged. "I know. What can I say? You are the only reason I'm here. Your guards escorted me out to await the call from my employers. I made sure they heard the entire fifteen-second interaction. I gave the Bratva the order and told them to call tomorrow night at 7:00 just as your guard instructed." She nodded toward the food on the tray. "Now be a good little billionaire and come eat your food."

He lifted away from the desk and stretched, drawing her eyes to the impressive form under the clothing. The sharp angles of his face and dark features were drawn. Judging by the dark circles under his eyes, he hadn't had much sleep. He made his way over to the conversation group and flopped into the huge bat-winged leather chair.

Closer, she could see lines around the corners of his mouth and noticeable tension in his shoulders. "Were you able to get aid to the victims?"

His head snapped up at her words.

She answered the question he spoke with his eyes. "Hannah."

"Ah." He reached for the beer and leaned back once again. His focus on the colored glass seemed reflective, so she patiently waited for him to speak. "The organization does a great deal of good when we can. Some areas are harder to reach than others. Navigating the political quagmire and bribes needed to gain access to the area the victims are in has been... trying."

Her stomach sank for the innocent lives caught in the crossfire of the political and religious posturing. "So, no relief has gotten to the victims?"

His shoulders slumped, accompanied by the slow shake of his head. He lifted haunted eyes. "An embedded journalist from the UK managed to get word out. The people who have survived are being hunted down. Our resources are at the border. While we wait for the political pressure and bribes to smooth the way, children are dying." He put the untouched beer down and sank back into the chair.

Taty was on her knees at his side before she realized she'd moved. Her hand touched his thigh. The muscle jumped under her hand. "It isn't your fault. You are doing everything you can."

He opened his eyes and gazed down at her. His hand pushed her curls out of her eyes. "Thank you. Sometimes it's hard..." His words trailed off. She leaned into his touch. His thumb grazed over her cheekbone.

"You are doing a good thing, David Xavier." If she hadn't been studying his face while she spoke, she would have missed the small flinch at her statement. The comment bothered him. *Why?*

Taty lifted onto her knees and slid her hand behind his neck, pulling him closer. She placed a soft kiss on to his lips before she moved away. "You should eat. Then you need some sleep."

David drew a deep breath and leaned away from her. He glanced at the covered dish and lifted his eyes. "What did you make?"

"Stuffed potato pancakes. There was ham and roast beef. I added Swiss to the ham and a soft white cheese to the roast beef, I'm not sure what it was, but the combination was pleasant." She stood and lifted several silver domes revealing the pancakes and a fresh chopped salad.

He motioned toward the food. "Will you join me?"

She shook her head. "I ate dinner. Plus, I sampled

as I cooked." A startling thought crossed her mind. "Oh! Serve me any portion. I swear I did not taint the food."

David's eyes slowly raised. "I didn't think for a moment you had. I was offering out of politesse."

"Oh." She moved to the farthest chair and curled into the cushions. He spread a napkin over his thigh. His knife and fork divided a pancake. He lifted a bite and sampled it. His eyebrows lifted and a smile tugged at his mouth. "You may cook for me anytime. Once again, the food is delicious."

She thanked him and watched as he began, with immaculate precision, to devour the food she'd prepared.

"What did you do today?" He asked as he reached for the beer. Taty thought about bringing a glass for him to pour it into, but he'd drank it out of the bottle last night. He lifted it to his lips waiting for an answer.

"Hmm? Oh, almost nothing. I wandered the chalet for a time this morning. I found the library again and selected a couple of books to read. Hannah and I visited for a moment while she was doing her chores. After dinner, I waited for your escort. When you sent the guard, I went outside and made the call. Then I returned to your room and waited. When you didn't come back by ten, I went looking for the kitchen. I knew the way to your offices because of the guards posted in the hallway. I asked them to bring me to you."

"I appreciate the thought behind the gesture, and I appreciate the food. I probably wouldn't have eaten if you hadn't brought it to me." He put his empty plate on the table and grabbed the second beer.

Taty watched him closely. His gaze roamed the room and found their way back to her. She moved her hand over her arm, and his eyes tracked her movement. She lifted her hand to her face and licked her lips. His eyes followed her tongue. Desire wrote itself across his expression.

She stood and slowly walked to him, sinking to her knees between his legs. Her hands lightly traveled from his knees to his thighs. Maybe, she was hungry after all. The dense muscle under the soft fabric clenched at her touch. She unclasped his belt and lowered the zipper of his slacks. He lifted when she tugged the material and the fabric shifted down out of her way. She traced his growing erection through the body-warmed material of his silk boxers. His cock hardened under her touch. She glanced into his heavily hooded eyes and offered him a shy smile. Her hand snaked in and pulled his cock out. She cupped him and pushed the foreskin down with one hand. A manicured fingernail smeared a small drop of pre-come over the head and down the underside of his shaft. The soft skin surrounding the hard core of his cock felt like warm velvet in her hand.

She lowered slowly and carefully licked the exposed head. She spoke to him but didn't lift her eyes. "I love your taste." His cock jumped in her hand

and pushed out another glistening drop of arousal. Her hand lifted the foreskin pushing it back up as her tongue delved into the folds around his cockhead. A low rumbling groan fell from above her. She glanced up to see his head pushed into the back of the chair. His hands gripped the arms of the chair, white at the knuckles. Taty worked his foreskin and shaft with her mouth and reached out to his hands, prying them off the furniture, placing them on the side of her head. She worked his length while his hands held her head gently.

She popped off him and dipped down, licking a stripe up the thick underside of his cock. "Use me. Let me help you feel better." Her eyes locked with his seconds before she took as much of him down her throat as she could. She held there and waited. David's fingers carded through her hair. Slowly he pulled her off. She took a deep breath and reveled in the feeling of his hands pushing her down again. It thrilled her to have him take control of his pleasure. His direction released her from the worry of not doing what he wanted. She moaned and worked her tongue as he lifted her head again. He wrapped her hair around his fingers and took control. Taty lost herself in the sensation. She worshiped his cock, working her mouth, lips and tongue to give him the most pleasure. His thighs shook under her hands. She used her bottom teeth to gently tease his shaft on her way up. He stopped her advance and pushed her back down as his hips lifted. His cock head sank into her throat. She held still, even though every survival instinct she had demanded she breathe. His strangled gasp and thrust sent his seed down her throat. He pulled out, allowing her to relieve her lungs as another rope of come filled her mouth. She sucked and licked until he collapsed back in the chair and pulled her away. He tugged her up into his lap. She laughed softly. She'd truly enjoyed making him come.

He chuckled. "Just so you know, laughing after giving a man a blowjob like that is considered a breach of etiquette."

She leaned away. Laughter bubbled out of her again. "I was thinking that I like the way we start. Yes? I've tasted you both nights. I'm... content."

He gently pushed her down onto his shoulder. "So am I." His deep voice rumbled under her ear.

"You need to go to sleep." She played with a button on his shirt.

"I can't. I'm waiting on a call." His words were low and muted.

"You'll fall asleep in this chair."

He took a deep breath and rubbed her back. "No, I'm allowing myself to relax for a moment." He kissed the top of her head. "You go back to your room. I'm not going to be able to leave anytime soon. Thank you for the food and your company." The phone on his desk rang, shattering the peace of the moment. She stood and watched him tuck himself back into his slacks and stride to the desk.

"Xavier." He looked back at her and winked. His

hand ran through his hair, and shifted his focus to his desk, searching for a folder. "No, we sent that envoy twice the required amount."

Taty turned on her heel and left the office. The guard who accompanied her was waiting in the outer foyer. He escorted her out of the wing. She strolled back to the kitchen to clean up the mess she'd made before she rambled through the mansion and headed to bed. Sometimes, if she tried hard enough, she could imagine a life when the Bratva was no longer her focus. *Sometimes*.

CHAPTER 15

Mike sat down, put on his seatbelt and leaned forward, rubbing his temples with his fingertips. The high whine of the plane's engines as they started pushed against the migraine that threatened to overtake him. He'd slept only a handful of hours in the last six days. The all-out civil war that erupted had thwarted all Omega International's humanitarian efforts. Not as much as one bandage had made it to the region where the conflict raged. The political minefields he needed to cross to get the aid into the country were close to impossible to navigate. The crisis only added to the pressure of maintaining the normal obligations that shrouded his persona of David Xavier in legitimacy. None of the duties could be shirked, and he'd be damned if he'd fail the real David by not getting those people the help they so desperately needed while still maintaining his cover. The stress didn't stop there. It was compounded by the fact that he was heading to New York to pay for and take custody of fifteen young women who had been kidnapped and violated in ways he prayed no one else would ever have to suffer.

He cast a distracted glance across the cabin. Tatyana sat across from him. She smiled at him and held his gaze. He could see the questions in her look. He closed his eyes, breaking the connection between them as the engine revved and the bird taxied. He felt the plane pause at the end of the runway, waiting for clearance, before the pilot released the brakes and catapulted the aircraft into the air.

He sighed and tried to relax in the huge leather recliner he'd dumped his ass into. Tatyana was an entirely different stressor. He had not seen her since the night she'd brought him dinner and a happy ending. The deep-seated guilt he felt about using her had been beating the shit out of him. He knew there was a line. He was on one side, and she was on the other, but dammit if she hadn't blurred it. He didn't want to like her. In fact, he'd rather hate the woman, because it would make it easier for him to walk away when she was arrested. But fuck it, something wouldn't let him hate her. The bottom line in the scenario was that he actually *liked* the woman. That realization made him half sick to his stomach. She was a part of the Bratva. The farce of her admitted lies aside, there was no escaping the fact that she was a criminal of the worst imaginable type. The initial security report he'd received confirmed everything she'd admitted to.

Stopping the Bratva was his mission. To do so, he'd use her to get to those bastards and then he'd walk away. The thought of that action hurt in a way he didn't want to take out or examine. He'd blocked her attempts to see him. He sent word through Hannah that he wouldn't be able to spare time for her. In actuality, he didn't have the time, but to ensure he maintained the upper hand, and his sanity, he couldn't let a replay of that night happen again. She'd been escorted to the plane by his security detail because he didn't leave the chalet until the last possible minute.

"Good Afternoon, Mr. Xavier, would you like a glass of cognac?"

Mike still had his eyes shut but smiled at the familiar voice. He opened his eyes and took the glass from the same flight attendant who he'd traveled with for the last year. "Thank you, Daphne."

"You are quite welcome, sir. We have a little over eight hours in the air. Your security detail, staff, and your personal assistant are in the rear of the aircraft and all settled in." She turned toward Tatyana. "May I get you something?"

Taty shook her head. "No, but I believe Mr. Xavier will need something to eat and then privacy so he can sleep."

Daphne smiled and glanced back at him, her concerned gaze running over him. "I will bring dinner up as soon as it is ready, sir, and I'll make sure the forward cabin is ready for you."

"Thank you. Dinner would be appreciated, but I won't be needing the cabin during the flight."

Daphne smiled, dipped her head and headed back to the galley that separated the elegant, spacious front cabin and the smaller area in the rear.

"You push yourself too hard."

"You assume too much," he responded and stared at her dispassionately. Her concern seemed genuine, and was an unwelcome presence, if it was real. Who knew with Tatyana? She was a consummate liar.

Her eyes narrowed, and she shook her head. "No. I don't assume the dark circles under your eyes. I don't assume the mornings I have breakfast alone knowing you have not returned to your quarters. I didn't assume when I watched the growing violence and heard the television reports of aid convoys being attacked or turned away."

"You are not at liberty to dictate my staff's actions. I do not require your concern. I can take care of myself." He took a long pull on his drink. Exhaustion battered him, and he would love to sleep, but there weren't enough hours in the day to maintain the illusion of his cover.

Tatyana unbuckled her seatbelt and moved across the cabin behind his chair. She placed her hands on his shoulders and started to massage them. He groaned, dropping his head forward allowing her access. "I would never assume to dictate your actions,

David. But anyone can see you are tired. Would a small power nap hurt?" Her fingertips found the tight muscles in his neck and kneaded them until he felt them loosen.

"At least take off this jacket and let me work these muscles. Your back is one big knot."

He couldn't agree more and the headache he was fighting killed any argument he might have had about it. Besides, after a quick massage, he could call Joel up to the front and work through any of the thousand outstanding issues. He unfastened his seat-belt, removed his jacket, loosened his tie and leaned back. Her strong hands found purchase on the tight muscles of his traps and shoulders and worked them slowly and carefully. The soothing ministrations drew several low groans of pleasure from him. His aching muscles relaxed by increments and he drew a deep breath. The drone of the engine and the feel of her hands on his back lulled him into a comfortable trance.

"You should eat."

He blinked. The gentle touch to his arm woke him immediately. He shifted around, orienting himself and focused on the tray in front of him. Dammit. He must have dozed off. He focused out the window and frowned. It was completely dark. His gaze sought his watch, and he blinked back a bubble of anger. What a waste of time. He'd been asleep for six hours.

Tatyana lounged in the adjacent recliner with a book across her lap. "I told your man not to wake you. If you want to be mad at someone, be mad at me."

He rubbed his face and leaned forward, stopping when his seatbelt tugged at his waist. He looked from the restraint to her.

"It isn't safe to not wear one while in flight. I fastened it while you were sleeping." She lifted a shoulder with an elegant shrug. "Sue me. Someone needs to take care of you."

He unbuckled his belt and stood to stretch. His muscles rebelled at the strain, but it felt amazing. He bent down and picked up the glass of ice water on his tray and downed it in one go. "How much longer until we land?"

"The flight attendant said the pilot had to deviate around a storm, so two and a half hours." Tatyana closed the book as she spoke. Her brown curls fell over her eyes. Mike rejected the immediate impulse to push them back. Instead, he nodded and headed into the front cabin. The queen-sized bed taunted him as he passed through the plush interior and made his way into his private bathroom. He had several suits hanging ready in the closet. He used the facilities, stripped and washed quickly. Wrapping a towel around his waist, he headed back to the cabin to dress.

Long, silky, naked legs caught his attention. His eyes traveled over taut muscles to the full curve of her ass where the perfectly matched dimples at the bottom of her spine fixed his attention.

Her curls shifted as she looked over her shoulder at him. "I thought maybe you needed to relax just a little bit more." Tatyana rolled over.

Mike's cock jumped under the towel. His body betrayed the punch of lust he felt every time he looked at this woman. He glanced at the cabin door to ensure it was locked before he dropped his towel and crawled over her body to settle his weight on top of her. The soft warmth of her curves and the heady smell of her perfume raced over his senses. At her neck, his lips found her pounding pulse. She wrapped her arms around him and arched up into his body. The woman was in-his-face-wanton and sexy as sin. He wrapped his arms around her and rolled onto his back, bringing her with him. Her curls fell into her face again. He ran his fingers through them, cupped her cheek and then lifted the small distance to her lips. He brushed her softness and whispered, "Entice me."

She smiled, placed both of her hands on his chest and pushed up. Tatyana stretched across the mattress toward the nightstand. His hand supported her waist and pulled her up and back on the bed after she grabbed a condom out of the drawer. She put the gold foiled square to her teeth and ripped the package. Her eyes flashed with a glimmer of humor before her tight ass cheeks wiggled against his cock. She leaned forward and kissed his neck and started a trail of nips and licks down his chest. A groan escaped him when she sucked his nipple into her mouth. Fuck, he'd never had a woman do that before. The sensation had a direct connection to his dick. It stiffened to the point of pain. Her body slithered down his as her lips tracked the valleys of his muscles. He grabbed the duvet and held on tight as her tongue traced the V from his hip to his cock. She laughed and slid to the other side, making the trek from hipbone to cock again.

His dick wept pre-come, and he hurt he was so hard. She circled the head of his cock with her tongue before she lifted away from him. He watched as she rolled the condom down his shaft. It shouldn't have been as erotic as it was, but then again, she followed the latex down with her mouth. His hands found their way to her hair. As good as she was with her mouth, that wasn't what he wanted right now, and if he let her suck him, he'd be done all too fast. He tugged her hair gently. She lifted those big brown eyes to him. "I want in you."

She lifted off his cock and smiled, sliding up his body to take his mouth in a kiss. Her hips lowered and ground her hot sex over his cock. They both moaned. Without breaking the kiss her hand sought him out and lifted his heavy shaft to her core.

She pushed up and away from him. His hands cupped her soft breasts as she lowered herself onto his cock. The slow, tight slide forced the air out of both of their lungs. She held his hands to her breasts as she slowly gyrated her hips. There was a distinct possibility that circling action caused his eyes to roll backward into his skull. Tatyana lifted and lowered, moving her hips in a serpentine motion, slow, steady and deliberate.

"You feel so good. So hot... and hard." Her thick Russian accent slid over his senses as his hands traveled her body. The sensuous dance on his cock pushed his endurance.

He slid his hands down to her sex and split her open. His thumb found her swollen clit and massaged the little nub in concert with her motions. Her hips stuttered, and her breath caught. She fell forward, bracing herself on his chest with her hands. Brown curls clung to her damp forehead and neck. Her lips were red and swollen. Her chest heaved with her rising passion. Mike drank in the debauched sight of her. It did little to quench his burning need. He cupped her ass and lifted her far enough to raise his legs and brace himself. He thrust into her, hard and demanding. A soft mewl fell from her lips. He pulled her down into a kiss that turned into shared breaths as he pushed them both toward orgasm. Her breasts slid over his chest on each upward thrust. She gasped and shouted something in Russian when she came, but he couldn't be bothered to translate. Her release triggered his as assuredly as an electronic blasting cap detonated a Claymore. He pulled her tight against him and stroked deep as his body spilled and sent shards of pleasure through him. He held her trembling body on top of his. Slowly, the noises of the aircraft came back into focus. He repositioned the duvet up and around her to protect them both from the forced air that provoked shivers from their rapidly cooling bodies.

Tatyana snuggled into his neck. "You feel more relaxed, yes?"

He chuckled and patted her bare ass. "No stress whatsoever."

She lifted away and gazed down at him. "You have much to offer a woman, David Xavier."

Mike's mind whirled. He hugged her down against his chest and glanced at his watch. How many days until he took possession of fifteen human lives and used Tatyana to help him barter for a meeting with the head of the Bratva? *Much to offer?* No, he was a mercenary. He'd chosen his life, and he'd lived it allied with strong men of equal conviction. Brothers, family, and friends. He didn't have much to offer a woman, but what he did have was built from the ruins of his childhood, and he was damn proud of what he'd done with his life. No, he wasn't a good man, but he was a man who would do his best to break the Bratva's grip on the innocent people they enslaved.

Jewell stared at the lines that scrolled across the monitor with more than a little disbelief. The amount of red-tape and bullshit they had to go through to legally access the computer systems of countless social service networks had paid off. She pumped her fists in the air as a sense of giddy triumph flooded her. They'd done it. Every last pixel floating across her screen was legal. She pushed to the front of her massive leather chair, sent the image to the middle screen and pulled one of the many pencils from her hair, and used it to tap the desktop. One, two… she flicked the mouse and opened a new document on the same screen… three, four… Jewell copied and pasted the pertinent information for each location… five and finally the sixth and final identified computer system.

"What is it?"

Zane's low rumble behind her no longer sent her through the rafters. He'd become an attractive, yet annoying, part of her world. If she weren't in such a good mood right now, she'd think of some scathing remark just because it was fun to watch his reactions. "We've identified six more intake IP addresses."

"Intake as in?"

Jewell scowled through a glance tossed toward the corner of the room where he always sat while she worked. "Intake as in my team built a sniffer software that has identified six more workstations which meet the criteria for people who are hunting and actively identifying possible targets for the Bratva's sex trade."

"Congratulations to you and your team." Zane's deep-voiced comment shouldn't have meant as much as it did. At least the man saw the hours her people put into making the magic happen. They were dedicated and the smartest programmers, hackers, and computer engineers in the country.

"Thanks. Could you take this down to Jason? I want to refresh the protocols and run the program one more time just to make sure no one slipped through." She held out the thumb drive.

"No, but I'll call a runner." Zane took the thumb drive and picked up her desk phone.

Jewell gave the man the stink eye. Whatever, she had work to do.

CHAPTER 16

The energy of New York City thrummed through Taty's body. Each city in Europe had a character and vibe all of its own. She should have expected New York to be the same, but the amount of traffic that pulsed through the city's arteries at two in the morning was unbelievable. Little market shops, restaurants, and even large stores were lit up. A current of yellow taxi cabs flowed through the streets like blood flowed through her veins. The limousine they traveled in had dark tinted windows, but she could still see out, and it was fascinating. A huge sign flashed, catching her attention. She leaned over David to see, forcing him to raise the tablet he'd buried his nose in as soon as they'd landed. "Times Square! We are in Times Square!" She bounced up and down in her seat and clapped her hands together. The thrill of actually seeing the famous landmark bubbled up and held her there, buoyant with joy.

David lowered his arms, trapping her over his lap. He powered down the tablet and placed it on the seat beside him before he cupped her ass. She twisted in his embrace, looking out the back window while draped over his lap. He effortlessly lifted her up and into a straddle position across his muscled thighs.

"I assumed you'd been to New York. I take it this is your first time?" His smile reflected hers.

"I've never left the EU." Her mood shattered and she turned her head to avoid his penetrating stare.

"What? What did you think about just now to make you so unhappy?" His fingers tucked under her chin and directed her gaze back to him.

"This isn't my assigned territory." She slid off his lap and tucked herself into the corner of the seat, keeping her gaze averted. She had no intel about the U.S. arm of the Bratva operation, that is why she had to get to the top of the organization. As much as she'd like to kill the bastards, in order to disassemble the entire organization, MI6 needed the name of the person running the Bratva.

The atmosphere thickened between them, dousing any happiness she had at seeing the famous city or its landmarks. They traveled in a lengthy, uncomfortable silence. Lights slowly strobed through the interior of the vehicle, casting an ominous glow across David's somber face. Tatyana glanced his way with frustrating frequency. The minutes stretched by.

Taty chased her thoughts around and around, but there was no magical solution to her problems. The unknown factor that David Xavier brought to her investigation, coupled with the fact she hadn't checked in with her handler, put her in a precarious position. She was operating without a net, but after eight years as an agent for MI6, she knew the protocols.

The car slowed and then stopped at the base of a towering building. She waited as David's security deployed. A team of four men departed the building and brought his security team's number to nine. Headlights glared through the back windshield. She saw Hannah, her husband Higgins, and David's personal assistant, gather at the front door and present identification. They were allowed inside while another traveling security team deployed. Saints above, that was fourteen guards surrounding the small area between David and the door to the building.

"Why so much security?" Taty glanced back at him when she spoke. He gave a distracted look out the window before he went back to the tablet he'd retrieved earlier.

"I have no idea. I leave security issues to those who know it. I pay people to ensure my employees and I are safe." He flipped through a screen on his tablet and sighed.

"You should pay more attention to your security and your surroundings. You never know when being observant could save your life." Her eyes strayed back to the men outside the vehicle. A team of four went into the building. She noticed the distinct bulge of weapons that were not visible in Switzerland. The American version of his security team appeared less refined, more... military. Finally, the men moved as one. She glimpsed the ear pieces and nodded in understanding. They were waiting for something to be cleared before allowing him to leave the secure environment he currently occupied.

A guard opened the door and extended his hand for Tatyana. She stepped out and tipped her head back, looking as far up as she could see. Buildings boxed in the sky, leaving only a murky blue-black smudge directly above her. David exited the vehicle and placed his hand on the small of her back, escorting her into the building.

Taty stutter stepped. The opulence of the chalet in Switzerland should have prepared her for this, but... no. A massive round table centered in the lobby held a floral arrangement at least six feet across and six feet high. The immediate fragrance of thousands of blooms swirled against her senses. The floor was a mosaic of interlocking ribbons of color that dazzled the eye. She took in as much as she could as they walked across the beautiful lobby. The far wall held three elevators and two doors. The door on the farthest side was opened by one of the guards. When they entered, they immediately were moved into an elevator with no control panel. Three guards entered with them. One removed a black card that he pressed to the wall. The elevator shimmied under her feet, and her stomach sank as they rose. The door opened seconds later, which surprised her. She'd thought David would have the penthouse, not an apartment on the lower floor. She felt David's hand on her back and moved forward behind the guards. When the behemoth in front of her veered off, she stopped and stared at the beautiful cityscape. She glanced back at the elevator and then ran her gaze along the solid glass walls that enclosed the apartment. To her right and the center, the city's lights were vivid and beautiful. The left was darker. She gravitated toward the windows as if she was a magnet and they were metal. They *were* in the penthouse. The elevator's speed was astonishing. "Why are there no buildings this way?" she asked as she tried to absorb the excessive affluence that surrounded her.

"Central Park. Come." He extended his hand, and she took it without a second's hesitation. He led her through a sliding glass door to the wide veranda. She braced against the cold. Her jacket did little to dispel the biting chill of the wind. He led her to the railing, and she gasped at the beauty of the park below her. During the day the view must be spectacular. Ambient lighting gave her indistinct allusions of trees and shrubbery lining walkways and vast expanses of grass. Pathways and streetlights lined the roads that surrounded the massive green space and glowed in shimmering patterns of white-blue luminescence. She wished the sun would rise in this minute so she could see the splendor she knew was hiding in the darkened vista.

Tatyana shivered and pulled her coat closed at the neck. He came behind her, wrapping her in his muscled arms. His body heat enveloped her. "How has having this much money not ruined you?"

His silence stretched between them before he answered. "My father and my mother weren't married. I did not have this wealth while I was growing up. As a matter of fact, before... my father introduced himself to me, I had very little. What I did earn, I sent home to my mother. No matter how successful I become, in my mind's eye, I'm still that bastard child. My mother suffered the fate of many of my people. She was an alcoholic. She died before... father."

"Is that why there are no photographs of you?" She turned in his arms.

"Partially. But mostly because the wealth I now control demands certain precautions." He dropped his head, and she lifted onto her toes. His slow, soft kiss ended far too soon for her liking.

With his arm wrapped around her, they went back into the apartment and through the grand living area. He opened the door to what she assumed would be where she would be immured until she was needed. Higgins and Hannah both worked in the room. She saw a man taking out her luggage along with David's. She glanced up at him questioningly.

He shrugged out of his wool coat and winked at her. Higgins appeared magically at his side to take the outer garment.

"Miss, I've unpacked your cases." Hannah extended her hand.

"Umm... thank you?" Taty looked at Hannah's empty hand, not knowing what the woman wanted. David chuckled and stepped behind her to remove her coat from her shoulders. He handed it to Hannah and the woman headed out the door along with her husband. The door shut behind them quietly.

"You want me to sleep with you? I thought you slept alone?" She glanced around the massive bedroom. Surely the bed was twice the size of the king-sized beds they had in the chalet. The enormity of the thing still couldn't dwarf the size of the room. She glanced at the floor to ceiling windows and out at the cityscape.

"I want you in my bed, among other things. My time here shouldn't be as regimented as it was in Europe. And since I have it on good authority you've never been to New York before, we may do some sightseeing."

Taty's head whipped around. "Really?" She scurried over to him. "May I see the Statue of Liberty? Yankee Stadium? Rockefeller Center? *Oh!* The Rockettes!"

He slid his hand behind her neck and stilled her undisciplined and completely regrettable requests. She blushed and dropped her eyes, embarrassed at the lack of focus she'd had since they'd landed. Perhaps it was the jet lag? She had no other way to explain away the impetuous remarks. She shuttered her enthusiasm and returned her attention back to the mission at hand. Use David to reach the top of the Bratva. Why in the hell was it becoming so damn hard to keep that focus at the front and center of all of her thoughts?

"We will have time to do a few things." He leaned down and tipped her head back to capture her lips. "But right now we are going to get some much needed sleep."

Tatyana nodded, not tracking because his lips moved against her neck as he spoke. He stepped away and winked at her. *What? What had he said?*

"Bed. Sleep. Now," he spoke as he started to disrobe.

Taty nodded and headed to what she assumed was the closet. Minutes later, she shivered as she slid under the silk sheets. She squirmed into David's warmth. He tucked her into his side and fell asleep within minutes. Taty stared out the massive window-like walls. If only there were a way she could get to the top of the Bratva without involving David. She drew a deep breath and mentally slapped herself. He was a criminal; she was just doing her job. Taty closed her eyes as his body warmth seeped into her. He was buying women, and no matter what happened, he'd have to pay for his transgressions. And yet, her instincts and years of experience were screaming at her to take notice. So many things did not compute on a basic level. The way David had worked to get help to the refugees. The utmost respect of his staff, from the lowest servant to his personal assistant, wasn't based in fear, or from what she could see, greed. She compared each thought to try to find a nucleus of redemption that she could attribute to this man... this criminal. She closed her eyes and drew a deep breath. No, it wasn't her place to find redeeming qualities, it was her job to stop the Bratva and the men who used them, including David.

CHAPTER 17

M ike's security team led him across the foyer and into his private elevator. The day had been a litany of legalese and projections. He'd have to study the information on the short-term decisions that were required and pray he wouldn't have to deal with the decisions for next quarter. If tomorrow's meeting went well, hopefully, he'd be back at the ranch, knee-deep in training issues while the real David Xavier made the decisions. He handed off his coat to Higgins and glanced at his watch again.

"I'll inform the lady you are home, sir."

"Thank you, Higgins." They had reservations at Nido dell'Aquila. The insanely successful Italian restaurant was almost impossible to get into. Almost. He accepted a glass of cognac and stood in front of the floor-to-ceiling glass panes overlooking the

cityscape. His mind worked the intricacies of
tonight's meeting. He would introduce Tatyana. That
would put her on Guardian's radar. He turned at the
sound of her heels. She wore a nude-colored dress
that floated around her in an iridescent shimmer. In
her dark brown heels, her legs looked miles long.

She stood still while he slowly crossed the room
and walked around her. He leaned in for a kiss.
"Beautiful." Her cheeks flushed at his compliment, or
perhaps with anticipation of another kiss. He didn't
care which.

"Shall we go?" He set his drink down and escorted
her to the door where Higgins and Hannah waited
for them. Tatyana gasped at the three-quarter length
mink cape that he'd ordered from storage for her to
wear tonight. He'd originally requested Higgins
purchase a warm cloak for her, but his personal
assistant suggested using one of the many furs that
had been handed down in the Xavier family. He'd had
it taken out of storage and cleaned today while he
worked. He took the cape from Hannah and helped
Tatyana into it, making sure her hair wasn't caught in
the collar. "I was tired of watching you shiver in your
designer jackets."

"It is beautiful." She ran her hand over the
plush fur.

"As are you." He guided her into the elevator.

"Where are we going tonight?" She exited with
him, and they followed his waiting security detail
across the foyer.

"An Italian restaurant that I've heard great things about. I've met the owner a time or two. Interesting man. A successful restaurateur with exceptional business sense."

He pulled her closer to him when they settled into the limousine. She bent and twisted to look out the windows, taking in the sights. It went against his nature to treat her like a prisoner, but to ensure she didn't contact the Bratva, he'd continue to limit her access to people and electronics. His security team watched her like a hawk, and the apartment had been swept for listening devices before they arrived. The sweep had delayed their entry this morning. The team would be actively sweeping the apartment again, right now.

They arrived at the restaurant, and Mike couldn't stop his smile at her wide-eyed expression. They were ushered to their table and seated. Drinks appeared without being ordered, and Tatyana gaped at him in surprise. "Why would they not ask what we want?"

"This establishment is different." He watched as she took in the environment. Each table was secluded from the others. "They know our drink preferences. I'm assuming Joel spoke to them when he made the reservations. The meal is selected and prepared by the chef, taking into consideration our personal tastes.

"We don't order?"

"No."

"You pay money so someone can tell you what to eat?" She watched as a waiter approached with a domed silver tray.

"I do." A well-timed procession of wait staff appeared. They cleared table settings and placed silverware. Glasses were filled. Delicacies were delivered, and the menu for the evening was explained before the staff disappeared in a graceful, quiet dance of serving perfection.

He lifted a blue cheese stuffed fig wrapped in prosciutto and drizzled with port wine sauce to her lips. She lifted an eyebrow suspiciously but opened her mouth taking a small bite of the delicacy. He popped the rest of the bite into his mouth and froze mid bite at the erotic moan that left Tatyana's lips. His cock jerked with interest when her eyes closed, and her tongue peeked out, cleaning a drop of port wine sauce from her succulent bottom lip. "Now I understand why you let the chef tell you what to eat."

"You need to trust me, Tatyana." He lifted another bite to her lips. An expression flashed across her face right before she opened her mouth and took the fig, her lips and tongue caressing his fingers in the process. His cock filled at the memory of what those lips could do.

"Mr. Xavier, it is so good to see you again!" Justin King's voice interrupted his desire filled thoughts. Tatyana's eyes popped open at Justin's words, and her face flamed crimson with embarrassment. Mike chuckled and wiped his hands as he stood. He shook Justin's hand while taking in the man's appearance. His slim cut suit was tailored impeccably to his frame. When coupled with the thick black frames of his glasses and his lack of pretentious attitude, his appearance might lead a person to believe the man wasn't one of the world's most successful restaurateurs. Yet, Justin's establishments were the hottest tickets in town. Politicians, the elite of society and everyone who wanted to be someone made it a point to be seen at his restaurants. He was not-so-secretly touted as the man with the Midas touch and had access to people and conversations that gave Guardian a very secret edge. To his knowledge, only Jason knew Justin was involved in Guardian's business. The way the other brother good-heartedly harassed Justin for not being part of Guardian, he could damn near guarantee it.

"Justin. Thank you for fitting me in at the last minute. May I introduce my companion, Tatyana Petrov? Taty, this is Justin King. He owns this and, what is it, six other restaurants?" He turned to Justin as he asked.

"Actually, the ink is just now drying on the contract for my ninth." Justin took Tatyana's hand in his and lifted it to his lips and in Georgian said, "It is a pleasure to meet you,' Tatyana."

Mike chuckled at the wide-eyed expression that hadn't left Tatyana's face. "You speak Georgian?"

Justin lifted away and winked at her, bringing a further pulse of color to her cheeks. "No. I've learned the phrase, 'It is a pleasure to meet you,' in about ten different languages, but I must admit, if it doesn't concern food, nothing else will stick in my muddled brain. English is hard enough to master. Wouldn't you agree?"

A wide smile spread across her face. "Wholeheartedly. The nuances of the English language frustrated me for years when I was studying it in University."

"You're a linguist?" Justin somehow managed to look embarrassed. "You must tell me did I get that phrase right? I practice each one to try to get the accentuated words correct, but the last Italian greeting I gave… well, suffice to say, I ended up very embarrassed when I inadvertently told a distinguished sixty-five-year-old woman it was my pleasure to eat her."

Mike barked out a laugh at the same time as Tatyana. Justin removed his glasses and pinched his nose in an excellent portrayal of mortification. He smiled and shook his head before he returned his glasses.

"Your accent is cute, and the words they were stilted, but you did well." Taty smiled up at Mike. The happiness on her face pushed past the mask she normally wore. She was breathtaking. With an effort, he turned away from her. Justin's raised eyebrow let him know that he'd seen whatever it was that transpired between them.

"Are you in town long, Mr. Xavier? I have a new chef that I'm bringing in from Spain. He'll put together the back of the house for my new place in Philadelphia. I'm having a small gathering at my apartment for a few select individuals Wednesday evening so Mateo can test one or two of his ideas on my favorite clientele's palates."

He weighed the invitation. He rubbed his chin with his hand as he considered the reason behind the invitation before it clicked. He dipped his head slightly and smiled.

"What time?"

"We will probably start with cocktails at seven. I anticipate the tasting to start at eight-ish."

He put his hands in his pockets and glanced over at Tatyana. "I'm sorry, I can't. I have a rather important business meeting that will have both of us tied up from late afternoon until at least seven."

"Maybe you can stop over after?"

"Unfortunately we will be traveling back over the bridge into the financial district from the Bronx."

Justin groaned. "With traffic that time of night, there is no way to make it back to Manhattan in time to enjoy the party. Maybe the next time you are in the city?"

"Perhaps." He shook Justin's hand. The man turned to Tatyana and bowed slightly. "It was a pleasure to meet you, Ms. Petrov. I hope to have the pleasure of practicing my greeting on you again."

"I look forward to it," Taty glanced at Mike, "but I

do not travel to the United States often. Perhaps you will come to Europe, yes?"

A half smile played on Justin's lips. "I'm rarely away from my restaurants. Perhaps one day in the future we will meet again. Until then," he spoke in Georgian, "I hope your life is pleasant."

Taty giggled as she spoke, "I hope your life is pleasant too, although that phrase you may need to work on. Your pronunciation was not so good."

Justin hung his head and sighed. "I told you I need to stick to food. Good evening." He moved on to the next table, the low rumble of his voice as he spoke with his patrons could be heard, although the words weren't distinguishable. Mike stared at her, determined to get back to the mission at hand, and that mission was to seduce the Bratva operative sitting across from him. Thanks to that little conversation, Guardian knew her name and knew the date and time he'd be in the Bronx. He watched her fidget under his unyielding stare.

"What?" She glanced at her dress.

"Entice me." His words tumbled out of his mouth before his brain engaged. She glanced out at the shielded tables before she picked up a fig from the plate and leaned over the table offering it to him. He bit the morsel in half ensuring his tongue swept the pad of her finger in the process. He watched a shiver run over her. "Are you cold?"

"No." The lust in her expressive eyes answered his

question before she swallowed hard and licked her lips. Her hands trembled slightly, and her breath came in shallow pants. All indicators told him she needed - no she desired - more, and that was exactly where he intended to keep her for the next forty-eight hours.

The waiters continued the well-rehearsed and expertly choreographed dance, removing plates, filling glasses and silently slipping away. The finger foods continued as if the entire dinner had been imagined and prepared for lovers. Mike deliberately teased Tatyana's senses with slow lingering kisses between courses. His cock hated the languid pace he'd set out for tonight's seduction, but for once while dealing with this woman, his cock wasn't doing all the thinking for him. The conversation with Justin brought the reality of his mission front and center. No, tonight's seduction was aimed at lowering every defense she had. He wanted her stripped bare, both emotionally and physically. He knew he was developing feelings for the woman, but if he could keep her off balance and looking to him to lead, maybe— just maybe, he could protect himself from the disaster that had been coming from the moment he decided to seduce her.

Mike put his finger under her chin and lowered his lips to hers, giving the briefest touch before he moved away. Her small sigh indicated her reluctance to end the kiss so soon. The wait staff floated in again, exchanging plates and glasses. The dessert was a classic, chocolate covered strawberries. Although the liqueur-infused, imported chocolate ganache, hand-decorated with white chocolate and edible gold leaf, were a far cry from the standard fare.

Strawberry nectar dripped across her bottom lip as he pulled the fruit away. He licked the sweetness from her kiss-swollen lips. "Are you ready to leave?" He whispered the question before he granted another feather-soft sweep of his mouth over hers.

"God, yes. Please." Her eyes closed momentarily. She pushed her cheek into his hand. He stood and extended his hand after he took the time to adjust his suit jacket to hide the obvious effects of the night.

She glanced around and tugged on his hand as he started to leave. "You need to pay."

He dropped his hand to her waist and guided her toward the entrance. "They have my information. I can't tell you the last time I've had to deal with a bill." He paused as their coats appeared. He couldn't help thinking of when he'd *actually* last paid for his meal. He had breakfast at the little diner in Hollister, South Dakota the morning before he left for this mission. Genevieve's homemade breakfast biscuits and cinnamon rolls were amazing. But as good as the food was, the little diner's friendly, homey atmosphere was what sold the place to everyone who worked for Guardian.

He swatted away the feelings of homesickness. He wouldn't allow himself to think about his wants or desires. There were too many innocent lives at stake for him to take his focus off the finish line. *Whatever it takes. As long as it takes.* The specter of Alpha Team's motto slipped through his mind as he waited for Tatyana to fasten the neck clasp of her fur cape. He'd bet his last dollar none of the team would think seducing a Russian mobster would fall into that parameter. He smiled at the fun the Wonder Twins would have with that thought. Mike shook his head and sighed. Dixon and Drake were his brothers. Annoying little shits, but brothers nonetheless.

Cold, brisk air filled his lungs as he exited the building, clearing his mind of any lingering thoughts of home. His security team appeared and escorted them to the waiting limousine.

"Well, he's definitely not gay." Tori cocked her head as she watched the video feed from the restaurant.

"What? Who said he was?" Jewell whispered as if the people on the monitor could hear them.

"Jacob didn't know for sure. Not that he cared. Shit, girl, would you look at that? Mike has got some moves." Tori had unconsciously lowered her voice to match her sister-in-law's volume.

"Seriously, how is this even the same man we knew?" Jewell nudged her with an elbow when Mike ran his thumb across the woman's cheek.

"I don't know. I wouldn't have recognized him if I

passed him on the street, that's for sure. The haircut, the suit... hell, even his mannerisms are different. He seems so relaxed, and he's actually talking to her... well, he was." Tori shifted her weight to her right hip and watched, mesmerized by the couple on the screen.

"Shit, this is like watching porn. He's making *my* princess parts tingle." Jewell stepped closer.

Tori mimicked her actions. Mike cupped the woman's neck and pulled her in for a long, slow kiss.

"Fuck me, that's *so* hot." Jewell sighed.

"What's hot?" Jacob asked.

Both women jerked around at his sudden presence *and* loud question. "Shit, you scared me!" Tori shrieked.

"Sorry, you must have been focused on the computer not to hear me come in,"

Tori stepped into her husband's rock solid chest. He enveloped her in his embrace and dropped his head onto her shoulder, peering at the video screen. "What in the hell are you two watching?"

"Mike and his date, a Ms. Tatyana Petrov. They're at Justin's newest restaurant in New York." Jewell filled him in as Tori turned in Jacob's arms so she could see the monitor. They watched as Mike leaned away from Tatyana and smiled. The couple exchanged some hushed conversation before he lifted one of the chocolate covered strawberries to her mouth. Both women sighed as Mike fed the fruit to the woman.

"I'm *never* going to let him live this one down. 007's got nothing on Mike." The absolute delight in Jacob's voice spun Tori around.

"No." She pointed at her husband and squinted her eyes.

"No, what?" Jacob blinked, looking cross-eyed at the finger suddenly an inch from his nose.

"No, you will not use anything you've seen on this video to tease or humiliate that man."

"I won't?"

"No, you won't." Jewell chimed into the conversation.

"Why the hell not? He knows he's being recorded!" Jacob pointed at the screen.

"Seriously?" Tori planted her hands on her hips and glared at the mountain of man-child she'd married.

"Well... yeah?" The confusion on his face was priceless, but she wasn't going to let him know that. The men of Alpha team were always razzing each other. They lived for it.

"No. That man is doing his job." She turned around and cocked her head as Mike stood and extended his hand to the woman. His excited condition was readily apparent before he adjusted his suit jacket. "Damn, she's got him hot and bothered." The words tumbled out of Tori's mouth unabated.

"Well, duh." Jacob snorted his retort and crossed his arms over his chest.

Both women turned to look at him at the same time.

"*What*? She's hot!" Jacob paused and blinked when he registered the expression on his wife's face. "But not hotter than you babe. Seriously, she doesn't hold a candle to you."

"Smooth, little brother. So freaking smooth." Jewell flipped the switch, turning the monitor off. "I'm going to start a background check on Mike's little Russian hottie. Come on, Norman." Jewell called over her shoulder to her bodyguard-slash-personal assistant. The man powered down his mini tablet and lifted away from the wall, following after Jewell.

Jacob watched them leave. "I thought his name was Fred?"

"It's Zachary... I think."

"Huh." Jacob closed the space separating them. "You know I only have eyes for you, right, baby?"

Tori flipped the monitor back on and hit several keys without answering. Finally, she found a camera view of the couple at the front of the establishment. Tori magnified the screenshot, so only the couple was visible. Mike put his hands into his pockets while his back was to the camera. "Well, I mean she is pretty, but *daaammmn*, would you look at Mike's ass? I never noticed how nice it was before. Maybe it's the suit."

"Oh, hell no." Jacob spun her around and dropped down, launching her over his shoulder. "*I'll* show you who has a nice ass, woman."

Tori reached down and grabbed his ass cheek. "Yes, dear, I agree you are the best ass around."

"Damn straight, woman." Jacob opened the door and strode into the hall.

"Works every time." Her laughter nearly obliterated her words.

CHAPTER 18

The sexual tension that ignited in the restaurant smoldered in the limousine on the ride back to the apartment. He pulled her tiny form on top of him, allowing the mink to drape over both of them. His hands traveled her soft curves of their own accord while he lost himself in her kisses. Her hand cupped his hard-as-diamonds cock. He grasped her hand and moved it away immediately. The woman had him so revved up he'd lose it in his pants like a horny teenager. Thankfully, the car parked at the apartment building before he did something that embarrassing. He gently pushed Tatyana back. Her lust-filled gaze and swollen, shiny lips made him groan internally. She ignited a passion he'd never felt before. His need and desire peaked. She was everything he'd ever wanted. Tonight he was going to turn off the voices in his head that told him he shouldn't want her because he did... God help him, he did.

The car door barely opened before he hauled ass out of the vehicle, nearly dragging Tatyana behind him. Her low sexy laugh brought a smile to his face. The knowing smirks from his security team would be addressed tomorrow. He pulled Tatyana into the waiting elevator and fused his lips to hers before the door shut. The mink was lost, and so was his wool coat. He somehow bunched the skirt of her dress up, grabbing her ass, gathering her tight against him. Taty shoved her hands between them. Her fingers fumbled with his belt and zipper. Lust, desire, want... hell, unrestrained need coursed through his veins like a runaway freight train. He pulled away from her succulent lips long enough to shed his suit jacket and tie.

The elevator door opened... or it had been open and his hunger had blinded him to the fact. He led her through to the entryway of the apartment. He lifted her, and she wrapped her legs around his waist. He pinned her against the wall, sending a framed painting askew. A rush of air pushed out of her with the movement. He kissed her hard before he pulled away the barest amount. "I can't stop. I fucking need to be in you."

"Yes. Yes, want you. Hard. Now." Tatyana wrapped her arms around his neck and bit his jaw line, before sucking away the sting. He released his straining cock from his boxers. He fought momentarily with the folds of her skirt until she groaned and bunched the material up around her waist.

"Thank fuck." He groaned before he slid into her heat. Rivulets of electricity rocketed through every fiber of his body. He lifted her small body easily. She fit perfectly against and around him. He pulled away from the wall and held her as he drove into her core. He thrust as if his life depended on it. The woman was a drug, and he was chasing his high. His balls drew up, and his mind blanked to everything except the woman in his arms. He pushed her back against the wall, lifted her legs higher and slammed home. His brain couldn't process her moaned Russian words, but he could and did understand her legs tightening around his waist and the way her body tightened and milked his cock. He braced against her and came inside her. The intensity of the orgasm nearly put him on his knees. They held each other tightly. The ecstasy lasted until he realized he'd just had unprotected sex. He tensed immediately.

Tatyana cupped his face in her hands. "Hey. I'm clean, and I'm on birth control. Nothing bad will come of this."

He shook his head. "I'm sorry. I…"

"I am an adult, too. I could have said stop. I knew we were protected and I wanted you."

He got it, he did. But, he'd seen what happened to Doc. The vicious woman that had used a pregnancy to bring the man to his knees flashed through his mind.

"Stop worrying. I do not want a child. I wear an IUD. You understand this?" Her Russian accent thickened slightly.

"I do." He shook his head, still not ready to stop his self-flagellation. It was fucking irresponsible and insane to have unprotected sex.

"Come. Shower with me." She headed toward the bathroom, dropping the dress at the door. It fell from her shoulders and pooled at her feet in a cloud. "Do bring condoms, David. I would hate to spoil the mood again."

Mike watched her small, supple body ghost through the bedroom door. Fuck, he was in over his head. He loosened his tie and undid the top button of his shirt. He'd lost his mind. "Stop worrying. Come shower with me." Tatyana's voice carried from the bathroom. He grinned and shook his head. He did need a shower.

David collapsed on top of her. His body weight prevented any thought of a deep breath, and God, she could use a deep breath. The man was phenomenal in bed. Actually, in and out of bed. Taty considered him the best lover she'd ever enjoyed. After the quick, hard and perfect fuck in the hallway, he'd brought her off three times before he allowed himself to finish. Her body ached in the most pleasant way. The man was a playground of solid muscle punctuated with slides of tender caresses and a seesaw of soft kisses. She had no idea a lover could be so selfless. The men she'd been with in the past were more interested in what they got out of the encounter than pleasing her. Then there were the men who tried but failed. The sheer number of times she'd faked an orgasm to get an inept lover off her was mind boggling. Men like David were rare, a lover who took care of her and had the sensual skill to drive her into a frenzy. He made her want to give him as much pleasure as she'd received—which was almost inconceivable.

David groaned, lifted and rolled to the side, allowing her lungs to expand. The flushed heat of their shared passion cooled quickly. He took care of the condom and reached for her, pulling her back into his side. Tatyana relaxed into the rock hard muscles and closed her eyes. Minus his freak out about the condom, the evening had been a storybook night. She felt like a princess who'd been rescued by the dashing prince and swept away from a horrible existence.

David's fingertips stroked her stomach. The caress brought her out of the orgasm induced stupor where she'd allowed herself to drift. His soft petting somehow became more intimate than the sex they'd just shared. He kissed her shoulder moments before his hand stilled and his breath evened out as he slipped into sleep. Taty's fingers dipped between David's as he slumbered. She longed for the connection she imagined, all the while knowing she could never really have it.

A small snore brought a small smile forward. God knew the man deserved a proper rest. From what she'd observed, he never stopped working and rarely slept. She'd overheard David and Joel going over his insane schedule for the upcoming week earlier this morning. The only oddity was the void in his schedule on Wednesday. His off-handed words with the restaurateur tonight confirmed that they'd take receipt of the fifteen women he'd ordered during that time. Taty tensed at the thought. Nothing about David, his actions or his business, would lead her to believe he was a criminal. One thing she'd learned from her training with MI6 and the Bratva was to watch and listen to absolutely everything. She'd been intensely focused on David Xavier since she'd been confined inside his gilded cage. His staff loved him. Everyone spoke of his kindness. The security teams respected him. She'd seen the deference with which they treated him it was an earned respect, not a token response. Some very important pieces to the puzzle of Mr. David Xavier were missing. The question was how in the world could she find the ones that would make sense of his actions?

David shifted behind her and rolled onto his back. Deep quiet breaths steadied once again. Taty glanced at his phone on the nightstand. She turned her head and glanced at him as he slept and then looked again at the phone. A glimmer of an idea breezed through her mind. The procedures for manipulating a home screen lock were plastered all over the internet, and she'd hacked her own phone to practice. *Anyone* could bypass the lock screen in a heartbeat, and with access to a computer, she could download his emails, contacts, and photos.

David had told her any activities on the electric devices he'd allowed her access to were monitored. But if she used *his* phone, his security team wouldn't know what she was doing. Or what she'd done, if she was successful. No, getting information to assist MI6 could blow her cover and jeopardize the goal of getting to the bastard at the top of the Bratva. But *David's* phone wasn't monitored. She could get in, get to her shadow account and get out within minutes. The small rectangle was a lifeline to MI6 and lay within arm's reach while David slept soundly beside her. Hell, she didn't even have to leave the bed. She could position the sheets up over her head so the illumination from the face of the phone wouldn't disturb him. The mental pros and cons battled against themselves in her brain for over a half hour before she finally made a decision.

Taty slowly reached over and laid her hand on the phone, pausing to make sure David's breathing didn't change. The small noise that the phone made when the metal back scraped the wood bedside table echoed through her mind. She froze, stopped breathing and listened to David's steady inhale-exhale rhythm continue. She slowly retracted her arm with the phone in her hand until it was tucked against her chest. She rested for several minutes. The digital numbers on the bedside clock changed, but thankfully, David's breathing hadn't. Taty pulled the silk sheet up toward her neck. Dammit! She gently tugged the sheets. David was lying on the excess material, restricting her ability to move it up. She waited a few moments and slowly scooted down under the material, stopping beside David's hip. Her senses filled with their combined scent. His muscles twitched as if he were dreaming. She waited long moments, listening to his breathing to ensure he hadn't awoken. Carefully, she turned toward him, using his body and hers to shield the light that would activate when she pushed the home button. She faced the phone as far toward the bed as she could and still see the screen to manipulate the lock. She carefully went through the six steps that would grant her access and quickly went to her ghost email via the private browser function. She hit the draft folder and read the messages her handlers had left her. They thought she'd been compromised. No, not good. She silently tapped out a message in response:

>Turtle *slowandsteady@rvanft.net*
    Rabbit,
    New runner found. Finish line visible. Race organizer within reach.
    Turtle

. . .

Taty backed out of the account, leaving the message in the draft folder. She hit the home button, locked the phone and planted it face down on the mattress. She was starting to perspire under the sheet, especially with David's body heat radiating next to her. A moment to still her racing heart and then she'd return the phone to the bedside table. She'd done it, she'd made contact, and it would be untraceable. She closed her eyes and said a small prayer that this mission would be over soon. The prayer couldn't hurt.

His hand carded through her hair. The movement froze her instantly. The soft touch ran through her curls again. In an instant, Tatyana pushed the phone as far away as she could while at the same time lifting up and over him. She licked his hipbone and was rewarded with a low groan. Under her, his body repositioned, and his legs opened, giving her access to his incredible cock. His musk and taste were undeniably more pronounced since they'd made love before he'd fallen asleep. Both hands found purchase in her hair. She made no pretense of subtlety and immediately took his soft cock in her mouth and fondled his heavy balls with her hand.

She listened to him moan her name softly and closed her eyes. The necessity of completing her mission was the impetus of this contact. Shame washed over her. She'd done so many things to bring the Bratva down, but this…

"So good." David flipped the sheet down, giving her fresh air and a visual of the man she was with. She hummed and worked his hardened shaft with her hand and mouth. Right now she'd give anything to find a way to vindicate this man of the crime he'd initiated in Switzerland.

He lifted off the bed, curling up to grab her under her arms. He pulled her up with him as he lay back down.

"Didn't I wear you out earlier?" His smile was sleepy and unguarded.

"You did." She lowered into a long lingering kiss. Her tongue and his danced in a slow, languid slide. She lifted away and smiled down at him. "You make me feel… generous."

"How so?"

"I want to give you more than I should." She spoke the absolute truth and hoped a miracle could deliver her from the actions she knew she'd have to take. A miracle that would end up with this man being innocent and not charged with human trafficking.

"I must admit, I didn't anticipate you, Tatyana." He traced her lips with his finger. David watched as his touch moved over her skin. His eyes slid up. "I fear you, my little enticement, have turned into something… unexpected."

"You don't like unexpected?" She lowered and kissed the tip of his straight nose.

He chuckled and rolled her over. Her calf hit the phone. She lifted her foot and pushed it toward the bottom of the bed while distracting him by pulling him down into a kiss. He broke away and trailed kisses down her neck.

"You didn't answer me." Her hands traveled over his shoulders and back, feeling the muscles move and contract under her fingers.

"My life is solitary, by design. Unanticipated factors are a liability. *You* are a liability."

Her stomach dropped at his words said between kisses. Tatyana threaded her hands through his hair and gently tugged to get him to lift up. "I am here to do a job. One *you* contracted." The weight of the truth fell like a hundred pound lead weight between them.

He lifted up to his elbows so she could see his face. He held her gaze for what felt like an eternity. "Oh, you are doing a job. Make no mistake; I know what you do and why you are here. Our destinies have crossed for a specific reason. But, I will regret when our time together ends. Perhaps in another life, there would be room for more, but neither of us are romantics or idealists. We both know the reality of our actions. You have your path, and I have mine. When the second deal is complete, we will be at our journey's end. I *will not* alter my destiny, and you can't alter yours."

She more than understood the harsh reality he'd just put into words. Hell, she'd lived it for years. The respite of their time together was just that. A blip on the screen as she sought out her target. Too bad he would be collateral damage. David's expression gave nothing away as he lifted away from her and walked into the bathroom.

Taty waited until the door closed before she scrambled to the bottom of the bed and fished for his phone. The damn sheet tangled around the phone. She lifted and pulled the material. The phone spun free from the twisted silk landing with a distinct 'thunk' on the thick carpeting. She lunged off the side of the bed, stretched out and hung upside down grabbing for the phone. Gravity was her enemy, and David's expensive silk sheets gave no friction to stop the slide. Taty arched her back and stuck out her hand to grab the footboard, but missed, landing face first in a naked heap on the floor beside the bed. The top sheet slithered down the side of the bed and pooled beside her. She groaned at the discomfort of David's phone pressed directly under her.

"What in the hell just happened?" David strode across the room wearing a pair of jogging pants and a t-shirt. Taty lifted her head while still lying on the man's phone. "I was going to follow you but got tangled up in the sheets."

A smiled lifted the corner of his mouth before it broke across his face.

Taty grabbed at the top sheet, suddenly conscious of her naked sprawl. "What? I've never been accused of being graceful." She draped the material over her and sat up, keeping the phone under the sheet.

David extended a hand to help her up.

There was no way she was lifting off the phone. She shook her head in an obstinate fashion. "No thank you, I'll get up by myself."

"Suit yourself. I don't know about you, but I'm hungry." He headed to the door.

"You are always hungry," Taty said the words to herself as she stood up. It took two seconds to replace the phone. She tried to walk while wrapping the sheet around her five or six times. She stumbled out of the bedroom toward the kitchen. David had a platter of meats and cheeses out and was searching through the kitchen cabinets. Taty scooched up onto a bar stool and watched the man. He moved with a fluid grace that someone with his bulk shouldn't be able to achieve. Looking at him in the dim light of the kitchen, his scars darkened. There were several that appeared to be knife wounds, and one that she could swear was a burn.

"We'll call your employers tomorrow. They will have three hours to arrive at the location I stipulate. I'll sort the details out with you in the morning."

"You are a fool, David. Don't go through with this." Taty watched as he built a sandwich the size of her head.

He glanced over at her and shrugged his shoulder. "I've been accused of worse. My reasons for doing this are not up for discussion." He dropped the sandwich onto a plate and headed out of the kitchen. Over his shoulder, he spoke, "I have work to do in the office. Don't wait up."

Jason stopped at his secretary's call. He glanced over his shoulder at the woman. How she ran in those heels, he'd never understand. "God, please slow down. I can't have you breaking an ankle. I'd be lost without you telling me which way to go."

"Stop laughing at me." Sonya swatted at his arm with a manila folder she was carrying. "I knew you wouldn't be back at the office anytime soon. I tried calling around but I'd either just missed you, or no one had seen you."

She fell into step with him as they approached Jewell's queendom. Jason paused to push in the security code to get them into the outer offices. As soon as he closed the door, Sonya brought him up to speed, "I don't know why, but MI6 has called twice. The agent's name is Spencer Churchill."

"You are shitting me, right?" Jason laughed out loud.

"Nope. Anyway, the man stated he needed to talk to you regarding the current operations against the Bratva."

"Holy fuck, please tell me he was on secure comms." Something as simple as a few unguarded words could cost several teams their lives.

"Yes. He wouldn't say what it was in regard to during our first conversation, but as soon as he made reference to our current operations with his second contact, I told him that I'd have you reach out to him. I also sent a request to Jewell to trace the call to ensure it originated at an MI6 switch. It did."

Jason scratched his jaw before he nodded. "Okay. I'll have Jewell hook me up with secure comms here and reach out to our new friend across the pond. Thanks for running me down."

"I won't make it a habit. Lord knows I abhor cardio workouts." She twirled on her six-inch heels and headed back to his offices.

Jason waited in the soundproof conference room. The light on the phone turned yellow and then green. A short chirp told him his call had been connected and the green light told him both ends were encrypted.

He picked up the handset. "This is Jason King."

"Ahhh… good evening, or rather, good afternoon, Mr. King. Spencer Churchill here. I'm a division chief for MI6. Recently I was made aware of an offensive being coordinated by your organization to take out the legs of the Bratva."

The man would have to be pretty high in MI6 rank structure to have that knowledge. Jason waited because he'd be damned if he was going to acknowledge the fact.

A huff of air came through the line before the man cleared his throat. "I have an operative that has been undercover for the last eight years. Turtle is close to identifying the top players in this game."

"So give me your operative's identity, and we'll work around him." Jason wasn't about to out his operative, but if MI6 would identify an ally, they'd work with the agent.

"I haven't been cleared to identify our asset. It was my hope that you'd be able to give me something to relay to the field to assist us in getting our assets in synch?"

Jason rubbed the back of his neck and shook his head even though the man couldn't see his mannerism.

"I'm not at liberty to disclose any information about operations currently in progress." Jason fell back on the line he'd used countless times with other agencies.

"Bloody Hell."

The clipped exasperation echoed Jason's sentiments. He knew the division chief was in the same position as he was. "Exactly my thoughts."

"Listen, mate, I'm stretching my authorization here. The last contact was today, or rather last night your time. They are close to identifying the head of the organization. I know you can't disclose anything, but for god's sake make sure there is no unnecessary bloodshed."

"We have the same objectives in mind, Agent Churchill. I'll do my best."

"That's all I can ask for."

Jason disconnected the call and mulled over the conversation. The MI6 handler had given him more than he'd expected. The MI6's agent's code name was Turtle. He'd get Jewell and her team busy working that tidbit of information before he got ahold of Joseph. He needed advice from someone who'd been in Mike and Turtle's shoes.

CHAPTER 19

Taty rode in the back of the darkened SUV followed by a large bus. That vehicle's windows were also blacked out. Transportation for the merchandise no doubt. She gazed at the men in the SUV with her. They were armed to the teeth. The weaponry instilled caution. It felt wrong and foreign. In all the transactions she'd supervised in Europe, there were no weapons allowed on the buyer or his party—ever. The men, including David, were dressed in worn blue jeans, polos and leather jackets. There was no way to tell who the buyer was.

"You will do all the talking when we arrive," David spoke to her over his shoulder. He was riding in the front passenger seat, not in the rear of the vehicle. She added another tactical kudo in his favor.

Taty met his eyes, wondering what he was planning. She cocked her head, questioning him without words. He handed her a phone. "You will inspect all fifteen. Casey and I will accompany you. You will not look at or talk to any of us, just do the inspection. If there are issues, you will use this phone, press and hold the number one. The line will engage. Speak into the phone when the line engages. If I move away from you, drop the deal. If I stay with you, continue on."

"Do you have the account information?" Taty pocketed the phone.

"It will be handed to you after you approve of the merchandise. You will let me know of anything that may be off with the transaction via the phone. Understood?"

The intensity of his stare shot through her. Tatyana nodded again and suppressed a shiver. This was the side of David Xavier she'd suspected when she'd first met the man weeks ago. This… savage, unrestrained, aggression that she'd seen only once before. Adrenaline spiked through her veins. She was hyper aware of all the men in the truck. The man, Casey, was dark skinned and had black hair like David. Both wore aviators and dressed similarly. Even if the Bratva had any idea what David looked like, it would be a gamble as to which man to…

To what? Taty's mind ticked off the possible reasons for the subterfuge. The Bratva wanted the transaction to go through. Jeopardizing the buyer would be asinine. The fifteen women would be the largest order filled to date, as far as she knew. Four was the most she'd ever delivered to one buyer, and the Bratva had been very pleased with that order. After all, who wouldn't want a cool twelve million dollars? But David was buying fifteen women at three million each? Forty-five million dollars with a promise of double that in a few months' time. No, the Bratva wouldn't jeopardize the payday coming their way. Unless... Taty glanced around her again as realization dawned like morning rays of golden sunshine. Kidnapping and ransoming David Xavier would give the Bratva access to hundreds of millions of dollars. That was it. That was what the precautions, the look alike guards, the similar dress and the phone were about.

"How do I explain your absence? You had me tell the Bratva you would personally inspect your purchases."

"Unavoidably detained by business. I sent you as my proxy. If they want the next deal, they will proceed."

They slowed and turned into a large compound. The gate stood wide open with no guards Tatyana could see. Her gaze traveled across the rooftops of the neighboring structures. The afternoon sunset, blocking the winter light, made the lot they bounced over dark and ominous. The SUV ventured around the corner of the cavernous warehouse and pulled into a large bay. Taty took in the scene immediately and noted the two vehicles parked facing them. One was an old bread truck, the other a dark sedan. The

SUV she was traveling in came to a stop, and the bus continued around, only stopping after the driver had it facing out of the building. Again, smart on many levels. Taty took a deep breath. She needed to make this deal happen. All her plans hinged on getting to the meeting where the bosses would meet with David. As if coordinated, all four doors of the SUV opened, and the men stepped out. She watched and waited. When David nodded to her, she exited the vehicle. The doors on the sedan opened. Taty stutter-stepped when she recognized the man who exited. Evgeniy Kuznetsov, the sadistic, evil, *toy trainer* smirked at her from a distance. "Where is the buyer, Tatyana?" he asked in his native language.

Tatyana shrugged and replied in English, "Unavoidably detained. He sent me to inspect and accept the order."

The man straightened and examined the set of towering armed guards who flanked her on the left and right. She knew instinctively the one on her left was David.

"Exactly who do you work for, my little concierge?" Again he asked in Russian.

Taty put her hands on her hips and spat back in Russian, "I work for the same people as you do, and I am following the order the boss has given me. I am doing everything I can to ensure these deals go through. Now, if you are done with the stupid questions, Evgeniy, I will inspect the cargo and get the boss his payment."

"Always such an ice-cold bitch, Anya. One day you and I will meet on my terms." The lecherous bastard had the audacity to lick his lips and adjust his cock in his pants. She heard an almost inaudible growl emanate from David.

"The only way you would get me was if you fucked my dead body, you disgusting pig." Taty turned on her heel and headed back to the vehicle, hoping that David and Casey would follow her. She heard their footsteps behind her and mentally cheered that they backed her ballsy move.

"Where do you think you are going?" Evgeniy yelled after her.

"Obviously you do not want this deal to go through. She lifted the phone David had given her earlier in the air, still walking away. "I'm calling the boss and telling him you fucked up the deal. Good luck with what little life you have left."

"Stop. The merchandise is here."

Taty stopped and turned around slowly. Evgeniy's face was blood red with anger, but she knew the threat had hit its target. She was above Evgeniy in the food chain now, and they both knew it.

"Bring them out. One at a time. After I inspect, they will be taken to the bus."

Evgeniy nodded to Thing One, who had been driving the truck. The thug nodded at Taty before he headed to the back of the van. The door squeaked open, and a series of small cries could be heard. Thing Two pulled a naked woman behind him. She heard Casey quickly suck in a sharp breath of air. Taty performed her duties—fourteen times. The young women were in poor condition, not even close to the quality the Bratva provided to the elite buyers. They were not acceptable, but she needed this sale to go through. At least the bracelets on their wrists showed that they had been examined by medical and were free from disease. No, she'd tell David to get the women examined. Nothing here was going as it should be. Taty waited for the last woman to be removed and cringed at the small bruised frame that emerged. Both David and Casey stiffened and shuffled at her side. Tatyana did not wait for the woman to be brought to her. She picked up the phone and hit speed dial one. When the phone engaged, she spoke. "One of the toys has been damaged. Soft tissue bruising and she looks malnourished. What are your orders?" She glanced at Evgeniy who shrugged as if to say *"Whoops."*

David did not move a muscle. She nodded her head as if she was receiving instructions. She formed a plan in her mind and hung up the phone. She motioned toward one of the guards that had been escorting the women to the bus. "You, pick her up and carry her."

The man lifted the tiny woman into his arms and held her close, allowing her to hide against his neck. The veins in his throat and forehead were pulsing with rage as she knew David's would be if she'd glance at him.

"You will not be paid for that one." Taty was ready for Evgeniy's reaction. He swung toward her, and she moved. She dropped and swept her foot, knocking him on his back. Two forty-five caliber Desert Eagles, one from each side of her, pointed directly at the man. Things One and Two were covered by David's security team.

"You'd better get your story right, Evgeniy. Damaged goods are never presented to the buyers." She held her hand up and snapped her fingers. A piece of paper was presented to her. She stepped around the piece of shit on the concrete floor and handed the paper to Thing One. "Tell the bosses exactly what happened here. We will hold him and his driver for ten minutes."

"You can't do that!" Evgeniy shouted. Casey planted a huge boot in the middle of the man's chest and ground out, "Just try to stop us, motherfucker."

Taty dismissed the Things and watched as the old truck rumbled out of the compound, followed closely by the bus. She slowly wandered around Evgeniy's prone figure. She looked at her watch and then took in the confines of the warehouse as if she had nothing better to do. The silence in the building was crushing. She could hear the traffic outside, sirens in the distance getting stronger and then fading. The sound of motors stopping and starting formed a white noise. Her breath formed cold clouds as she breathed. Her heart bled for the poor naked women who had been transported like chattel in the freezing weather. God only knew what David was going to do to the women, but she prayed they would be clothed and fed… treated humanely at least for a while.

She glanced at her watch again and nodded. For the first time, David spoke, "Go to the vehicle." Taty turned and gave him a look of disdain trying to keep his identity a secret. "If I wanted the help's advice, I'd ask for it."

Evgeniy's arm shot out and grabbed her boot, yanking her leg back and down. She fell hard on her hip and elbow. The unguarded plummet sent a lightning bolt of pain through her shoulder and tore a scream of pain from her.

Mike flew into motion when the son of a bitch on the ground scrambled and grabbed a gun from behind his back. Casey dropped to cover Tatyana as he'd been instructed to do and his training and experience took over. He kicked the man's hand, dislodging the weapon, and dropped onto the Russian's chest. The driver's side door to the sedan opened. He twisted, recognized a threat and shot as Evgeniy's driver raised an automatic in Tatyana's direction. Mike jerked back while he was firing as he moved when the bastard below him grabbed his firing arm and twisted, trying to dislodge his gun. He knew the shot hit the motherfucker, but he had no idea if he'd taken the son of a bitch out. He countered the piece of shit's maneuver, and they grappled for a few seconds. Evgeniy twisted and reached for his gun. Mike rounded on him with an elbow to the cheek. Blood and teeth sprayed from the man's mouth, but the bastard wouldn't stop. The Russian bucked up and twisted. He slapped the man's arm away and dug the barrel of his forty-five into the man's temple. He wanted nothing more than to splatter the fucker's brain onto the cement. "Move a muscle, and you're dead."

"I'm already dead."

Mike saw a flash of metal and reacted, shifting to try to cover his core and vital organs. He felt the blade as he squeezed the trigger of his weapon. His reflex muscle spasm was a reaction to the searing pain and imminent threat, not an intentional kill.

Casey was beside him in an instant and Tatyana was there a second later. She held her arm against her stomach. "David, don't move. The knife is lodged in your hip."

He pushed off the dead man and grabbed the knife. He pulled it out and threw it away. Lifting up, he stood with Casey's help. What a fucking mess. He'd told Casey he was paying ransom on the women from Russians who'd kidnapped them. The man picked his most trusted men and briefed them on David's cover story. They'd bought it hook, line and sinker. Thank God. He surveyed the spray of brain matter against the concrete and winced at the pain of the stab wound as the adrenaline ebbed from his system. "Casey, get us out of here and close this place up. Don't let the security company come back here for at least twenty-four hours. Get me back to the apartment." If Guardian were on the ball, there would already be a team covering this building, and they would have had eyes on the situation. Jacob's people would clean up the mess. The warm seep of blood darkened his jeans and ran down his leg, soaking into his sock. He needed a doctor. The wound wasn't the worst he'd ever had, but he needed to stem the flow of blood and the damn thing probably needed stitches. He could do it himself... if there wasn't any muscle damage.

"You need a doctor." A very pale Tatyana carefully cradled her arm.

"Broken or dislocated?" He limped toward the SUV while putting as much pressure on his wound as possible.

"I don't know."

They somehow managed to get into the rear of the vehicle. Casey and the others piled in and tore out of the building. Mike glanced back before they turned the corner and thought he saw someone in black tactical gear slip into the warehouse.

He withdrew the phone Taty had been given by her bosses. She handed him the one she'd used to stage the call earlier. "Call them. Tell them what happened. Find out if it was an intentional trap. Tell them I wasn't there, my people have briefed me and that I'm pissed. I want to meet with the boss, soon, and I won't take no for an answer."

Taty nodded, activated it and hit redial and put it on speaker phone. "You were told never to call."

"Evgeniy tried to kill me today."

"Evgeniy?"

"Yes. He died for his troubles."

"You are in New York?"

"Yes."

"You met with the American storekeeper, Daniel, to complete the transaction?"

"No. Only Evgeniy and my two escorts were present."

"All dead?"

"No. The escorts have the account number."

"They were not your contacts. They were not to be at the meeting."

"They were who was present."

"Our client is… well?"

"Our client did not attend. He sent me."

There was a pregnant pause. "Evgeniy acted on his own. The escorts have not contacted us with the account information."

"The client paid in good will. I do not know if he will deal with us again. The merchandise was sub-par. One of the toys was badly damaged. All were in poor condition."

"We will call you back."

"No. The client will not allow it. He will give me the phone when he wants to initiate contact."

"The circumstances are regrettable. You will use everything at your disposal to ensure the rest of this deal is successful or you will follow in Evgeniy's footsteps."

The line went dead.

Taty dropped the phone to her lap after shutting it off. He took the device and pocketed it. He groaned and leaned closer to her trying, to alleviate the pain in his hip and upper thigh.

"You need a doctor, David."

"There will be one at the apartment when we arrive." At least he hoped Jacob would send one. No, he knew one would be on the way. The team was definitely providing high cover, and even the small glimpse of the bus driver and attendant told him Guardian had his six. Hell, his team had his back, and that felt damn good. Mike shifted again and grimaced in pain. The fucker had perforated him.

"How? You did not call anyone."

"Don't ask questions I won't answer, Tatyana." The traffic over the Brooklyn Bridge was chaotic on a good day. Today wasn't a good day. There was a traffic accident between a minivan and a delivery truck that took out two lanes and the stupidity of people who slowed down to gawk at the twisted carnage brought things to a crawl. He had to move so his leg didn't bend at the hip. He did the only thing he could and lay across the bench seat with his head in Taty's lap. Her good hand wove through his hair and started a rhythmic sweeping motion. He focused on the movement and the sounds of the city outside the darkened windows of the SUV.

Ember King rubbed the small of her back. Junior was causing some serious discomfort, and she was just seven months pregnant. Joseph's voice rumbled through their home. Grabbing her freshly made tea, she padded into the office and settled down next to the fireplace. Joseph turned and gazed at her, raising his eyebrows in question. She made a soft, pffft sound and waved him back to his conversation. You'd think she was made of paper-thin china or something. The man hovered. Those two helicopters over at the landing strip had absolutely nothing on Joey.

Ember lost herself in the latest book from The Warden. Damn that woman could write. Her vamps were alpha, sexy and macho as hell.

"What are you reading?" She jumped and twisted, looking back at him. His soft words whispered in her ear scared the shit out of her. The man was a freaking ghost. Seriously, how did he still sneak up on her?

"Dammit, Joey, you really need to make some noise. One of these times you are going to scare this baby out of me!" Ember regretted the words immediately. The laughter in his eyes disappeared.

"No. I didn't mean that. Honestly. I'm fine, the

baby's fine, and you can sneak up on me anytime you want to."

"I didn't think." His whispered words were low and apologetic.

Ember grabbed his hand. "Come sit with me." She waited until he moved onto the couch with her. "I love you. You are quite possibly a worry-wart, but I'll excuse that because I love you. Now, tell me what the phone call was about."

"Work."

Ember sighed at the singular word. Yep, that was her husband. A man of few words. Hell, she'd be happy with a few words—a few words more!

"And…" She snuggled into his side and smiled as his hand caressed her baby bump possessively.

"I need to leave in a couple of days. I'll be gone a week, tops." His voice rumbled through his chest and against her cheek.

"Work as in what you used to do or what you do now?" She knew something big was happening. Keelee was her best friend, and she got the 411 about Doc leaving to take care of some business. She'd hoped Joey wouldn't be called into whatever was going on.

"Work as in tying up some loose ends so the family is safer."

"The Russians?"

"Mmm."

"Promise me you'll come back to us, safe and in one piece." Ember put her hand over his and moved it to where Junior was pushing his foot out. He didn't answer, and that drew her attention from her soon to be son, to the man she loved more than life itself.

"I made you a promise to never lie to you."

"You did. After Aruba. Rat bastard."

He chuckled and kissed her temple. His five o'clock shadow prickled against her skin. "I will do my job. I'll protect my family, and I will come home."

Ember swallowed the emotion his words engendered. What he hadn't said weighed on her more than what he had. "All right. We'll be good here. I have three other doctors at the hospital, and Junior won't be here anytime soon."

"We should decide on a name."

Ember smiled and moved Joey's hand again, chasing her rambunctious baby as his foot moved in her womb.

"We've narrowed it down to two names. Blake or Lincoln. Which do you like best?"

"Blake."

"So 'B's?"

Joseph shrugged. "I like the name."

"Blake King. That sounds like a solid name."

"So you'll stop calling him Junior?"

"I don't know. Joseph Junior has a ring to it." Ember squealed when Joey's fingers drifted to her rib cage and started tickling. "Stop, or I'll pee my pants!" She held his hand and drew a deep breath. With the baby sitting on her bladder that threat was more imminent than she'd like to admit.

"When do you leave?"

"I'm flying out with Doc tomorrow morning."

Ember threaded her fingers through the touch of gray at his temples. "Well then, Mr. King, you'd better love me like crazy tonight."

CHAPTER 20

J ason King pushed his way through the door
to the ops center. It was a fucking family
reunion without the alcohol. Jacob and Tori
worked the displays while Jewell typed fran-
tically on the workstation in the corner. Joseph and
Jared lounged in the theater seating, sandwiching
Jasmine between them. Jade was still undercover and
Justin… well, his talents weren't coming out to play
in this scenario. Jason straddled the aisleway and
crossed his arms over his chest. The bus and the SUV
carrying Mike and the Russian operative entered the
warehouse. From the helmet cams of the positioned
team, there was a visual of the garage door they'd
entered and… yes, the front door of the bus. He
watched with everyone else. The minutes ticked by
before movement drew every eye. Jasmine's hiss of
air was the only sound when the first woman was led
to the bus door, hands tied in front of her and naked.

Jason looked at the weather conditions and hated the bastards even more. Fucking ten degrees outside without the wind chill and the motherfuckers delivered the women naked.

Jason barked out, "Are they outfitted to receive the women?"

"Yeah, Adam has it handled. He and Ember have a team from the ranch ready to go not far away. Nobody knew what to expect, so they have enough equipment to take care of any contingency."

"Dixon and Drake have supplies on the bus?" Jason needed confirmation.

"Don't know. They drove in this morning and fell in behind the SUV. It doesn't look like they are letting Mike's men into the bus, so I'm sure they have something going on inside." Jacob pointed to the screen where one of Mike's men stopped short and handed off the woman. There was no visual of either twin. They were playing it smart. Jason took a breath and fixated on the screen.

Jared leaned forward and cast a look at his sister. "Jewell, is the system working?"

"Yeah, we're ready to go." She glanced over at Jason.

"Send it." He gave the command while his eyes stayed glued to the warehouse doors.

Jewell hit the button and three other screens illuminated. Jacob and Tori launched into action and Jared, Joseph and Jasmine stood to take in the spectacle. Two takedowns on known Russian Mafia positions and a raid at a bordello operated by the Bratva started within seconds of each other. The operations were timed to distract the Bratva's leadership and keep them off balance. This was the second series of attacks on the mob today. The timing could have raised suspicions if they hadn't terrorized the fuck out of the Russians earlier. The raids and takedowns diverted Jason's attention for a few seconds. He let his brothers deal with the necessities of the operations. His focus was at the location where the head of the snake was being positioned. They had no plan B. Mike had to get to the leadership.

"Shit." Jason's words pulled Jewell and Jasmine's eyes to the screen. Mike's man carried a small... ah hell... was that a child? Jason's stomach rolled in disgust. He watched one of the Wonder Twins reach out for the girl. The men on the screen flinched at the same time looking toward the back of the warehouse. Dixon or Drake scooped the girl from the man's arms and headed for the bus. The door moved shut behind him.

The old bread truck that the mob had transported the women in raced out of the warehouse with their bus on the old vehicle's ass. The van turned left, and Guardian's bus turned right.

"Put that bus on a map and track it," Jason demanded as he kept his eyes on the warehouse.

"Shots fired!" The team leader at the Bronx warehouse broke radio silence. "Archangel, do we move in?"

"Negative! Position for entry but stay out of sight." Jason watched the screen and chanted beneath his breath, *come on... come on... come on...* The SUV screamed out of the warehouse. "Go! Secure the site and report."

Jason watched the team. Waiting for information was the single worst part of his job. "Archangel. Two down, not team players. Evidence of a fight. A fuck-ton of blood splatter. The primaries may be injured."

"Get Maliki to the apartment."

"Working it. A coded UHF message will go out in about two minutes," Jewell said as her fingers flew over the keyboard.

Jason rubbed the back of his neck and drew a deep breath. They were doing things the old fashioned way and it sucked, but they had the equipment pulled out of mothballs. The fucking Bratva had super hackers. No problem. They'd operated in decades past. Newer didn't always mean better.

He couldn't worry about Mike until he knew the score. He glanced at the red dot that represented the bus. It was traveling through the Bronx. The duress signal had not been activated, so the twins were taking care of business. He turned his attention to the side screens. "Report. The Operation in Helsinki is over. Three in custody." Jacob glanced over at Jason as he spoke. "One of ours is down. A bullet wound to the abdomen. It doesn't look good."

Fuck. Jason moved to the next screen, Jared briefed him on the status. "Miami op is winding down. Twenty-seven being held in locked rooms. The teams are reporting most are drugged, a few are in bad shape. Locals have ambulances on standby, but they need more. The teams are working with Miami-Dade and the FBI. The fucking Bratva lost a big operation tonight."

Jason nodded and carried on to the third operation.

"The team in Chicago is reporting both members of the Bratva committed suicide after the initial breach. It's all on the helmet cams." Jason's eyes narrowed at Joseph's words. "Why? What is so important about operations in Chicago that they would die rather than surrender to us?"

Joseph rubbed his five o'clock shadow and glanced over at Jason. "Maybe they'd been programed to do that? I mean, if they worked close to the bosses or with sensitive information, we can assume they would have a mandate. I've seen situations where an operative is caught, and their families are summarily executed."

Jason lifted his glasses up and pinched the bridge of his nose. "All right. Jewell, we will need everything on those two. Ram a microscope up their digital asses and give me everything since their mom and dad conceived them."

"On it." Jewell never turned away from the keyboards in front of her.

"Tori, let me know the second that bus makes it to the compound."

"I will, and we have three teams tracking it looking for tails or anything that is out of place or suspicious." She glanced over her shoulder, "Jewell, I need access to Brooklyn's traffic cams and the traffic signal grid."

"Yeah… coming your way."

Jason heard Jewell's response as he gazed at the pictures coming out of the brothel. He watched as the team leader reached down to open a trapdoor found under one of the beds. "Oh, fuck. No way." Jason leaned forward as if that would help him see down the hole.

"What is that?" Jasmine asked.

"Coke or H," Jared replied. "Whatever it is, the amount is insane." They watched as brick after brick of the substance was hauled out of the hidden compartment.

His watch buzzed, reminding Jason of a meeting. He silenced his notification and took one last glance at the screens. "I want status updates on all four situations every thirty minutes. Jacob, get me a medical update on our downed man in Helsinki. I need to pull his folder and contact family if he has any."

"Roger that, it will be in your inbox before you get to your office."

Jason took a deep breath and turned away from the events on the screens. While these missions were important to him personally, there was so much more coming down the pike. The evil of the world never rested.

~

"Mr. Xavier, we have security from the apartment on the comms. There is a doctor requesting access."

He opened eyes that he honestly didn't remember closing and found Casey's concerned mug looking at him over the front seat. *On comms... shit.*

"Any names given?"

"No sir, the doctor declined to provide any information other than you have a standing appointment."

Good, so no damage would have to be mitigated by the telephone call if it were monitored. He nodded and swallowed hard clearing his throat. "Let him in."

The semi-permanent furrow in Casey's brow deepened, but the man relayed his instructions. The truck struck a huge pothole and Taty gasped sharply. Hell, he did too.

"Sorry, sir, ma'am. I'm trying to take the fastest route. It isn't the smoothest." Thomas, the driver and a member of his primary security team, spoke for the first time today.

He let out the breath he'd sucked in and nodded. The trip had already lasted almost an hour and a half. The wound on his hip had stopped bleeding, but he knew it would rip open as soon as he moved. Tatyana had to be in excruciating pain, but the woman didn't complain. Not once. A dislocated or separated shoulder was one painful bitch to deal with. A fact he knew from an experience involving a helicopter,

Dixon and Drake, and no seatbelt. Damn, he missed those two buffoons.

"Sir, we're here." Casey's voice nudged into his thoughts.

He nodded and lifted up. He felt the denim of his jeans rip the dried, clotted blood away from his wound as he shifted. He grabbed his hip and waited for Casey to open his door. Four guards in suits and wearing comms equipment sprinted out of the building and joined Thomas, Casey and the rest of his primary security team. The men built a human wall around them as they limped across the sidewalk and through the lobby. More of his security were posted at the lobby entrances and elevators, which ensured they would not be seen by any other residents. He made it into the private elevator and leaned against the wall. Tatyana looked a hell of a lot worse than he felt. From the pallor of her skin and the black circles under her eyes, he feared she would pass out any second. He glanced at Thomas and nodded toward her. The man's eyes followed his, and the guard reacted immediately. He watched as Thomas moved over and carefully wrapped an arm around his woman. *What the fuck? My woman?* Mike forced his gaze down to the blood stain on his jeans to ensure any emotion in his eyes was shielded. How in the hell could he consider a criminal, a Russian mobster, as his woman? No. She belonged in prison. Full stop. Although, she'd done one hell of a job handling every piece of crap that flew her way today.

The woman was a quick study. She'd improvised and swung at each curveball she'd been thrown. As soon as he could, he'd get Casey to give him a rundown of the Russian portions of the conversation. Even with the advanced tutelage he'd received, his ability to follow the language at the speed Tatyana and Evgeniy spoke was tested. One of the primary reasons he'd chosen Casey's team to be his security for the mission was the man's fluency in several Russian dialects.

He limped out of the elevator when it opened. He got three steps before Maliki Blue grabbed his arm, swung it around his neck and took the majority of Mike's weight as he assisted him to the bedroom.

"Dammit, dude. It never ends, does it?" Maliki commented as they hobbled along.

"Take a look at Tatyana." He directed the doctor toward where Thomas was helping Tatyana.

"Is she bleeding like you?" The doctor snapped the question at him.

"No," Mike admitted. He didn't see what the issue was. He'd been injured worse than this before. Maliki damn near dragged him to the bed and wasn't too gentle about it either.

"So you suspect she has internal injuries?"

Maliki had him lie down on the bed. He groaned at the wave of nausea that accompanied the sudden movement from lateral to horizontal. "No. She has a dislocated or separated shoulder."

"I'm fine. Treat him." Taty's voice behind him was shaky but determined.

Maliki left the side of the bed and grabbed his bag. "How about both of you shut the hell up. Let me use the medical degree I earned to determine who to treat first."

Mike did a double take at the doctor's verbal volley. He'd met Maliki several times and spent a couple of weeks at the training facility with his team. He was Foxtrot team's doctor or rather *had been* their doctor before Jacob dissolved the team. He unbuttoned and unzipped his pants at the doctor's command. Maliki instructed Thomas to escort Tatyana to a large chair. The man did a quick assessment on her before he returned and carefully pulled Mike's jeans and boxers down over his injured hip.

A low whistle sounded, and Mike lifted his head to see the damage. The knife wound looked jagged and ran about five inches before it went deep and stopped. *Oh fuck, that's going to leave a mark.*

"When was the last time you had a tetanus shot?" Maliki gloved up, pulled out a drape, rubbing alcohol, betadine, gauze and other things he was all too familiar with but would rather forget.

"I'm up to date." Mike reached down in front of Maliki shielding his hands from Taty's view. He used American Sign Language to spell out:

Undercover. My name is David.

Maliki nodded and grabbed a syringe. "Sorry, David. This isn't going to feel good, but I need to clean that wound out and see what I'm working with." He glanced over his shoulder and snapped at Casey. "I need towels and a couple of big plastic trash bags." Mike watched Casey head out of the room. Maliki busied himself with the prep of his equipment until Casey returned. Mike was unceremoniously rolled to maneuver the plastic under him. He grunted as he righted himself again.

Maliki chuckled and bent over before he signed:

Quit being a baby. You've stubbed your toe and hurt yourself worse.

He huffed a laugh and responded:

Your bedside manner sucks.

Maliki lifted his eyes and winked before he filled the syringe with sterile water. "All right, David, be a good patient and hold still."

He dropped his head and let the doctor clean and stitch his wound. The fucking Russian hadn't done too much damage, and Maliki had been correct, he'd been hurt far worse. Having nothing better to do while he lay there being sewn back together, he reviewed everything that happened in the warehouse.

He arched his back and looked past Maliki. "Evgeniy was trying to screw over your bosses?"

Taty's face was as pale as a country snow bank. She cast an eye at the men in the room. Mike took a deep breath. "My security team won't talk, and the doctor is a trusted employee."

Maliki lifted his head and arched an eyebrow

KRIS MICHAELS

before he went back to work. Taty drew a shaky breath. "It is the only thing I can think of that makes sense."

Mike batted that around for a moment. "Will the escorts know what to do with the routing number?"

"Doubtful. They are not the sharpest tools. I think maybe they saw a way to escape. They will be found and... taken care of."

He palmed his phone and made a call. He watched Maliki place a bandage over the wound.

"Mr. Xavier's office, Joel speaking."

"Joel, the account I had you activate this morning, has there been any activity?"

"One moment, sir." Mike heard the telltale tapping of keys and mouse clicks before a few moments of silence. "No, sir."

"Good. Transfer all assets from the account to one of the other offshore folders. I'll call later with further instructions."

"Very well, sir. Will there be anything else?"

He looked down at his wound and over at Tatyana. He trusted his staff, but only to a point. Shit was about to get real on this mission, and he needed to contain the people who had information —any information about today's events. The security team that he'd taken to the warehouse had been handpicked and given enough information to believe they were assisting the women, not buying them for sex slaves. Casey and his team were solid. He'd talk to Jacob and Jared about recruiting them

234

when this op finished. They'd flourish in Guardian's organization.

"Sir? Will there be anything else?"

"Yes, give Higgins and Hannah three weeks paid vacation somewhere nice. It started ten minutes ago."

"As you wish, sir. I'll have them rejoin you in San Diego?"

"That is fine. I'll meet you there, too."

"Excuse me, sir?"

He drew a deep breath. This was it. He needed to pare down to the bare minimum so there would be no collateral damage if things went south. Joel knew if he was told to take a vacation that Guardian's operation was getting close to an end.

"Joel, when was the last time you were on vacation?"

"Well… ahh… I can't actually say, sir."

Mike chuckled. "After we get the offshore accounting rectified, cancel all but the most essential meetings, then you are on an all-expense paid vacation starting tomorrow. If I need you, I'll call you on your personal cell."

"But sir… are you sure?"

"I am."

"Very well, sir."

"Goodbye, Joel."

"Goodbye… and sir? Thank you."

"No, thank you. For everything." He pushed end on the conversation as the doctor lifted his shredded boxers back over his hip. He groaned as he stood.

Damn, he felt like Danny Glover in that old *Lethal Weapon* movie… he was getting too old for this shit.

Maliki headed over to Tatyana. "So, beautiful, can you tell me exactly what happened?"

He stifled a growl of irritation at the doctor's flirtatious conversation,

"Someone grabbed my leg. I fell. I landed on my hip and my elbow."

Maliki looked at the two security guards. "Gentlemen, I think we can handle it from here."

Casey and Thomas immediately searched out Mike for confirmation. "We're good."

Thomas headed out, but Casey stood his ground. He left Maliki's side, allowing him to examine Taty, and crossed the room toward him. He leaned in and whispered, "Mr. Xavier, you aren't *just* a businessman. I can recognize one of my own. What the fuck happened today?"

He leaned away and stared dead into Casey's eyes. "I'll need a translation of the conversation. I couldn't keep up."

Casey stared back. Mike could see the questions in his eyes, but the man simply nodded before he turned toward the door. He said over his shoulder, "Yes sir, I'll get on that right away."

He headed toward the closet to put on clothes that a switchblade hadn't shredded. Maliki called to Casey and asked him to stay for a moment. Mike heard the word dislocated on the way out of the room. He *didn't* want to look at Taty as he left. He *didn't* want to go to her and comfort her. Shit, he couldn't show her any weakness. They fucked. That was all there was to the relationship. He used her to get to her bosses, and she used him for... fuck, who the hell knew what her end game was? The woman was a tangle of lies and deception.

He made an awkward and protracted affair out of changing his boxers and sliding into some athletic pants. Taty's startled, pain-filled scream had him clenching his hands into fists. That would be Maliki reducing her dislocated shoulder. He counted to three hundred before he walked back into the bedroom. Taty was on the bed, and Maliki was holding a sling with Velcro tabs.

He carefully put the contraption on her and handed her a small vial of pain pills. "Take one now and then one when you want to go to sleep. There are four in here. If you need more, have David call me. Your hip and elbow are bruised and will be stiff and sore. If the pain doesn't decrease, we can take you in for an x-ray, but I'm confident nothing is broken. Keep your shoulder iced." Maliki pointed toward him and smiled. "He's got it down to a science, so if you have any questions he can't answer, have him give me a call."

Taty swallowed the pill with the water he gave her and then reclined against the stack of pillows. He walked out of the bedroom toward the front door with Maliki. He looked around to make sure they were alone before he signed:

What are you doing in New York?

Maliki responded:

I'm freelancing. After all that has happened...

Mike nodded and asked:

How were you notified to come here?

Maliki's hands flew in a flurry of words:

I was on standby and notified by personal courier this morning to wait at the coffee shop around the corner. There was a pre-arranged signal if I was needed. Why all the old school methods on this? Are the comms compromised? I've been out of the loop for a couple of months.

Shaking his head he signed:

This op only.

Maliki nodded and looked around, appearing to see the grandeur of the apartment. "Nice digs."

He laughed quietly and shook his head. "Understatement of the year, my friend."

Maliki's smile slid off his face, and the haunted look Mike had seen one too many times in one too many faces appeared, prompting him to give the guy some encouragement. "Don't give up, Mal. It gets better."

The man's eyes snapped toward him. "Does it?"

"Yeah, I can guarantee it. You'll never be able to forget what happened, but you will learn to live with the ghosts." Mike clasped him on the shoulder. "If you need to find me, you know how. I'll always be around to listen... when you're ready to talk."

Maliki's eyes averted, and he drew a shaky breath.

"Yeah, okay. Thanks. Keep that clean. You know the drill."

"Yep."

"Stitches come out in ten days."

"Yep."

"You're not going to have a medical professional do it for you are you?"

"Nope."

"Typical."

"Yep."

"Take care Ch… David."

"You too, Mal."

CHAPTER 21

Taty knew she was waking up. She was at that stage when the pain was creeping into her consciousness and pulling her away from sleep. She turned her head and groaned. Her body ached. She blinked her eyes open and looked over to the other side of the bed. It was empty, and David didn't appear to have been to bed. It was completely dark except for the twinkle of lights from the cityscape visible outside the massive floor-to-ceiling windows. Taty held her breath as she lifted up into a sitting position. Her hip barked a sharp reminder of its injury, but the shoulder and elbow weren't too bad. Of course, she hadn't tried to move them either.

She slid from the mattress and landed on the soft carpet on her good leg. The trip to the bathroom was an awakening of aches and pains, but she'd suffered through worse. The initiation into the Bratva hurt a hell of a lot more than her current bumps and bruises. She flexed her fingers in the sling as she walked out into the living area of the apartment. The gas fireplace was lit and cast a glow around the room. She searched for David and almost missed his silhouette against the far bank of dark windows.

"Can't sleep?" She headed toward him, carefully navigating around the furniture. He glanced over his shoulder at her before he returned to whatever vigil he was holding. "No."

"When will you contact the Bratva? They will be expecting their pay." She stood next to him and looked out over the vast cityscape. Towering buildings twinkled in the distance. She'd seen pictures of some of them, but the names escaped her.

"We will call in the morning."

"What will you do?" Taty wanted him to say he was going to walk away as much as she needed him to say he was going to go through with the next purchase. The difference between want and need, in this case, was too slim to measure. She'd lost perspective. David was a man she cared for... in some fashion, as crazy as that seemed.

"Is the merchandise safe?" She'd never let herself ask that question before. It was safer not to know, especially if the answer was something she couldn't live with.

"I'm assuming they are. I told you I did not purchase the women for myself. I'm working as a broker." David turned toward her. His expression was calm, but his body was tense. She'd never have noticed if she hadn't lived with him or lain with him. He was a master at masking his emotions, but his body language—he either didn't realize it betrayed him or he couldn't modify it.

"Will you pay for the merchandise?" She left his side and went to the large overstuffed couch and lowered herself slowly into the cushions. She waited until he looked at her and patted the black leather beside her. David strode across the floor as if he hadn't been knifed only hours earlier. He did, however, hold himself carefully when he sat next to her.

"I will pay for fourteen. Three million will be deducted for the young one who was damaged as you stipulated. I have the new routing numbers."

"And you are going to purchase again?" Taty leaned into him with her good shoulder. His arm lifted, and she settled next to his warm, bare chest.

"I've been thinking about that. I need a sign of good faith. They say they were not part of the situation today. I don't have reason to believe them. I will keep the order but I demand a sit down with the head of the Bratva, and we will talk—face to face."

Taty tried desperately to calm herself. She closed her eyes and mentally relaxed each portion of her body from her feet to her neck. When she'd completed the mental exercise, she rolled her head and looked up at David. "When will you meet with them?"

David gazed out the windows. His fingers drew aimless patterns along her arm. The soft caresses were surprisingly vivid against her injured arm. "I haven't reached a decision on time and location. We will contact them tomorrow. You will remain here as their liaison until we meet, then you can return to your life."

The disappointment that pooled in her gut shouldn't have been there. She was within reach of the end of her mission. David would no doubt hire the best lawyers, or maybe relocate to avoid prosecution. Rich people did not go to jail for the crimes for which lesser people languished. That is why MI6 had started this operation so many years ago. The evidence against the ranks of the Bratva was documented and ready. Taty shivered at the memory of Evgeniy's brain splattering across the concrete. It wasn't the first time she'd seen someone killed. Hell, she'd killed people under the auspices of the Bratva's requirements, but it still amazed her how simple it was to make a person cease to exist.

"Are you cold?" David's words cut through the haze of her thoughts.

"Hmm? Cold? No. Just thinking about today." She drew away from him. "Was today the first time you've killed someone?"

David shook his head. "I told you I haven't always been the heir to this fortune. When I lived the other life, I served my country."

Taty leaned back against him. "It never gets easier."

"You've killed before?" David's fingers didn't stop moving.

"Not by choice, but I have defended myself and my cargo. I may not be a good person, but I take care of what is entrusted to me." It was one of the few things she could do to help the poor souls that flowed through her fingers.

"So you've killed for the Bratva."

"No. I killed to live." There was a difference. If David didn't see that, well, that was on him. She knew, and that let her sleep at night.

"I understand." His quiet words floated like a feather in the night, but the affirmation carried so much more weight than the simple words implied.

"Do you miss your mom? The one who raised you?" The question lingered. Neither of them moved except for David's fingertips over the skin of her upper arm.

Finally, he answered, "I mourn for the loss of the mother I wished she could have been."

"She disappointed you?" Taty lifted her eyes to look at his profile.

He seemed to consider his words carefully before he spoke, "She was disappointed by life, by me, by circumstances. I loved her. Disappointment is never an emotion I felt when I thought of my mother." David smiled sadly and chuckled. "On her good days, she was amazing. I will always remember her smile

KRIS MICHAELS

and laughter. The bad times were harder. She was simply my mother. The good didn't outweigh the bad. She was both, and I loved her."

"Your father? How did he meet your mother?" It was an obvious question. How did a man of David's father's worth meet a poor woman?

"She worked as a maid. He was an attractive man, and my mother loved him."

"He was married?"

David nodded. He withdrew his arm and stood up carefully and walked over to the bar. "I'd offer you a glass, but with the painkillers..." He shrugged and poured his cognac into a snifter.

"Have you eaten?" Taty asked. The man was a bottomless pit. He shook his head and looked down at the tawny liquid. "I have no appetite tonight." He took a sip and walked back, joining her on the couch. "What was your childhood like?"

His question made her think. She blew out a lungful of air in a sigh. "I had a perfectly normal childhood. A mother and father who loved me. A little sister who annoys, you know?" David smiled and nodded, so she continued, "I went to university. I have an ear for languages. I was there when I found out my sister was..." Taty ended her narrative abruptly. She'd almost told him the truth. She swallowed and cast him a weak smile. "She was taken from us. My mother and father were heartbroken. They died within a year of her loss. Father had the... brain tumor. Mother died because my father and sister had gone. You understand?"

"Brokenhearted?" His word was correct. Her mom had shriveled to a husk of the woman she'd been.

"What was your favorite toy growing up?" She nudged him when she asked, trying to lighten the mood.

"Ah… well we were very poor, but I had a wooden butterfly yo-yo. I could make that thing do some pretty amazing tricks. We didn't have a television, but the liquor store down the street did. I'd go there and watch when I could. Mostly, I read anything and everything I could get my hands on. I guess it was a way to escape a pretty shitty childhood. But, when you don't know anything else as a kid? I believe I was content, if not happy." He glanced at her. "What about you? What was your favorite toy?"

Taty screwed up her face as she concentrated. "I think my doll, Natasha. I would play for hours with her. My momma made clothes for her out of scraps. I pretended I was here in America and that I lived a glamorous life. Did you have any pets?"

David chuckled. "Nope. Not until I was much older. Now there are two dogs who have claimed me. I can't go outside my home in… Colorado without tripping over them."

"You don't bring them with you?" The man had enough money to bring his pets with him.

"It wouldn't be fair to the animals. They are happy

where they are. Making them follow me around the globe would be selfish."

"You like this home in Colorado?" She concentrated hard in the pronunciation of the strange word. She had only a vague understanding of America's western states. "This is where people are cowboys, yes?" She twisted as far as she could and gave him what she hoped was a sexy look. "I would like to see you as a cowboy."

David drew a long breath and blew it out slowly. He leaned over and kissed her softly. "I'm a businessman. Nothing more. That home was before my father entrusted his empire to me. I haven't been back since I took over and, at this point, I don't have any idea when I will go back."

"But you will, yes? You will return to the two dogs that make you happy and the memories that put a smile on your face?" For some reason knowing that David could be happy was important. Maybe after he finished his jail term, he could live in this Colorado and be happy.

David stood and extended his hand to her. "It remains to be seen. Now, you need a pain pill and some sleep."

"And you?" She let him assist her off the couch, trying not to hiss as her hip pulled when her leg straightened out. The muscles were tight under the bruising. She had no idea how he was walking without a noticeable limp. From what she'd seen, his wound was much worse than hers.

"I'll be making arrangements to pay and meet your bosses." David lifted her hand to his lips. "Good night, Tatyana."

He turned and walked into his office. The door closed with a snick, and then the lock clicked into place and so did she. It was a sharp reminder that she was not welcome or needed. That thought hurt when it shouldn't even be a consideration. She nodded to herself while staring at the door. She closed her eyes for a moment and silently wished to anyone who was listening that her bosses would agree to the meeting so she could end this case and escape from David Xavier without losing her entire heart.

Dixon carried the tiny woman off the bus. She'd lost consciousness about ten minutes into the drive. He'd provided blankets for the other women as soon as they passed the front divider of the bus. They were drugged, but a few had begun to cry. He tried to remain as calm and unobtrusive as he could, but the women were terrified of him. He fucking wanted to kill the bastards who'd done this. He carefully laid her down as the medical teams swarmed the stretcher and headed toward the other women Drake was helping off the bus.

He stepped back and watched the medics' orga-nized chaos turn into a dance of salvation for the dazed women. "He's has got to succeed." Drake's voice cut into his thoughts.

"You heard the gunshots."

"Yeah."

"Has he checked in yet?" Dixon watched a couple of female technicians try to calm one of the women who had just lost it and started screaming. Fuck, what a mess.

Drake waited for the woman's screams to abate before he spoke. "No. The team on site found two dead bodies and a lot of blood."

"Dammit. Any idea if the security team he has is any good?"

"I'm assuming he knew how to pick a team, but fuck, who knows. The radio message went out to send the doctor to his cover location just in case." Drake was driving so he'd been monitoring the UHF channel they were using. They changed channels every fifteen minutes and alternated how they traveled the bandwidth. Old school, but with a digital wizard tracking them, they were taking a page from the 1960's.

"Is Adam here yet?"

"No, they sent Maliki Blue." Drake dropped that bomb like it wasn't a thing.

"Fuck, like *he* needs to be involved with another op." Dixon's stomach turned at the thought of what that man had been through.

"He was available."

"Doesn't make the shit right."

"Yeah." They turned at the same moment and headed out of the secured location. Their mirror movements freaked most people out, but Dixon had always been in sync with his twin. That symmetry had saved their lives more than once.

CHAPTER 22

M ike palmed the cell phone in the pocket of his coat. The carriage he and Tatyana rode in made the most of the rare sunshine-filled winter day. The sudden upswing of temperature allowed the owners of the carriages to earn some money. As soon as the cold weather returned, the horses would be stabled per the ASPCA's mandate. He glanced at the old mare that plodded along pulling the ornate carriage. She should have been put out to pasture years ago but, then again, he had the distinct feeling the same could have been said about him.

The last month had been difficult. He'd let the woman beside him sway decisions and take his focus off the mission. Last night he'd slept on the couch in the den because he needed the separation to maintain a clear head. The connection he'd inadvertently formed with Tatyana had somehow grown hooks and dug deep inside him. Hours of meditation had cleared his head… to a point. Dammit; he'd revealed more to this Bratva underling than he had to any other person on the planet. Even Jacob, Doc and the Twins didn't know about his childhood. They'd never presumed to ask and he sure as hell wouldn't volunteer that information. His relationship with Doc and the Twins was tight while at the same time —distant. They each had things they didn't want to bring up. Jacob, on the other hand, hell, they were all part of the King family and accepted as the people they were without question or limitation. Alpha team would always be his first family, but the Kings and now Frank Marshall were as much a part of who he was as his old team members were.

He lifted off the carriage bench seat and slipped a hundred to the driver. He mumbled his request, and the man nodded his head. The carriage stopped, and he assisted Tatyana out of the coach. His leg ached, but nothing more than the normal pain of being stabbed. He chuckled and looked away from Taty's questioning glance. How does one explain that this was his fifth time being stabbed? You didn't.

He pulled the phone out of his pocket and walked her over to a bench about a hundred feet from the carriage. "Are you ready?"

"Yes."

She'd been reserved today. He couldn't blame her. Hell, he'd kept her captive, and he'd used her body— not that she hadn't been willing, but still. Mike held her arm while she sat on the bench. The fur encompassed her body so she wouldn't be too cold. He put his hands back in his pockets and carefully surveyed the people around them. His security team had been pre-positioned. There wasn't any reason to be overly concerned. His mannerisms were habit from far too many years of danger, and before that, it was survival instinct. He watched her lift the phone and drew a deep breath. This was the moment. The entire mission hinged on the way this conversation played out. He glanced around one more time to assure himself there was no one close by before he sat down next to Taty. He leaned in so he could hear the Russian exchange between Taty and her boss. He'd instructed her to go slow and to repeat anything in simpler words if he indicated she needed to do so.

"We've not received payment. The escorts' numbers were not correct."

Taty glanced at him and bit her lip. The anger in her superior's voice wasn't disguised. The man's American accent was clear and distinct—at least to her.

"I have the routing number. The customer didn't want the escorts to access the money." Taty rattled off the numbers. There was a distinct pause. "It is short three million."

"As stipulated, the last toy was damaged. Evgeniy's sadistic tendencies cost you dearly."

"Our people did not find him where you indicated he'd be." Taty's eyes popped to him. He nodded indicating he knew the body had been moved. He could practically see the gears turning in her head. She had to be wondering when and how he'd made the corpses disappear. Her eyes narrowed as she spoke to her boss. "The client took care of the debris." Mike nodded again.

"Our client is resourceful."

"He has resources far beyond my limited comprehension, sir. He wants a face-to-face. The incident has left him concerned."

"He need not be."

"Sir, he is listening. He has directed me to ask and I quote, *'How in the hell does a competent businessman lose complete control of his people and resources during such an important transaction?'* He wants an explanation as to why the European storekeeper was selling toys in America."

"He understands Russian."

"He does if I speak slowly."

"Due to the short timespan given, and number and purity of the toys purchased, we had to combine stock. The storekeeper and the escorts traveled with the stock to ensure they were controlled in a proper manner."

Taty glanced over at him. He made a motion with his hand indicating he wanted her to continue.

"The meeting will take place in one week. The client proposes a neutral location, one that cannot be compromised by either party. You will be allowed to determine the time of the meet."

"Security?"

"The client would like to remind you he is a businessman. He will leave his security and requires you to do the same."

"We will take this into consideration."

Taty shook her head and launched into rapid-fire Russian. He concentrated and caught most of her clipped monolog. "Sir, this is an ultimatum. You, and whomever the 'we' you include when you speak, will meet with our customer or he will find another vendor. The product was far beneath our standard. One was completely broken. One of his men was badly wounded. He can wash his hands and you have nothing, no way to link him to the transaction and no way to stop him if he spreads words to his very rich friends to avoid our product. This meeting will give you what you need. I will be with him. I do not believe there is any pretense other than wanting to know who he is doing business with. The man is too rich for his own good. He may be persuaded to expand his support to other areas the Bratva has interests in. It would be stupid to ignore this ultimatum."

Taty's eyes had closed during the speech. Her hand shook as she held the phone out. He popped his neck trying to rein in his anger at her tangent. He led her to believe his Russian was at an elementary level, but he understood she was setting him up, dangling him in front of the Bratva like he was a carrot. Regardless, the words she'd fired off to the mystery man at the other end of the line could not be unsaid. If she cost him his shot at the top of the Bratva, he'd turn her over to Guardian with a smile on his face.

"Call us with the location. We will set the date and the time."

"No sir, time only. He will set the date."

The silence held again. "Agreed, and Tatyana?"

"Yes, sir?"

"You will leave with us. Nobody speaks to us with such disrespect without paying the price."

"I understand, sir."

"I don't think you do."

Taty handed the phone to him. He powered it down and pulled the battery, sliding his hand into his pocket. The phone slipped out while he simultaneously palmed a small metal case. He leaned forward, removing his hand from his pocket in a natural movement. "What did you say to him when you went off in that rapid-fire conversation?" His hand slid down the far side of his leg. He slid forward, too, and bent at the waist to look at her as his hand slid under the front rung of the bench. Hopefully, it would look as if he was using the bench to steady himself. He felt the metal container as it magnetically pulled against the metal bench joint.

"I explained he would be throwing away the chance of a lifetime." She glanced up at him. "He wasn't happy." He stood and extended his hand to help her up. She unfolded slowly with only a small grimace. His hip throbbed like a bitch. He could only imagine how Taty was feeling. She refused to wear the sling Maliki had left for her. He knew from experience her arm had to be weak and aching.

"So it would appear. The threat at the end I understood. Don't worry, if all goes right, I'll require your bosses to allow your stay with me to continue. That would alleviate any need to explain your choice of words."

They walked slowly toward the carriage. Just before they moved within hearing of the driver, she asked, "And if things don't go right?" She slowly turned to him.

Mike shrugged with a casualness he didn't feel. "Let's just hope they do."

Her beautiful face wore a look of vulnerability that pulled at his gut. He turned and guided her to the carriage, reminding himself once again the woman was a master manipulator, a liar, and a criminal.

"This can't be right?" Jewell ran the coordinates again and looked at the map. She felt Zane's presence behind her. She glanced over her shoulder and pointed to the map. "It is the middle of the fucking Indian Ocean!"

"Stop swearing. It doesn't become you. That's the Maldives Republic. The man is a genius. There are over twelve hundred islands. We know which one he is going to, the Bratva doesn't."

"You aren't my mother. I can say whatever the fuck I want to say. I knew it was the Maldives. It is just a shit place for a meet because I have no surveillance there. I need to get this to my brothers." She turned and bumped into Zane. He caught and steadied her. Jewell growled in frustration. "Move out of my way, Walter."

His hands slid down her arms before he side stepped and fell in beside her. "You need to eat. You haven't had anything since breakfast."

Jewell snarled something crass and slammed the door open. She'd just thought she needed to eat something, but she'd be damned if she'd do it now. Zane's overbearing act had been driving her crazy for months. She'd been able to run the others off, but this man... uggg!

She strode through Jason's office and waved off Jason's secretary's effort to stop her.

"What the fuck, Jewell?" Jason's head lifted from the paperwork he had in his hands.

"I want Rockford here fired," she motioned over his shoulder at Zane, "and I have the location for the meet." Jewell flopped into the huge chair in front of Jason's desk.

"No. He is the only one who will put up with you. I'm giving him a fucking raise, and his name is Zane." Jason placed the paper he was holding down and leaned back in his massive desk chair. "Where?"

"The Maldives Republic." Jewell dug in her pocket for the coordinates she'd used in her office. "Here."

"The man is a fucking savant strategist." Jason turned to the huge map of the world behind his desk. He ran the longitude and latitude the old fashioned way. "Okay, we don't have a date or time?"

Jewell shook her head. "TBD."

Jason turned and pushed a button on his phone system. "Sonya, please come in here."

"Right away, Mr. King." The tiny woman teetered in moments later with her tablet. Jewell was amazed the woman didn't break an ankle on the six-inch heels she was wearing. Jason waited until she sat in front of him to begin. "All right, we need to bring everyone in. Sonya, get ahold of Jacob. Tell them to get Doc here. I'll need a rundown of all available assets, personnel, and machinery. Due to the location, I'll need specific locations and status on all air and watercraft at Guardian's disposal. Jewell, do a complete back brief on this location. I want to know if a gnat scratches its ass on that island. As a reminder, all of this is done old school. Nothing goes out on any electronics. I'll be damned if I'm giving that hacker any indication of where my family will be."

Jewell's stomach growled. Damn, she was hungry. She popped a look at Zane. The smug ass lifted an eyebrow at her. She stuck her tongue out at him and turned back to her brother. "Roger that. We've got the next three operations ready to launch on the Bratva's assets. Do you want them to continue?'

"Hell, yes. If we keep sniping at their ankles, they won't be looking at the fist that is about to knock them the fuck out."

CHAPTER 23

The remote island in the Maldives that David Xavier owned was the perfect spot to lure the head of the Bratva. Guardian could set up before anyone knew they were going to the island. If the Bratva brought firepower, he trusted his team to have a plan. He just needed to keep the bait on the hook. He glanced over at Tatyana and sighed. As a Bratva operative, she was no doubt hiding too much, and he didn't want her to be the reason his mission failed. There were too many times that one plus one didn't equal two when the woman was involved. He really should just sit back and let the course of events play out, but he cared for her. It was irrational and against his every resolve, but his feelings for this woman were there. He couldn't ignore them anymore.

"Taty, come over here please," He called her over

to him, and instead of letting her sit beside him, he positioned her so she straddled him.

"We need to talk."

"About?"

"When we started this—arrangement, you had your goals, and I had mine. The lines seem to have blurred."

"What lines?" She settled on his lap and his cock thickened.

He pushed the brown curls that were always flopping into her eyes from her forehead. The two things she'd been adamant about today were that he be allowed to meet with the Bratva and she would be present. He needed answers, so he took away one of the two things she seemed to want. "I have decided you will not be going with me to the meeting."

Her body tensed immediately. A look of fear flitted across her face. "No! I must go. I know you will do what you can to keep me out of harm's way, but there are reasons I must attend."

Warning flags flew through his mind at the vehement plea. "Why?"

She closed down. He watched as her expression shuttered. She shrugged and looked down at her hands that were on his chest. "Please, you cannot leave me here."

She leaned in and tried to kiss him. He pulled back. "Why? You've lied at every turn. You jeopardized the meeting this morning when you went off script."

Her head whipped up at that comment.

"Yes, I speak your language better than you assumed. You told them to use the upcoming meeting to trap me into future transactions." He grabbed her wrists and held them securely. "What do you have to gain from being at my meeting with the Bratva, Tatyana? What do you gain?"

"I gain nothing." She wouldn't look at him. Those expressive brown eyes were focused on his chest.

"Liar."

She popped her eyes up and shrugged. "Think what you will."

"I rarely do anything else. You are a puzzle. You state you want revenge, yet you do everything in your power to ensure this deal continues. Your quickest revenge against the Bratva would be to ruin the transactions. Instead, you continually ensure nothing interferes with them." Mike held her wrists firmly in his hand, and when she pulled away, he used his other hand to cup the back of her neck. "No, you will stay here until I figure out this conundrum you've given me." He gave a gentle tug and brought her down against his chest. Her tense little body failed to relax into him.

"So, if we eliminate all other considerations, you need me to meet with the Bratva, and you need to be present. Why?" He was thinking out loud and didn't expect an answer. His hand traced a line down her back and returned in a mindless caress.

"You don't know where the meet is, you are

secluded, so working with someone in the Bratva to collude against the leadership is doubtful, especially as three of your closest known associates are now dead." He assumed the two escorts who had the routing numbers had been eliminated. It was logical. His mind cut to the seclusion bit of the puzzle. He hadn't ordered a report from his security team. Damn, he'd dropped the ball on that one, but they would have alerted him if she'd tried to make contact with anyone. "Why do you want to meet the leadership of the Bratva so badly, little one?" He continued to run his hand up and down her back. His grip hadn't lessened an iota on her wrists. The woman was strung as tightly as a guitar string. His words were hitting home. The problem was he didn't know why, but he would figure it out. He'd give Guardian three days to mobilize and set up before he reached out to the Bratva with the location and date. He'd use a dead drop again to send the information and recordings of the telephone conversations he'd taped. Due to the time to travel to the Maldives, Guardian would have at least five days to set up. Was the mouse following him... or was the mouse leading him? He wasn't too certain.

Taty turned her face into his neck. "I need to be there, David. I do not want harm to come to you. That is the truth, and I swear it on my family's graves."

He didn't respond. Hell, he didn't know for a fact that she had a family. Everything she said last night could be another elaborate lie. She lifted enough to kiss his jaw. Fuck, the woman was using sex to distract him, and she was one hell of a distraction. He made a mental note to request a report from security in the morning. Her tongue trailed down his neck before she nudged his shirt collar aside with her nose and started to suck on his collarbone. Her tongue and lips were pulling up a bruise, and his cock was beating with the thump of his heart behind his zipper. He didn't release her hands when she tugged. Instead, he pushed her away. "You can't use sex to distract me, Tatyana. I will figure out what game you're playing."

Her face was flushed and her eyes hooded. She licked her lips and spoke in Russian, "No games tonight. I need you. That is the truth. Please, be my lover for the night? Just be with me. No lies, no pretense, no tomorrow. Just now, tonight. Just us."

She leaned down hesitantly, slowly dipping before her eyes sought his out. Her open need lay naked before him.

He released her wrists and cupped her face in his hands. "No lies."

Tatyana nodded slightly.

"Bedroom." He helped her to stand, her hip obviously still sore from the hard fall she'd taken. She looked over her shoulder at him as he lifted off the couch and followed her. Her shirt dropped by the steps leading from the great room. He watched as her skirt followed at the top of the steps. The soft pink lace of her bra trailed in her hand at the bedroom door. He glanced at it as he entered. She stood by the bed. A massive black and blue contusion mottled her perfectly toned outer thigh. Mike ripped off his shirt at the door and unbuttoned his slacks, making quick work of them. He crossed the room and dropped at her side. His lips and tongue trailed the edges of the bruise. She ran her hand through his hair as he turned her to face him. He carefully lifted the elastic of her panties away and slid them down her legs making sure not to abuse the damaged muscle. He pushed her back, so she was trapped between the bed and him. He licked and nipped her hipbone. Her shudder and small gasp filled his senses as much as the delicious taste of her skin. Mike dipped his head lower and concentrated on her sex. God, the woman was a feast. Her body's reactions to his touch defined bountiful. Her shivers and gooseflesh, her excitement wetting his fingers and tongue, all called to him as much as the delicious sounds with which she filled the room. Her hands clenched his shoulders, and her thighs tightened in small convulsive jerks. She was close. He lifted slightly and found her clit. She jumped at the slight touch of his tongue and cried out. Mike smiled against her hot flesh. He flicked that bud repeatedly with his tongue and added his fingers. She ground against his hand, gripped the back of his head and demanded more from his lips. He refused, keeping the steady flicking of his tongue against her sensitive, swollen flesh.

Tatyana bucked against his fingers. Words in a language he couldn't decipher pierced his sex drugged haze. She was begging. It didn't matter what language she spoke, the meaning was clear. Mike moved closer and sucked her clit into his mouth. The pressure and suction pushed her over. Her fingernails dug into his shoulders as she exploded. He remained on his knees and held her through the orgasm.

Mike lifted; his hip complained, but not enough that he'd change his plans. He dropped kisses across her freckled nose. She still clung to his shoulders as she recovered her breath. Finally, she chased his mouth. He kissed her deeply before spinning her and pushing her shoulders down to the bed. She folded in half, standing beside the bed, her chest resting on the tall pillow-topped mattress.

He shucked his boxers; his hard, angry cock slapped his stomach. He grabbed the nightstand drawer and retrieved a string of condoms, ripping out the first in the line. He suited up and drove home. Her searing hot core closed so fucking tightly around him. God, the feeling of this woman was divine. Mike held her hips and gazed at where they joined. He closed his eyes when he'd seated himself completely within her. His hands traveled up her spine. "Lift your leg." He helped her fold her leg up on the mattress and then followed suit with her other leg. Still impaled on him, she was now high enough. He pulled her up, so her back was against his chest. She'd be too short to hold like this if he hadn't had her on her knees on the bed. He tugged her close. Her arms reached back to circle his neck. He let his hands discover her body. She pressed back with her hips as he thrust forward. Fuck, he wasn't going to last if she kept that up. He dropped his hand and massaged her sex in concert with their movements. She lost her rhythm and folded forward. He caught her and lost any thought of control. Her moans and shuddering clenches enticed him into that void, one where he couldn't stop even if he tried. He grabbed her uninjured hip and pounded into her heat, demanding his release. He roared through his orgasm. He fucking couldn't do anything else. He caught himself on straight arms to keep from falling on top of Tatyana and shuddered when he pulled out. After dealing with the condom, he helped her find the middle of the bed and flipped covers over both of them. He rolled onto his side and folded her into him—his bandaged hip be damned.

His hand petted her arm. He wanted to be able to tell her the truth, to warn her to run away or to keep her locked up so she couldn't be found. Fate had conspired to fuck him royally. He listened to her steady breathing as she faded into sleep. Somehow he'd screwed up and fallen in love with his enemy. He gazed out the floor-to-ceiling windows. The one woman strong enough to stand by his side stood on the opposite side of the divide between good and evil, and there was no way to bridge the gap. His heart might not recover from this devastation.

Jasmine King glanced at herself in the full-length mirror. Not bad. She could rock this flight attendant uniform. Granted, the color wasn't her favorite, but the scarf was nice enough.

"Shit, darlin'. Tell me you have a nurse's uniform in that closet, too, and you'll knock two of my top ten fantasies off the list." Chad came up behind her and pulled her back into him.

"Not so fast, cowboy. This is for work." Jasmine turned her head to the side asking for and receiving a scorching kiss. God, her man could kiss.

"Work? What work?" He asked between panty-melting kisses. Jasmine turned in his arms. "Remember that Russian threat?"

Chad straightened. His face hardened, and he nodded.

Shit, this probably wasn't going to go over well. "I'll only be gone a week or so."

Chad dropped his arms and took two steps back. Oh, he was pissed. She could see the anger radiating off him. Dammit, she should have laid some groundwork, but she wasn't given much time, and those kisses fritzed her brain.

"What exactly do you think you will be doing?" He ground his teeth as he asked.

Jasmine held up her hands in supplication. "Support only. I'm on board the aircraft our inside guy is flying to the meet on. Dixon and Drake are flying it. If shit hits the fan, we are to provide an escape route."

"Have you told your brothers?" Jasmine's stomach fell. No, she hadn't told anyone yet.

"Not yet," Jasmine admitted, "but flying this early won't be an issue."

"I'm not worried about you flying, Jazz! What happens if you get into it and something happens?"

"I won't let that happen!" She would never jeopardize their baby!

"Neither will I. If you don't tell Jason, I will." He crossed his arms over his chest and glared at her.

"*Do not* throw an ultimatum at me." Jasmine squared off with him.

"I have just as much say in this as you do. That is my child you're carrying."

"No shit? Here I thought I got pregnant from an alien insemination!" Jasmine flung back. "Look, I have to go. These bastards have attacked my family, for fuck's sake they attacked *us*, and now that we have a chance to take them down, I am going to be there. This child will not be safe unless we eliminate *that* threat. They know who we are, Chad!"

"So you just made the call without discussing it with me?" His anger hadn't abated one bit.

"No! They just found out about it yesterday. When I was last in Washington, Guardian was still working the lower level targets. This was overnighted to me. I just got out of the comm center not more than an hour ago. I was going to tell you, but you were writing music in the den. I'm not leaving until tomorrow night. I'll fly from here to LaGuardia, and then I'll jump on a plane and fly to wherever we're going. I'm going to be making food, serving drinks and keeping an eye on Mike's escape route. I swear I wasn't going to just leave! I wouldn't do that."

Chad stared at her and shook his head. "I'm flying with you to New York." He lifted a hand before she could speak. "I love you, and I'm telling you I'm not happy. Not by a long shot, but I won't stop you. You don't get a say on my following along. I'm calling Jason, and I'm letting him know we're expecting. That is nonnegotiable. I will be given a location where I can go that will be close but won't compromise your mission. I won't be across the entire fucking globe from you and our baby."

Jasmine mentally ferreted through his demands as she melted into her man's arms. She could deal with his restrictions. She needed to call Jason first to ensure brother dearest didn't tell Chad the rest of the story, but yeah, she could live with Chad being somewhere close by. Besides, nobody ever said you couldn't have the honeymoon before the wedding. Hell, she was having a baby before the wedding. Jasmine relaxed and closed the distance between them.

"Deal. I'll call Jason right now and let him know."

She snuggled into his neck and drew a deep breath as he pulled her closer to him.

"Don't think for a second I don't know you're working an angle, sweetheart. When I figure out what it is, I'll make the punishment fit the crime."

She lifted away from him, and pointed at herself and innocently batted her lashes at him. "Who? Me?"

He struggled to hide a smile and failed. "Yeah, you." He shook his head and dropped his lips to feather against hers in an enticement she could never resist.

Huh, maybe she'd call Jason later.

CHAPTER 24

The report on Tatyana's internet usage gave him nothing. She hadn't logged onto the computer he'd authorized her to use. From the report, he determined when she was left in the apartment by herself she'd binged *Supernatural* on one of the subscription channels. For a microsecond, that thought made him happy until he realized she'd never sit with Amanda, Keelee, and Ember drinking wine and watching the show that was the women's answer to the men's weekly poker night on the ranch.

He leaned forward and rubbed his temples, trying to massage away the stress and pain of the last twenty-four hours. The door to the study stood open, and he could see the open doorway to his bedroom. He'd left her sleeping about thirty minutes ago. The niggling ominous feeling that surrounded his connection to Tatyana had grown into a raging storm. At least in his mind it had, and that was unacceptable.

Mike stared at the desk blotter. He was missing something in this situation. The warning flags were everywhere, but he'd be damned if he could figure out what was happening. And the kicker? The temptation in the bed not sixty feet away was definitely working an angle. But what, and how? Fuck, what he wouldn't give to pick up the phone and call Jacob or Doc. He chuckled to himself as he threw his Mont Blanc pen across the desk. Hell, he'd even enjoy Dixon and Drake's continuous banter, but wishing for impossibilities wasn't getting him any closer to figuring out this riddle.

He half-heartedly thumbed through the IT security reports. The documentation outlined sites visited and data usage. As a comm specialist with Alpha team, he knew what he was looking at, but nothing seemed out of place. At least it made him feel like he was doing *something*. He gazed moved from the next-to-non-existent report on Tatyana's usage to his own electronic trails. The encrypted business emails were tagged with a five digit precursor indicating there had been no attempt to hack into David Xavier's life. His eyes caught on one line and backtracked. That one event didn't show encryption. He picked up the phone and waited for his chief of security to answer.

"Yes, sir?" Casey's voice drew him away from the line that stuck out like a sore thumb.

"I'm reviewing the IT report you sent up. There is one instance where it shows I utilized my phone but I didn't log onto my secure server. Reference number: X2573. Tell me what your system shows on that transaction."

"One moment, sir."

He heard the tell-tale tap of keys as he waited.

"It says you accessed an IP search engine the night before last, just before midnight. The trail from the search engine leads to a small email server in… it looks like the UK, but I'm not a computer genius."

Son of a bitch. She'd used his phone and made contact with the Bratva. There was no other explanation. "Is there any way to determine what was done at that site?"

"Honestly, there could be, but this is the limit of my knowledge. I can call in my computer expert if you need me to, sir," Casey offered.

"No, it doesn't matter anymore."

"Yes, sir."

He hung up and leaned back in his chair. He stared out the open door and blew a lungful of air out trying to come to grips with what had happened. Tatyana had contacted someone the night before the European team of the Bratva ambushed them. Had she arranged the entire situation? Hell, it could all be an elaborate mind fuck. The Bratva bosses act like they don't know what is going on. She sets the entire thing into motion with one email. The knife wound at his hip contracted when he moved. She gave the routing number to the two men identified as her team members back in Bern. Fuck. If true, she'd played him like a concert violinist. All right. Time to make a game plan and stick to it. The woman had shown her hand, even though she didn't know it yet.

Mike grabbed the phone again and hit Garrett's direct line. "'Sup David."

"I need to work out. Meet me in the gym." The muscle in his hip complained at the thought, but fuck it; he'd work his upper body with weights until he couldn't think. He dropped the phone and headed out of his office. Tatyana walked out as he exited as if she'd just woken up. Right. He'd bet she'd been standing in the doorway listening to his conversations with Casey and Garrett. She blinked owlishly at him. He couldn't help but notice she wore the shirt he'd thrown onto the floor last night. The damn thing dipped almost to her knees. Nothing he said right now would go well. He was too pissed. He passed her by with a small nod of acknowledgment. It was an all-out effort to get to the gym and reduce some stress.

"Well, that was rude. What did I do to deserve the cold shoulder?" Her words trailed after him. He stopped and ground his teeth, trying to control the aggression she had heated to a rolling fucking boil. He purposefully relaxed his shoulders and turned around with a carefully blanked face.

"That is exactly what I'd like to know, Tatyana."

She palmed her face with both hands and rubbed.

As if she'd been asleep. Yeah right, she wasn't going to fool him. Not any longer. His gut churned, with anger and self-derision. How could he have fallen for the woman's ploy? Well, the ruse stopped now.

"What are you talking about?" She replied after a huge yawn that seemed real. No, fuck that. He wasn't going to give her the benefit of any doubt. Not anymore.

"You used my phone and made contact with someone in Europe, and the following morning we were attacked, and a man was killed. I doubt that little event was a coincidence." He sneered, and let her see the anger that seethed just below the surface of his rigidly maintained calm.

Her hands dropped to her side. Her stunned look appeared authentic. "No…" She shook her head side to side as all the color drained from her face, leaving a deathly pallor in its wake.

"Yes. Not too surprising from someone who sells people for a living."

"At least I don't *buy* them! What are you doing with those women? What perverted things are they going to have to endure because *you* bought them for your sick bastard friends?" Taty's eyes flashed as she spit the words toward him.

"I guarantee those women will receive far better care than the Bratva gave them. Those fifteen lives are now safe, warm and being respectfully treated. Can you say that about *any* of the others you've kidnapped and sold into slavery?"

Her gaze fell to the floor, and her body seemed to collapse upon itself.

"I didn't think so," he growled savagely. "How many times have you replaced 'toys' because the fucking owner killed them? Where do you get off being offended? You. Set. Me. Up. I was supposed to die in that warehouse, wasn't I? Or maybe you were planning on kidnapping me and killing the men that worked for me? I don't know what your end game is, but I do know one thing—you're a criminal of the lowest sort. You have no conscience, no morals, and very little remaining value to me..." Mike's coldly enunciated words faded to a hoarse whisper at the end. He silently chanted a mantra to fill the hole opening in his soul. *She's the enemy. Tatyana is the enemy. The woman is my fucking enemy!* He pivoted and stalked out of the apartment, ignoring her shell-shocked stare.

CHAPTER 25

T hree days… well, thirty hours to be exact, since David had left the apartment and not returned. The fact his phone was monitored as well as the devices she used kept eating at her. Why was *his* phone monitored? From everything she'd gathered from his staff and his security team, not to mention the way he traveled and moved around the city, he was a very private man. The only explanation that she could think of was that maybe he was paranoid. But to monitor your own interactions? She'd gone around and around on this problem almost exclusively because she wouldn't allow herself to think that he'd leave her here while he went to the meet. Besides, he needed her as a conduit to the Bratva… unless he bypassed her and called them directly. But that didn't make any sense either and only added more to the thoughts swirling in her head. David didn't want any interaction with the Bratva that could be recorded. He'd controlled every aspect of the business proposition and the meet through a third party—her.

Tatyana retreated into the corner of the huge sectional, hugged her knees to her chest and gazed over the cityscape. It was a very nice view—for a prison. She had television, food, music and even liquor, but other than that, she had no contact with the rest of the world. The security guards outside her door ensured that remained constant.

Using her fingernail, she played with a loose thread at the hem of her jeans. Artisanal distressed designer jeans for which she'd paid far too much money. Tatyana looked out the window but didn't focus on the view. She ached. Her soul ached with the desire to tell David the truth, but she couldn't, not with the head of the Bratva so close. The documentation she'd amassed would put them away for the rest of their lives, but to do that, the people at the top needed to be identified. Then, and only then, would the bastards be prevented from hurting anyone ever again. Had she sold her soul to the devil? Yes. Without a doubt, she had. The faces of the countless men and women who had been bought and sold with her assistance sickened her. Before David summoned her into his life, she had a plan if she made it out of this operation alive. She'd find a small corner of the world and withdraw, regroup and try to figure out how to live a life outside the Bratva. But for now, the scum that wielded power and made the decisions within the Bratva needed to be eliminated. That one thought had become her mantra. But now, because of one man, she sat in a penthouse cage and considered throwing all that work, all the sacrifices and all the lives out the window. *All of that because she loved him.*

The realization, surprisingly, hadn't been an earth shattering moment. The small things he did, the way he worked so hard to get the people in need aid. His quiet strength and innate goodness had surrounded her. No, David Xavier had consumed her. She stood and sauntered over to the view of the massive green park. She shook her head and closed her eyes. This wasn't about her. It never had been. She couldn't throw away the years of work. She owed the successful conclusion to this mission to the people who would never be found.

The front door to the apartment opened. David crossed the space between them. He wore a black bespoke suit and red silk tie. His eyes were as cold as the most northern reaches of the Arctic. She inhaled deeply and mentally braced for whatever he wanted.

He handed her the phone. "Call them. Give them these coordinates and this date. They will call back in ten minutes and give me the time of the meet. If they do not, they will lose my business, and they will lose you."

Tatyana hesitated as she reached for the phone. Her eyes flitted up to his. His acidic tone confirmed that David thought she'd betrayed him. She lowered her eyes and opened the phone before she pushed the recall button and waited.

"Yes."

"Are you prepared to copy?" Tatyana asked.

"Affirmative."

David's body tensed as he cast a sharp glance at the phone.

She related the longitude and latitude of the meet and the date. "You have exactly ten minutes to call back with the time for the meet. If you do not, our client will walk away for good, and he will kill me."

"You are replaceable. The client, however, is not. We will call back."

David took the phone from her and headed toward the door. Taty called after him, "You can't even spend ten minutes in my presence?" He didn't even turn around before he soundlessly closed the door behind him. His expensive cologne still lingered in the air. She shook her head and took a deep breath. David's stoic stance beside her when she said that he would kill her hadn't altered in the slightest. She'd hoped hearing the words would cause a reaction, but there'd been none. She closed her eyes and wished he had as much compassion for her as he did the women he'd acquired earlier in the week, but he considered them victims. In his mind, she was a criminal... which was ironic because he was a criminal for buying the women.

Looking at her situation was disheartening. Honestly, it was quite grim. The Bratva didn't care if she lived or died. David, it seemed, didn't care either. She'd given her heart to a criminal, and it seemed she meant nothing to him. No, she wouldn't succumb to her circumstances. She'd worked too damn hard, and sacrificed too much to catch these bastards.

The door opened again. David strode across the room and extended his hand. The phone vibrated in his palm. She picked it up and answered it.

"One o'clock in the afternoon. The merchandise will be moved from us to you after the account number has been received."

David shook his head and whispered, "The account number will be given after an inspection by you and only after a face-to-face between them and me."

Taty relayed his words exactly as he stated them.

"Agreed."

The line went dead. She handed the phone back to her jailor. His expression gave her nothing to go by. No emotion whatsoever.

"Get packed. Clothes for three days only. Security will come for you within the hour." He turned on his heel and headed out the door.

"I'm no more a monster than you." Her words were a last ditch attempt to somehow bridge the chasm that stood between them.

He stopped and drew a deep breath. His massive shoulders under the tailor made clothes lifted and then dipped. He turned and stared at her for a moment. She couldn't utter a sound. His gaze held her spellbound. The pain in the man's eyes seemed to seep through his body. "I have killed people who deserved to die. I was the sole judge and the executioner. I did it because if I didn't, more would die. My culpability isn't in question. It never has been. I am what I am. Some would call me a monster, some a mercenary. I consider myself a man who is doing the best he can."

Taty snapped up that piece of information and clung to it. "David, I promise you that I am doing the best I can also. Have I done things that make me a monster in some people's eyes? Yes. Without a doubt. Whatever you think you know about me, I know deep inside you sense the truth. I'm doing the best I can, and I'm sorry for the lies and deceit, but it would seem both of us live in that web."

She panted, trying to settle her nerves. That was as close as she could push telling the truth to him. She'd regret his arrest. But she'd never regret the time she'd spent with him. He nodded once and left. Taty looked down at her hand and then back at the door. He'd left her the phone. If they were tracing her activity, they'd know she reached out, but they wouldn't be able to know to whom before they left New York. Thirty-seven seconds later the longitude, latitude, date and time were in the draft folder of the ghost account for her handler. There was nothing sent. Nothing traceable. She wiped the browser history, turned off the phone and dropped it onto the couch. MI6 now had the information. How they could get there and get set up in the short amount of time they had was yet to be seen, but she'd done her part. Whatever happened, she'd risk everything to see it through.

Jason looked up from his desk at the sound of Sonya's heels clicking on the hardwood of his office floor. "You have a secure call waiting. Your friend from London."

Jason nodded and waited until she exited the office. He picked up the encrypted line. "King."

"Ah, Mr. King, Agent Churchill here. I'm calling to let you know I'm going to be going on a holiday." Jason's eyebrows raised. He had no idea what the fuck the man was talking about, but he'd play the game.

"Thank you so much for letting me know. Where will you be going?" Jason turned and looked at the large gold leaf map of the world on his wall as he spoke.

"I've been saving for eight years, and I finally pulled together enough money to buy a ticket to the Maldives. Us public employees don't make the money you private security types do I'm afraid."

Jason's body clenched as his eyes went straight to the Indian Ocean. "Really? If you're interested, we always have openings. I've never been to the Maldives. I hear it is very nice."

"I hear it is an excellent vacation place, and although there are hundreds of private islands I'm headed to one of the more populated areas. Just going to kick back and let someone else drive me around. I've gotten tired of being in charge of every detail every day. Time to relax."

"Sounds like a plan. When are you leaving?" He glanced at the last report from Jacob. They'd hit the ground yesterday and were ninety percent done with the technical countermeasures for the island and had identified and fortified the defensive positions.

"Oh, I'm leaving tomorrow. I'll be floating about in the Indian Ocean relaxing by the day after tomorrow."

"Excellent. You enjoy yourself. That project our organizations were going to collaborate on can wait until you get back.

"Perfect. I'll talk with you later."

"Enjoy your vacation, Agent Churchill."

"Indeed. It was a long time coming."

Jason closed the line and dropped his head into his hands. Okay, that bit of information was off-putting, to say the least. Churchill was probably stretching his authority by contacting him in the first place. If anyone ever discovered the information he'd just relayed... well, Guardian was always looking for good agents. The man would have a place after he was fired. Jason considered the map while he thought. Whomever his counterparts in the UK had on the inside had the straight scoop. At least MI6 wasn't going to jump into the op and fuck things up. He glanced at his watch. Dixon, Drake, and Jasmine should be landing at Dulles within the hour. Tomorrow morning they'd load up with Mike, Ms. Petrov, the security team Mike traveled with and a Guardian flight crew aboard David Xavier's Boeing Business Jet 2 for the long flight to the Indian Ocean. The Wonder Twins and Jasmine would be passengers for the twenty-four hour flight. Double D would pilot the luxurious pontoon plane that normally resided at David Xavier's private island. The aircraft would be ferried over and ready to launch whenever Mike required it. Jason hated waiting for a courier to bring him the last message drop from Mike indicating the time of the meet, but there was no way they'd risk the operation so close to the end game.

He turned back to his desk and peered at the cipher key. He used the book to compose the coded message to Jacob. Louis L'amour's, *The Sacketts.* They'd all grown up reading L'amour's westerns, and this one was a particular favorite of all the brothers. Even if the hacker intercepted electronic communications between Jacob and Jason, he'd have to have the key to the cipher, and there wasn't a chance in hell this book could be identified. Jewell's team would bounce the origination of Jacob's signal around the world in case the hacker was watching. Jason crossed his fingers that the countermeasures Guardian employed would give them time to ensure the Bratva were taken down.

Jacob, Doc, Joseph, and five hand-picked Guardian operatives were on the ground. Jewell, Zane and a three-man team of IT specialists were en route to the area and would be airborne during the meet. He'd arranged to get her on a Boeing E3 Sentry that was doing exercises off the coast of Thailand. Simply pour some money into the Thai government's coffers and presto, the ride materialized. He was getting damn good at PFM. Pure. Fucking. Magic.

CHAPTER 26

M ike waited for the limousine to come to
a stop and watched his security deploy.
His attention focused on the team at
the aircraft. He recognized several of the men as
Guardian personnel. He'd brief Casey and Thomas
on the mission and his true identity as soon as they
were airborne. Tatyana shifted beside him. He flicked
a glance toward her. He'd lose her in two days. Hell, if
he was honest, he'd never had her. He'd meditated
countless hours during the last three days trying to
find peace in this situation, but there was none. The
fates had well and truly fucked him over. The one
woman who could complete him, the one strong
enough to walk beside him or even allow him to *lean*
on her was going to prison for a very long time. His
heart would be locked up with her. Pain, remorse,
and regret battled each other while love ripped his
heart out.

The trek onto the aircraft took less than a minute. At the sound of familiar voices, he glanced back at the passenger seating area and immediately breathed a sigh of relief. Jasmine and the Wonder Twins were visiting as if they didn't have a care in the world. He chose a seat facing the rear of the aircraft. He watched as his security crew made introductions and settled in.

When they were airborne, the flight crew that Mike had employed for the last eight months started service. Tatyana excused herself to the bedroom for which he was immediately grateful. Her absence gave him the opportunity to communicate with his Guardian brothers without being observed. He dropped his hand down and used rudimentary ASL to communicate with Dixon, who had a direct line of sight to where his hand began spelling out words.

Good to see you, brother.

Dixon dropped his hand after a stretch.

All on schedule. Team in place. Mission a go.

He relaxed for the first time in over a year. He was with his family. He was with Guardian once again.

Pull my security team aside. Brief them. Flight crew not to know. He trusted his crew, but they didn't need to know what was going on, nor did they need to be involved.

The woman?

He hesitated to answer. His eyes locked with Dixon's before he signed the word he couldn't speak. **Bratva.**

Dixon stared at him for the longest time before he signed again. **Friend or Foe?**

He drew a deep breath and shook his head. **Foe.** He intentionally averted his gaze. The conversation was over, at least as far as he was concerned. Dixon, Drake, and Jasmine would corner his security and brief them. He had one last thing to do before they landed in the Maldives twenty some hours from now. Mike called over Daphne and whispered his instructions before he headed into the bedroom. As well-meaning as the twins were, he didn't want any interruptions, and he wouldn't put it past either of his friends to come into the room on some made up pretense if they thought he was making a mistake. Interruptions were not welcome or needed. He had one day left before this mission and his time with Tatyana was over. If she was willing, he'd spend it making memories with her.

The bedroom was vacant, and the bathroom door was shut. Mike took off his suit jacket and tie. He could hear water running as he undressed. He had no right to assume she'd want him, especially after avoiding her for the last three days. Time away from her in a forced separation allowed him to focus on the mission and to come to grips with what was to come. The meeting was stacked in Guardian's favor. That was reality. But he'd survived too many missions when the odds were in favor of one side, and the results were catastrophic. Tomorrow both the Russians and Tatyana would be in custody or he, even with his Guardian advantage, would be dead. He could see no middle ground. Tatyana could never know that Dixon, Drake, and Jasmine were Guardian. She couldn't know that the rest of his team and probably the remainder of the King clan waited on that island for them. He couldn't tell her that she'd be arrested and sent to jail, and he sure as fuck couldn't tell her that he loved her.

On that thought, he draped his clothes over the built-in rack. The door opened and Tatyana stutter-stepped when she saw him lying on the bed. He dropped his hand to his cock and gave it a long slow stroke. Her eyes traveled over him and the strip of condoms that lay beside him before she leaned against the door jamb. "Presumptuous."

"I am." He wasn't going to deny it.

"Why do you think I would do this with you?" Taty lifted an eyebrow and waited.

"Because whatever else this is, we *are* good together. We belong together. In a little less than twenty hours we will never be together again."

He watched those expressive brown eyes as she took in his words. Her hands traveled to the button on her skirt but stalled before she opened it. "So you've decided to let the Bratva take me?"

He shook his head. "No, they cannot have you; but then again, neither can I."

Tatyana dropped her skirt and lifted the white shirt over her head, her lace bra and thong barely covering her most intimate areas. "I wish there were another way." She leaned down to the bed and crawled up his body. Her hair flopped into her eyes and out of habit he reached up and pushed the riot of curls out of her face.

"This is it, Tatyana. You have your destiny; I have mine. I will not allow the Bratva to take you with them, but you and I have an expiration date. You knew it when you first enticed me. I knew it when I requested your presence in my chalet. This isn't a surprise to either of us."

"I want to close my eyes and make a wish."

He pushed the curls back again before he asked, "What would you wish?"

"To be free, of my past, of my obligations… of everything except you."

Mike saw the sad smile and traced her bottom lip with his thumb as he cupped her face. "We can be free, if only for tonight."

She licked the tip of his thumb, stilling the movement and locking his eyes on her mouth. Taty's eyes closed and he gripped the back of her neck and brought her down to him for a kiss. She halted millimeters before they touched and whispered against his lips, "For the first time in my life, I regret my past decisions."

"Regrets change nothing." No matter how much he wished they did. He regretted her involvement with the Bratva. He regretted she would go to jail. He regretted his part in that process. But what he regretted the most was there was nothing he could do to stop it from happening short of blowing this mission. That could not happen. Period. Tatyana and her bosses had ruined too many lives, yet, he mourned her loss deep within his soul.

He pulled her down. Her full, soft breasts brushed against his chest, her scent enveloped him, and her kiss filled his senses. With one hand he unhooked her bra while the other angled her to deepen their kiss. He broke the connection for a moment and made quick work of the condom, moving to focus on giving her pleasure. He needed her to sense, perhaps to even know, that he was making love to her. Tonight she wasn't in his arms because the mission demanded it. She wasn't an affair or a quick fuck. *Hell, his life was a self-imposed crusade against casual relationships.* No, here and now, he needed his hands and his body to speak the words that could never pass his lips.

Mike rolled her over and moved the bra out of his way. He started his memorization of her beauty at her delicate collarbone and ever so slowly mapped the contours of her skin, the dips of her taut muscles and the soft swells of her breasts. Lost in the pursuit of something he could never have, he poured every emotion he couldn't acknowledge, every hope he'd never see come to fruition, and every dream that would die when she was arrested, into the way he worshiped her body. Time was irrelevant. Only this intimacy mattered.

Her hands traveled his back and shoulders and

did a dance across his chest almost as if she were memorizing him as well. His cock screamed for relief long before he found her hot core. He entered her gently and gradually, taking every moaned word and storing them in his heart. He held her close to his body and made sweet, slow love to her. The one thing he couldn't do now was look into her eyes. He couldn't let her see how much he loved her. That was a power he could never give an enemy, no matter how true it was. Thoughts faded and his brain slowed until he was lost in nothing but the sensation of Tatyana. He felt her body tighten like a bow before she bit into his shoulder and released a muffled cry. He felt his balls pull up, the tingling in his spine morphed into an electrical storm that zapped through him and nearly blinded him with its intensity. He knew at that moment everything he was losing and damned the fates for the tortuous taste he'd been given.

He fell to one side and hugged her into him after he'd disposed of the condom. Her lithe little body tucked up against his as if she was made for him. He held her close and ran his fingers through her silken curls.

"I don't want to say goodbye." Her words were whispered against his shoulder where she lay.

"Then we won't." He uttered other words without thinking. He hadn't spoken the old phrases he'd learned in at least twenty years, but they fell from his lips easily.

"That was beautiful. What language was it?"

Tatyana's head shifted on his shoulder so he could see her eyes, or rather the flop of curls that fell over her eyes. Instead of brushing them back he kissed her on top of the head and pulled her back into him. "Lakota Sioux. Roughly translated means have a good journey."

"But you said something else, too, didn't you?" Her hands traced the muscles of his arm.

"I did. It is just a term of familiarity." Mike lied, he'd told her he loved her, but it was an indulgence he couldn't repeat in English or any other language she'd understand.

"Say it again?"

He repeated the endearment. He tightened his arms around her when he spoke the words again.

She yawned after mimicking him perfectly. Mike nodded and held her as the drone of the aircraft's engines lulled her to sleep. Mike cast an exhausted glanced at the digital clocks embedded into the wall of the aircraft displaying the current times in New York, London, Moscow, and Beijing. In a little over twenty-four hours, events would seal his fate and hers. He hadn't slept more than two or three hours in the last forty-eight. They'd tracked her use of the Russian phone, but without being able to reach out to Guardian, they'd hit a wall. She'd contacted someone again. The last time the results of her call in advance of their meeting to free fifteen women had been disastrous, but this time he'd ensured he controlled every aspect of the interaction. As soon as they finished this mission the data was going to Jewell and her team so they could take down whoever was on the other end of the communications. They would be able to identify who she'd contacted and add it to the list of crimes that he had firsthand knowledge of her committing. That list was extensive. Human trafficking would garner the most penalties, but extortion and attempted murder were on that list if they could prove she'd set them up at the warehouse. He closed his eyes and hoped they couldn't prove it, but knowing what he did, there was no doubt. No matter what her last communication was, Guardian would be in place and waiting. There wasn't a force on this earth that would stop the men on that island from finishing this mission. He adjusted Tatyana's weight against his shoulder and made no further attempt to stay awake. He needed to be ready when they hit the island.

"We may have a problem." Dixon and Drake had briefed Mike's security team and had outlined the events of the next twenty-four hours while Jasmine had distracted the current in-flight crew.

"Chief." Drake acknowledged his brother's concerns.

"He *is* involved with that woman." Dixon knew Mike White Cloud. The man would do his job or die trying, but the addition of the woman was a wild-card. If there was a chance his judgment had been compromised, it could mean the difference between all of them making it out of the next assignment alive or losing a team member.

"Figured as much when they headed into the bedroom. Think he's using her or is she using him?"

As usual, Drake was tracking along the same lines. "I don't know, but my gut tells me Ms. Petrov is more than just an assignment for him."

"Shit."

"I concur."

They looked at each other. Things could get messy, and there was no way to get word to Jacob and the men on the island that there were emotions involved.

"If we get the chance, one of us needs to talk with him. Find out where his head is located." Dixon watched Jasmine talk to the flight attendant about the coffee maker on the aircraft. With some sixth sense that he was watching her, she looked over and winked at him. The woman was a damn good personal security officer. It was Guardian's loss when she signed on to be Chad Nelson's head of security and soon to become his wife. But they were happy, and Chad was a stand-up dude.

"No, we know where his head is, we can't question that. He's proven himself more times than a man should have to... I'm more concerned about what is happening with his heart." Drake leaned back in his chair and lifted his feet, stretching out on the reclining seat. They were the relief aircrew and needed to get their crew rest, although that would be a long time coming. They both hated it when others had control of the stick. Sleep wasn't an option. They'd flown tired before. Too many times to count, actually.

"It would fucking suck if he finally found someone only to have her be part of something so vile."

"Suck? Suck isn't even close to the right word, man. Try eviscerate. If his heart's involved, it will shred him, man." Drake rolled his head toward Dixon.

"Yeah." That was the truth.

"I couldn't imagine being in love with your enemy. Hell, we have enough heartache with someone who is supposed to be on our side."

"God, ain't that the truth. She doesn't even know we are alive."

"She knows it. She just chooses to pretend we don't exist."

"Yeah, thanks. That does wonders for my ego."

"You're welcome." Dixon chuckled but cast a look of longing out the aircraft's window. They'd found out the hard way that matters of the heart were controlled by a fickle bitch who loved to laugh when you thought you had a plan. They'd both developed feelings for the same woman, which didn't surprise either of them. What they were going to do with that wasn't clear. They both wanted the same woman, but she didn't give either of them the time of day or a second of consideration. Which sucked times two. Hell, she occupied way too much of their thoughts, and neither of them had even been intimate with her. With as messed up as their situation was, he couldn't imagine where Mike's mind was right now.

CHAPTER 27

Tatyana closed the bedroom door and glanced around the forward cabin seating area of the plane. Both of the extra pilots who flew with them appeared to be sleeping, but the dark haired flight attendant was awake and reading a magazine.

"Hi. Couldn't sleep?" The woman smiled over at Tatyana as she sat down.

Taty smiled back. "No, I guess I have a lot on my mind." She reclined in the chair and looked out the window. The pitch blackness was punctuated by the red strobe light of the aircraft's navigational lighting seconds before the flash of green from the other side of the plane illuminated the night. It wasn't annoying enough to pull the shades on the windows, but enough of a distraction that she could lose herself in thought as she focused on the lights.

"Care to talk about it?"

Taty blinked and shook herself back into the conversation. "Ahhh... no, thank you."

The beautiful woman shrugged her shoulder and gave her a sad smile. "I get that. I used to have a high-stress job."

"Used to have?"

"Yes, I worked too many hours." The woman chuckled and then shook her head. "After a time all the travel starts to build up and becomes less than ideal. I was home maybe two months out of the year. It was difficult, and maintaining a relationship would have been impossible with my schedule and his."

"So you just quit?" The conversation was benign, and it kept her from thinking about tomorrow's events.

"No, we figured out a way forward together. Sometimes those walls that seem so damn high aren't when you work toward a common goal. We loved each other and did what we needed to do to be together. The choice to leave what I was doing was simple really."

Taty considered the woman's words. "True, but sometimes those choices aren't yours to make." Taty focused on the darkness outside the window. David had made love to her tonight. She was certain that he felt the same thing as she did, yet she couldn't tell him how she felt. Tomorrow she'd perform the final act of the drama in which she'd been cast. Her testimony alone would put these animals away. There was nothing to do but survive the day. Once she could identify them and witness the transaction between David and the bosses, she would have the final and crucial piece of evidence that would allow MI6 to lock the bastards away. Unfortunately, the same evidence would convict David. Even if his lawyers somehow managed to keep him out of prison, sooner or later he would know it was her actions that identified him to the authorities.

"I'm going to make some tea. Would you like some?"

Taty blinked back to the conversation. She shook her head and returned her gaze to the darkness outside the aircraft. The DNA of the victims she'd been a part of selling was safely hidden. Only the fifteen women that David bought would be unaccounted for. She closed her eyes and rubbed her brow. They needed to be found. MI6 and whatever agencies they teamed with in the United States might be able to flip Casey, David's Chief of Security. It was possible they could offer him a plea deal to testify against David. Yes, that could work. He had to know where they were taken, at least initially, because someone had to arrange the bus and drivers. Who else but him? She filed that piece of information away.

She shivered against the forced air pushing down on her. The only place she wanted to be right now was sleeping next to David, but she'd snuck out of the room, not willing to deal with a final goodbye. They were over. Forever. Reaching deep inside, Taty clutched at every thread of determination she could muster and drew a deep breath. It was show time, and David wasn't cast as the hero; he was a criminal, and he'd be taken down with the rest of the scum she'd hunted for eight years.

Taty nodded to herself once and glanced at the small galley where the tall brunette flight attendant chatted with one of the other passengers. She would have no happily ever after like that woman. Her destiny had been written nine years ago when her sister was abducted. She was Tatyana Petrov, elite European concierge of the Bratva and an undercover agent with MI6. She had the internal strength to see this mission to its end, even if that end destroyed her life.

CHAPTER 28

M ike's body was strung as tight as a bow with an arrow loaded, pulled back, and at the ready. He could feel the adrenaline coursing through his veins. It was a rush unlike any other. The anticipation of a fight mixed with a healthy dash of resignation and a thread of tightly controlled fear. The fear that trickled through him was of the unknowns that plagued the entire mission. He'd never go undercover again, of *that* he was certain. When he worked with Alpha team, he'd been part of a carefully crafted and meticulously maintained unit that fed upon the strengths of each other. He missed that ironclad insurance policy—the knowledge that no matter what happened during an engagement he could predict with certainty what his team would do and how they would react. In this assignment, the unknown variables outweighed the known factors, and that led to trouble any way you sliced it.

He glanced at the myriad of seaplanes parked at the pier. He strode toward the end where Dixon and Drake were doing a pre-flight inspection. Tatyana hadn't said a word to him since she slipped out of the bed after he made love to her. The resignation of that loss weighed heavy, but he pushed it to the back of his mind. He needed the distraction of his emotions to be gone. There was nothing he could say to her at this point that would matter. His actions in the next two hours would destroy her world, but then again, he couldn't stop what was about to happen. The fucked up truth was he'd live for the rest of his life knowing the woman that completed him was a criminal, a sex-slave trafficker and, if the suspicions were correct, a murderer. The accusations against her completely violated his perception of her. His mind couldn't reconcile the wildly diverse halves that made her whole. Being so close to her, perhaps he couldn't see or sense the true nature of the woman. Mike frowned at that thought. He'd like to think he was an excellent judge of character, but...

They settled into a sixteen passenger seaplane. The smell of the sea and the warmth of the sun did little to divert anyone's focus. Tatyana's brow seemed creased in determination. Whatever she'd done, he'd deal with it. He leaned back in his seat after Jasmine ensured they were strapped in and Dixon and Drake fired the engines. He closed his eyes and focused on the myriad of events that could transpire on the island and his actions to this point. He'd left Casey and Thomas at the hotel in Malé, against Casey's vehement arguments. As bodyguards, his personal security team did not have international credentials and were not on Guardian's payroll, so getting them further entwined in the dealings of this mission wasn't going to happen, no matter how much Casey bitched.

After Tatyana had slipped out of the bedroom cabin last night, he studied a map and photographs of the island he had on his phone and used the time alone to meditate on the events of the next twenty-four hours. Unfortunately, he was walking into this situation blind. He had no firsthand knowledge of the island or the enemy and even though he could guess what Guardian would do to prep and guard the meeting—that too was an unknown.

Thankfully, he did know that Jacob would be somewhere close. He had no doubt his six was covered by the best. Even if shit went south, his team would protect the women involved in the transaction. Dixon and Drake would have charges planted at the entrance to the dock by the time the other planes landed, and with Jasmine in the mix, the people the Bratva left as guards were going to get one hell of a surprise. That beautiful woman could kick ass and take names with the best of them. They'd catch the bastards at the top or, if necessary, eliminate them. The Bratva was about to implode and take Tatyana with them, and he was the one who was going to push the detonator. Fuck. His. Life.

The flight was an up and down affair. Not twenty minutes after takeoff, the aircraft set down on the crystal blue waters of David Xavier's private island. They were right on time. Off the starboard side, two other seaplanes circled to land. One was a passenger aircraft. The other appeared to be a larger cargo craft, probably where the women were being held. He waited for the plane to dock. Drake hopped out to secure it to the metal tie-off anchored into the wood piling. Jasmine and Drake secured the passenger door before Mike extended a hand to Tatyana and began the long walk down the pier.

"Do you know how this will happen?" Taty spoke as they headed up the walk to the palatial house.

"We will meet over there." He pointed toward sheltered outdoor living area off the side of an Olympic-sized swimming pool. The area was secluded from direct view of the dock and defensible if necessary. Mike used a hand at her waist to steer her in the right direction before he continued, "After our introductions, you will proceed to the plane to check the cargo."

"And then?"

"After I conclude my business, you will depart."

"You are not leaving?"

"No, this is one of my many homes. I will remain here. Our association has run its course."

"I'm sorry to see it end."

He made an unintelligible sound. He wished he could believe it, but the woman had lied to him since the day they met. The only thing he knew for certain about her was that she was the other half of his soul. *Fuck, no. That line of thought was off the table. Forever.* The second call proved she was working her agenda and no matter what, he was either a bargaining chip, leverage, or bait. Little did she know, Guardian assets now surrounded her.

"Why do you doubt this?" Tatyana stopped at the top of the long staircase that topped the length of boardwalk from the dock and looked back at the planes as they maneuvered toward the tie offs. They watched as the passenger plane docked. Two men in dark business suits exited the first aircraft. He guided her into the area he knew the Advon team had somehow wired for sound and video. Taking down bastards like the Bratva required hard fucking evidence.

"They will be armed." She cautioned him unnecessarily.

"No doubt." He acknowledged. He had a Glock 43 in a concealed holster at his back, an automatic strapped to his ankle and a large knife strapped on and ready. If the bastards came to play ball, they'd play, but if they came to take him hostage or kill both him and Tatyana, well he would introduce them to Satan himself.

"I need a weapon." Tatyana squared up and looked him in the eye. She had intestinal fortitude.

"You don't." His mind flashed to the file he received on her. She was linked to three murders. Mike didn't doubt for a minute she was able to kill. He could see the hard resolve needed to take a life in her eyes the day they met.

"They will kill me."

"They won't."

"How can you be so sure?"

"Call it intuition."

Tatyana lifted an eyebrow at him and then started a careful scan of the surrounding area, obviously looking for the reason he wasn't concerned. Let her look. He knew Guardian's equipment. She'd never find it.

As she strolled around the lavish outdoor living area, he glanced to his left and then to the right wondering where his team was set up. No doubt they were deployed close, watching and listening. There was no way those slimy bastards were getting out of this without paying the price for their crimes.

He went through the scattered seating areas to the massive outdoor kitchen and opened the large stainless steel refrigerator. It was full of ample selections of beer, soda, and water. He grabbed a water and offered one to Tatyana.

"No, thank you."

"Nervous?" He glanced down the wooden walkway to the two men traveling to meet them. The one on the right tripped his alarm bells. There was something eerily familiar about the man's gait.

"Actually, no." Her voice held a note of determination.

"You've never met them before?"

"No. I was not important enough."

"But you are now?" He gazed at the men as they strode forward. They weren't close enough to distinguish facial features. Instinct told him the one on the right was deadly. The way he carried himself and the way his arm arched slightly away from his left side revealed he was carrying at least one weapon. Mike gave the figure another hard glance. A growing sense of foreboding bubbled up from deep within him. The man was familiar; too fucking familiar.

"Yes."

Tatyana's answer to his forgotten question didn't draw his attention. He lost sight of the men as they followed the walkway. His mind flashed through the thousands of men he'd met or seen, or fucking pointed a gun at. Tatyana moved from beside him and stood to his left. He noted the transition because it took her out of the line of fire. The sound of shoes on the walkway coming around the corner drew his eye. Every muscle in his body tightened as recognition slapped him in the face. His enemy, the one who was selling humans like they were no more than groceries was a brother—a Guardian.

Darren Kowalski stepped into the sheltered area and removed his mirrored sunglasses. All six-foot-six inches of the man abruptly tightened with the same recognition.

"Ski, it's been a hot minute." He moved slightly to ensure every weapon he was carrying was accessible.

The man's eyes pinged from him, to Tatyana, to the egress points of the outdoor living area. His partner, an older softer version of himself, pulled up short at Mike's greeting.

"You know David Xavier?" The older man asked, obviously trying to catch up. He could see Tatyana's head whip around to him as if asking the same question.

"This isn't David Xavier, Uncle. I don't know what his real name is, but he is a member of Guardian's lauded Alpha Team, he goes by the handle of Chief." Darren crossed his arm over his chest bringing his hand closer to his weapon. A corner of Darren's mouth lifted in a smirk when he mimicked his movement. "That haircut must have hurt like a bitch, huh?"

He shrugged. "This gig is a drastic change of employment for you, isn't it, Ski?"

Kowalski laughed, bright and loud. "Hell, those are the most words I've ever heard you say."

The older man shot a look at Tatyana. "You knew we were being set up?"

"No, he *is* David Xavier." Tatyana shot looks between the three men, her confused gaze landing on Mike. He gave her a lifted shoulder in response. She wasn't the concern right now—Kowalski and his uncle were.

"I didn't know you'd left Guardian." Mike remembered the last time he'd seen Ski. Alpha and Tango teams had been utilized to extract two men, a high-ranking diplomat and an oil mogul, from a hot zone the stupid motherfuckers had been warned not to go into. The entire mission had been mired in freezing rain, and Tango team had lost one member. Francis Lloyd was hit by shrapnel and lost most of his leg. Ski carried the man out and refused to allow anyone to take over, even after Lloyd succumbed to his injuries. They'd served together in the Army and joined Guardian together. That happened just over eight years ago. He hadn't seen Ski since.

"Why would I stay? To get myself killed? I don't think so." Darren cast a glance around the outdoor room again. "Where is Alpha?"

He smiled. "Not here."

"I see. So should we just get this over with?"

"We will leave." The older man started to turn, but Ski caught his bicep and shook his head without moving his eyes from Mike.

"We will not be allowed to leave, Uncle. This is a trap. There is no reason to run. Guardian will have us surrounded by now. The question is, do you want to spend the rest of your life in jail or would you rather go out like a warrior?" Ski's eyes silently challenged him.

He shifted slightly before he spoke, "Today is a good day to die."

Mike dove to the right, tackling Tatyana and dropping them both behind the bar as he unholstered his automatic. He tossed her the Glock 43 and prayed like hell he wouldn't get a bullet for the effort. He rolled through the small space and came up firing as he lunged again hard to the right. Ski had taken cover at the end of the bricked-in grill. His uncle wasn't in Mike's line of sight. Mike fired three shots, sending chips of brick and mortar flying, causing Ski to duck and dive behind the low front counter of the outdoor kitchen. A bullet from his left hit the wall just past him, driving him down to his stomach on the tile flooring. He scrambled in a low crawl to the corner. Tatyana moved to her left in a crouch. He saw Kowalski's uncle draw a bead on her just as a volley of bullets rained down around him.

"On your left!" He yelled out the warning just as he was spun around by a bullet that slammed into his arm. Mike heard several shots and prayed Tatyana had moved fast enough. He worked his way down the back of the couch and stood, taking aim at the uncle.

Ski hit him in a flying tackle. The grip he had on his gun failed. His hand was wet with his own blood, and the .45 went flying when he was hit. He rolled through the impact, and both men came up in a crouch with knives ready to engage. His knife was in his left hand. Not his dominant side, but he'd practiced countless hours for this very contingency. There was a barrage of gunfire down by the docks, and he heard the shouts of his team as they rushed to his assistance. His eyes locked with his opponent. Ski had the same training as he did, and they both knew the next few seconds would determine who lived and who died.

He feigned right and dove left, low and under Ski's slicing jab. Mike grabbed the man's ankle while deflecting a second thrust. He strained with his injured arm, whipped around with an elbow to Ski's knee and yanked the fucker's foot off the ground. Ski's body slammed onto the hard tile. Ski kicked sharply at his thigh. He deflected the blow and blocked a wild swing of Ski's knife when the man attempted to right himself. Mike grabbed the man's wrist, twisted it violently and pushed forward, driving the man down again. His good arm pinned Ski to the ground, but he couldn't hold him down with his injuries. Mike did what he had to do. He kicked hard, landing a blow on Ski's jaw. That kick would have taken out most men, but Ski knew to move with the force of the blow, and he did, freeing himself from the armbar. His legs were taken out by a sweeping kick. He went down hard and hit his head in the process. Ski was on top of him in a second. The sounds of shouting and shooting surrounded them, but his only focus was the knife that was now angled toward his throat. Mike grasped the hilt with both hands, forestalling the weapon's descent to his vulnerable neck. Ski pushed all his weight into the struggle. Clarity hit him at that moment. He had a counter move and executed it. His body bowed up as he pushed the weapon over his head. Ski's weight and the momentum initiated by his unexpected launch off the ground sent him forward onto his right shoulder. Mike rolled and pinned the man's arm under his knee. He rammed all his weight behind a right hook to Ski's jaw. He powered another and then a third before he felt Ski go limp.

Mike pulled the knife out of the man's hand and looked up. Jacob and Doc were in the corner huddled over someone. A man he vaguely recognized swooped in, turned Ski over and secured his hands with a double pair of zip ties. He drew a breath and looked for Tatyana. His gut clenched as his eyes caught a flash of color between Jacob and Doc.

"Fuck! Get me my pack now!" Doc was doing compressions and counting. Another man ran in with Doc's pack and started whipping out equipment. An electronic defibrillator hit the ground, and the two men placed the patches on Tatyana's chest. Jacob stood and swung an assessing eye over the area. He strode over and held out a hand. Jacob helped him up, but his eyes never left Tatyana. Her small form jumped as Doc and the man worked to start her heart. "Doc will do everything he can, Mike."

He nodded his head and watched as her small body jumped again. The men scrambled after that. "She's back." Doc's hands flew to a bullet hole as he directed the other man's action. "Get a stretcher in here and tell them to get a plane fired up. We need to get her out of here."

Doc sent a quick glance toward him. "You okay?"

He could only nod. He stared at the tiny form on the floor. His mind raged with fury. He reached for his weapon while his eyes searched the area for the fucker that shot his woman.

"Stand down." Jacob's warning barely registered.

Doc was in his face with that damn eyepatch pushed right into his personal space. "Mike, I have to go with her. Mitch will take a look at you as soon as we get her stable. I *will* take care of her." He blinked trying to formulate a response. He pushed toward her, but Jacob held him tight.

"You'll just be in the way. Trust Doc to take care of her."

"You don't understand, Skipper." He pushed against his friend trying to free himself.

"I understand more than you think. We have to take her in, Mike. Let Doc do his job, so she has a chance of mounting some kind of defense. If we don't stay out of the way, you'll lose her forever." Jacob whispered the words so only he could hear them.

"What am I going to do?" He watched as Jacob's people brought a stretcher in and they transferred his lover onto it. They were out of the area within thirty seconds.

"Live one day at a time." Jacob pulled him into a bear hug.

CHAPTER 29

Mike drew a deep breath after the stretcher carrying Tatyana was taken away. A crush of unimaginable anguish intensified with each step the medics took. Every fiber in his soul demanded he stay with her and yet he knew in his heart she was already lost to him. Any armor he'd tried to put in place against this moment crumbled into dust. He watched until he could no longer see her. The finality and loss consumed him. Doc would do everything humanly possible to ensure the woman survived. However, he'd already started a mourning process. He mourned the life he would never have with the only woman he had ever loved. He drew another breath, pulled away from Jacob, and finally took in the devastation around him. Fuck. "Where is the older man?"

Jacob had been watching and assessing him. He remained quiet for a moment before he nodded toward the green expanse covering the back acreage. "Ran to the interior. He's probably looking for the team the Russians sent to the far side of the island when they landed."

He rolled his shoulders and hissed at the burn of his upper arm. "Yeah, Didn't think he'd come alone." Jacob slung his M-4 around his back and tugged his first aid kit out of one of his pockets.

"Get your shirt off." He reacted automatically to his Skipper's order. They'd done field care for so long, having his team leader bandage his bicep was second nature.

"The uncle?" Mike's mind was still with Tatyana. He could hear a sea plane powering up. Dixon and Drake would break the laws of physics to get her to a hospital. They knew he had feelings for her. At least, he assumed they did. No, knowing the twins, they knew it.

"Joseph and Jared are out there." Jacob lifted his arm, and he pulled in a sharp breath of air at the movement. "Stop whining." Jacob reprimanded him with a gentleness that came with familiarity. "It's just a through and through. Not even near the bone. You'd think you've never been shot before."

Ski moaned, drawing both of their attention to the floor. "Did he say anything? I hit the ground running as soon as I recognized him. I wasn't listening. Too worried about getting here in time to save your ass." Jacob wiped away as much blood as he could with the gauze he had before he started wrapping a tight compression bandage around Mike's upper arm.

"Should have been closer," He grunted.

Jacob snorted and shook his head. "I was one hundred yards away. Any closer and I would have been in your fucking lap. This last year softened you that much? What did he say?"

"Fuck you too." He smiled through the insult. God, it was good to be back with people he knew and trusted. "He knew he wasn't getting out of here. He stopped the older man from trying to run and chose to fight. I don't know why, but the whole resignation thing was almost like he wanted to get caught."

Jacob uprighted a bamboo lounge chair and pointed to it. "Sit your ass down before you fall down."

He bristled at the command. "I'm not going to fucking fall down, Skipper." He caught movement in his peripheral and blinked to try to focus on the three men walking through the lush tropical foliage behind the house. Damn, his vision was fucked up. Maybe he hit his head a little harder than he thought.

"Yeah, I know. Sit your ass down anyway, my friend." He looked at the chair and watched as Jacob uprighted several more. Ski groaned again and moved against his restraints before he stilled. He sat down and pulled his arm away from his body.

"What you said about Ski not wanting to leave. Tell me about that." Jacob took off his comms mic and sat it on the armrest that Mike's uninjured arm wasn't using.

"Are we on with Archangel?" He needed to know his audience.

"No, there is no transmission out. Jewel is circling somewhere above us at thirty thousand feet and has us shut down tight. This is so we have your gut instincts on record."

He nodded and cleared his throat. "I'm not sure why, but something felt off when Ski just folded. Accepted that we had him surrounded without any surprise. He did a fucking wonderful job at trying to kill me, though, I'll give him that."

Jacob cocked his head and listened for a moment. "Jason got word that there was an MI6 operative high up in the Bratva."

Mike drew that statement inside and turned it around. MI6 had someone inside? With all the intel he had, plus whatever the MI6 resource had acquired, there was no doubt Ski and his uncle were going down. Unless… "You don't think he's the operative for MI6 do you? Skipper, that fucker was not acting. He was going to kill me."

Whatever Jacob was going to say was interrupted by Jared and Joseph as they escorted Kowalski's uncle back into the seating area. "Fucker is quick for an old man." Jared pushed the man into one of the chairs. The Russian bounced back up, and Joseph slammed the cuffed man down again, none too politely. The Russian's sweat stained face bulged against a makeshift gag. Mike's lip twitched. The man's designer tie was never going to be the same.

"The rest of the Russian's team?" Jacob looked directly at Joseph when he asked. Joseph smirked as he replied, "They won't be a concern."

"I guess I need to rephrase that... are any of them left alive?" The older Russian's eyes cast fearfully toward Joseph. Joseph held up his vicious looking blade and then casually wiped the blood from the shining metal on the back of his uniform before he placed it back in its sheath. The man walked over to the refrigerator and got out a bottle of water ignoring his brother's question.

"I sent Hanson and Berube out to find what is left of them and to tell Temple to bring the boat around for the prisoners." Jared relayed the information before he sat down across from Mike. "As soon as we get all this shit settled, we need to do a full debriefing. I'll need the recordings of all conversations with the Bratva to include with a statement about the involvement of the Concierge. She's notorious, and it will be a good thing when she's off the streets." Jared stood and turned toward the dock. "I'm going down to help Jazz and Thompson deal with the ladies on that aircraft." Jared turned back before he left. "It is good to see you again, my friend."

He nodded. It was good to be among friends although Jared's comment about Tatyana pushed yet another stake through his heart.

"She'll live." Jacob's words punched through his

thoughts. He lifted his eyes to meet his Skipper's. "She means something to you?"

He held Jacob's gaze while he clicked every plate of armor he could around his dying heart. "No, nothing." His spirit screamed in pain at the blatant lie he'd just told his best friend, but the rotting wound eating his soul couldn't dent his determination to never reveal how much this mission had cost him.

Temple strode into the area and grabbed the older Russian, breaking up Mike's pity party. "I'll come back with Thompson for that one in a minute, Alpha."

He watched the younger man escort the Russian out as Mitch came in with his medical pack. "I did a quick visual of the ladies in the cargo plane, sir. I didn't see any immediate distress, although, like the others in New York, they appeared to be under the influence of something. The stewardess from the plane has them all wrapped up in blankets and is directing the men down there like a taskmaster."

Mitch unwound the dressing and started cleaning his wound. The sting of alcohol brought him back to the present with sharp stinging clarity. Temple and Thompson came back for Kowalski while Mitch was packing his wound, which hurt like a motherfucker.

"We can do the interviews later. We have the head of the serpent, and over the last few months, we hit the distribution arm hard. Give Jared's people time with these two and the Concierge, and we will be able to close down this disgusting business once and for all. You're coming home, my friend." Jacob stood and walked over to where Joseph was standing, leaving him to Mitch's care. He looked down at the $15,000 watch he wore and then past it to the hand-crafted leather shoes. He was going back to South Dakota, but would the training complex ever be home again? He closed his eyes and blocked out the sounds around him as he called up an image of Tatyana and focused on the vision of her beautiful eyes. His life was as empty as when he'd left over a year ago. The abyss he felt now was more than a fissure in his soul, but there was nothing he could do to repair it.

CHAPTER 30

The utility gray walls and fluorescent lights added to the maze feeling of the underground levels at Vauxhall Cross, the renowned building better known as MI6 Headquarters. The *James Bond* mystique had earned the agency acclaim as a high-tech wonder, but this level consisted of cement, closed doors, and continuous questions. Tatyana yawned and scrubbed her eyes. The caffeine she'd lived on since she'd been released from the hospital had failed about two hours ago. She was crashing. The adrenaline, anxiety, and nerves were expected and had worked in her favor, especially during the countless hours of interrogation. She'd been interrogated, as any deep cover operative would need to be, but after five days of questioning and seclusion, she was ready to move on. To what, she had no idea, but rehashing the last eight years had been excruciatingly painful. Eight years of her actions and decisions were dissected and second-guessed. She'd managed to deal with the constant accusations of alternative decisions until her handlers had mentioned David Xavier. She'd lost any sense of decorum at that point.

Thank God she'd played off the defensiveness as a reaction to the injuries she'd sustained on David's island. Tatyana's arm ached even after downing the painkiller the staff doctor had prescribed. It had been eight years since she'd seen a doctor for any reason, so the hospital stay had turned into a myriad of tests, procedures and boxes MI6 ticked off to ensure their asset was healthy. Tatyana rolled her eyes as she glanced down at her useless arm pinned to her side in a sling. The bullet the older Kowalski had shot at her shattered her shoulder and damaged the muscle. According to the specialists that had been paraded into her hospital room, she would never regain full function of her arm. Seemed like karma for the last eight years had come around and bit her in the arse, and it chomped down hard.

Taty waited in the small room listening to the heating system cycle on and off. Over the course of the last eight years, she'd convinced herself she did the best she could within the confines of her cover, but the relentless questions seemed to reinforce the fact she'd failed miserably, even though she'd succeeded in reaching the top of the Bratva. Another agency, one that employed the man portraying David Xavier, had succeeded in taking down the top of the organization. Taty prayed that the information she had documented and the DNA she'd been able to save from the victims would help prosecute the bastards. Her handlers made it seem her efforts to reach the top was all for naught.

Taty wiped at a tear that fell. Everything she'd done, the people she'd... No, she wouldn't lose it here. Not in front of the people who sat in judgment now. Where had they been when she was making life or death situations? Damn them for their sanctimonious discernment years after the events and outside any stressors. Since being released from the hospital, a cloak of depression had settled over her. The overwhelming sense of guilt made it hard to breathe, impossible to sleep and brought the 'what ifs' to her thoughts almost constantly. Almost. When the thoughts became too much, she'd pull up the one memory in the last eight years that made her smile— David. Taty shook her head. No, he wasn't David. The younger Kowalski had called him Chief. Her handlers had informed her the man was a member of Guardian Security. The international company, the world's largest private security firm, had seemed to rise out of the mist in the last six years.

The man's single operation had lasted just over a year, and in that time he and his organization saved almost fifty women and brought the Bratva to its knees. What had she done? She'd become a pawn in the Bratva's organization while trying to reach the top. She'd killed, sold people and lost herself in the swirling cesspool of the Russian underworld. Maybe her handlers were right to question the entirety of her mission. Exhausted, Tatyana dropped her head to the laminate tabletop. David... oh, what she wouldn't give to have his quiet strength next to her now. She wanted...

The door opened, but she didn't open her eyes or lift her head. She needed another pain pill, maybe two... a drug induced sleep would be better than the exhaustion she was fighting.

"Are you Tatyana Petrov?" an American voice asked. Taty nodded her head but didn't lift it from the tabletop. She simply didn't have the energy or the desire.

"My name is Gabriel. Mike White Cloud works for me." Taty rolled her head and cracked an eye open. The dignified man in the bespoke suit wasn't what she expected. He was over six-feet tall. His dark hair had gray at the temples, but the man was hard and physically fit. He reminded her of David. He stood beside the table and stared at her as she took inventory of him with the one eye she'd expended enough energy to open.

Taty waited, but the man didn't speak. Whatever, she didn't know a Mike White Cloud nor did she care to be introduced to him. She closed her eye, rolled her forehead back down to face the table and drew a deep breath. The ache in her shoulder pulsed down her arm and back. She really did need another painkiller.

"It would seem he believes you are a criminal," the deep voice spoke again.

"He needs to find a place at the end of the queue. I understand it is quite long." Tatyana finally lifted off the table and carefully slumped back against the uncomfortable gray metal chair.

The man pulled out the chair across from her and sat down. He placed his hands on the table and steepled his fingers. His index fingers tapped for several seconds while he stared at her. Taty knew this game, and it was one she was damn good at playing. She closed her eyes and waited. If he wanted her to speak, he needed to ask a question.

"I don't believe it is. While debriefing from a mission as long as yours can make you question your actions, you are not a criminal, and you don't deserve to be treated as one. Your organization has provided the information you brought out with you from your op. The evidence and your testimony will pin human trafficking charges against at least fifteen extremely wealthy and powerful men. When people are cornered, they will strike out. Since you are the only one that can put those men together with the Bratva and the crimes they have committed, my organization believes you will become a target, from not only those men but any remnants of the Bratva that are still functioning—although the risk of the latter happening is very small. Between Guardian, MI6 and all the other organizations around the world, I have every confidence we have stopped the Bratva."

Taty opened her eyes and blinked several times. Well, dammit. She hadn't thought that far into the future. Yes, her testimony would be the stake in the heart of the soulless bastards that bought those people. She weighed the information and shook her head. The Russians would be stopped, but what about the Asians, the American Syndicate or the flood of humans being shipped out of the war-torn areas of the Middle East? The Russian sales were just a drop in the bucket.

"I'm offering you a place where you will be safe. No one will be able to reach you."

Tatyana looked at the door and back at the man. She knew what her organization had planned. She'd be stuck in some safe house and moved as needed until she was no longer useful. Then she'd be dismissed. Her shoulder would prohibit her from working.

"Mr. Churchill has worked diligently to get the Home Office's permission to assign you to me until the trials are over. As I'm sure you are aware, your current disability will not allow you to continue in service to MI6 as an operative."

Tatyana nodded but didn't speak. She didn't need to, and she wasn't one to add words if they weren't needed.

"My God, you and Chief are going to make one hell of a pair. Worse than Frank and his one grunt sentences," the man mumbled.

"Chief?" Taty sat up and winced at the sudden

movement. She didn't know who the hell Frank was, but that was irrelevant.

"Yes?"

"You are from this Guardian?"

"Guardian Security is my company, yes."

Tatyana's soul screamed for her to ask about the man that had become so necessary to her in such a little time. Was he well? Was he injured? The last time she'd seen him he was locked in a life and death struggle with the young Russian. She knew the Russian was in custody but was David... Chief, all right? Was he married? Did he love another? Could she ever be a part of his life? Was anything they talked about true? Was she just a mission to him or did he feel something for her?

The man, Gabriel, cocked his head at her and then looked around the small room assessing her accommodations. "I have the authority to take you with me, now. You may remain with MI6 or sign this." The man withdrew a neatly folded paper from his pocket and pushed it across the table to her.

Tatyana used her one functioning hand to open the paper. "This is my resignation from MI6." He nodded and extracted a second paper. Tatyana read the writing and immediately read it again. An offer letter for employment within Guardian Security as a consultant and an instructor of foreign languages at someplace called The SD Annex. The salary was exorbitant, even considering the dollar to Euro conversion that she had to do in her head. She put the paper down and lifted her eyes to the man across from her. Was this some sort of trick? There was no reason or rationale for this type of offer. "Why?"

Gabriel leaned back in his chair and narrowed his eyes at her as if he was determining whether or not to answer her question. "Because someone I care for put his life on hold for over a year to help bring these bastards down. In the process, he found someone important to him. As far as he knows, you are a criminal, and he'll never see you again. Now, you have a decision to make. If he means nothing to you, if you were just doing your job, stay here. But, if you feel anything for that man, sign those documents, and you'll be on your way to him." He leaned forward. Even with the table between them the man's aura filled the room and made her feel small and insignificant. "But know this: if you have any malice or ill intent toward that man, I will make sure you regret signing."

Tatyana shivered at the man's tone. She'd been around many powerful men, but the absolute authority this man radiated solidified his threat. He'd make her regret any such ploy. She looked at both papers as they moved slightly from the forced air heat that was warming the sterile room.

"Will he want me there?"

"If he doesn't, you will be relocated and the employment offer still stands."

"Why are you doing this? I understand that your employee has served you well, but this is a little over the board, yes?" Tatyana leaned back and cradled her arm. Her head pounded with the same heartbeat she felt radiating with the pain in her shoulder.

"He is more than an employee to me. He is family." The man leaned back and watched her carefully. She had the distinct feeling he could not only see every secret she'd ever hidden, but he could read her thoughts, too. A hint of a smile lifted the corner of his mouth and an eyebrow raised. *Oh my God, that was freaky.* Taty gulped and dropped her focus to the papers. A simple choice, but one that would change her life forever. If there was even a minuscule chance Dav... Chief would be happy to see her, she'd go. She positioned the sheets closer and scanned them again before she lifted her eyes to the man across from her. "Mr. Gabriel, would you happen to have a pen I may borrow?"

CHAPTER 31

"Chief." Frank Marshall's gruff voice interrupted his contemplation of an amazing view. The sun was setting, casting a golden hue across the pastures that spread out as far as the eye could see. Cows slowly meandered, eating the first green shoots of spring. They were in the middle of calving season. Frank, his ranch fore-man, John Smith, and several new hands that he'd yet to meet, had ridden out and brought in four of the cows that always had issues delivering and penned them up next to the barn.

The cool breeze of the early evening brought a chill to his skin. He'd lost track of time once again. He'd been doing that since he'd been back. The Wonder Twins had done a great job of running the facility, but were more than happy to hand the reins back to him. Their primary interests were physical training and taking on random projects. The latest

339

was a solar powered heating system for the water troughs and stock-pond, which wasn't new technology, but getting an old rancher to embrace the idea was a major project in and of itself. Listening to them pitch the idea to Frank had been hilarious. They never shut up, and Frank didn't do much of anything but grunt, yet the writers of the classic Three Stooges movies couldn't have scripted the dialog any better. He raked his gaze over the pastureland. God, he'd missed this place and yet...

"Frank." He acknowledged the man as he stepped up and sat his ass on the top board of the fence alongside him.

"You know I ain't one to butt in."

"But you're going to do it anyway." He chuckled when the man grunted an affirmative sounding noise.

"Yup. What happened out there?"

Shit, the man didn't mince words. Well, neither did he. "Fell for the wrong woman." He knew Frank would keep his confidence. The man was as close to a father as he'd ever had.

"Huh." Frank fished in his pocket and tugged out a bag of taffy. The little diner in Hollister had taken to selling it by the cash register. Damn stuff was good. Frank offered him a piece, so he took it.

"Yeah." He popped the confection into his mouth, folded the little square of wax paper and put it in his pocket. They didn't litter on the ranch. Ever.

"Took me forever to find Amanda… after." Frank busied himself folding his own square of wax paper.

"True, but you deserved to find happiness."

"Huh."

Ever the conversationalist, Frank ended his thought there. He gave Frank a sideways glance. "Huh, what?"

"You said that like you think you don't." Frank turned his head and stared straight at him.

"I'm not ready." He worked hard, gave Gabriel and Jason an honest day's work… more than that, actually. But he was even more withdrawn than he'd been before. Right now he didn't want to see what the others had. He needed time to heal, and he wasn't about to do that in public view.

"Huh." Frank fished for the bag again and drew another piece of candy out for each of them. "Life's just like a horse. Get bucked off. You get back on. You deserve happiness, too." He handed the taffy over as he spoke.

He shrugged his shoulder and fiddled with the peppermint taffy now in his hands. He didn't believe it. "Guess we'll see."

"You visit your kin when you was gone?"

He shrugged. "Got no kin. Mom is dead, never knew my dad."

"Damn good thing you got us then." Frank let out a long breath. "Been blessed. Got me one hell of a family and I figure you to be a son, just the same as those two whirling dervishes."

KRIS MICHAELS

He chuckled at that. The description fit Dixon and Drake. Frank gave him a rare smile. "You deserve the love of a good woman."

"That's the problem. That woman I fell for? She wasn't good. She's a criminal and everything I did last year put her behind bars, probably for the rest of her life."

Or he assumed she was there. Doc had told him that she'd made it out of surgery, but Interpol had taken her into custody. That was over two months ago. He'd made numerous inquiries about her, her condition and her case, but none had been answered. He'd given his deposition, and he'd testify when it came time. He didn't know how he was going to deal with seeing her again—as her accuser.

Frank rubbed the back of his neck and groaned. "Don't figure you give your love none too easy. Had to be something there."

"Nothing that can change her fate or mine." He fought daily to keep that thought front and center, or he'd go fucking insane.

"Dammit, son, this conversation needs more than taffy. Let's go get us some brown liquor."

He shook his head. "Thank you, but I'm good here. I need to process, to be alone."

"Don't like that idea."

"I know."

The drone of a jet engine shattered the silence. "Gabriel?" Frank asked as they both turned their eyes toward the complex's runway.

Mike drew a deep breath and jumped down from the fence. "Shouldn't be. He's in Europe. The last of the supply transports arrived about 2:00. Unless you and Amanda are expecting a visit?" He eyed the G6 as it descended in its approach pattern. It wasn't the aircraft the King family used when visiting the ranch. He watched as Dixon and Drake left the ranch house en route to the landing strip.

"Nope." Frank took off his cowboy hat and raked his hand through his salt and pepper hair. "Kids ain't due anytime soon."

The Wonder Twins disappeared. "They'll handle it." He headed toward the barn and Frank fell into step beside him. The man grunted his affirmation.

"Dinner is in thirty minutes. Don't make us wait for you." Frank turned and headed toward the house.

He'd heard Frank admonish his family in that tone too many times not to smile. "Roger that." Chief glanced at his watch to make a note of the time.

He wandered to the stalls and fussed over the horses while his two dogs followed at his heels. He loved the animals, and they seemed to sense he needed the peace of being alone with them, because every one of them, even Keelee's cantankerous gelding, nudged him gently when he approached. He stopped at Chance's stall. The sorrel had one eye and was scarred from a fight he'd had with a barbed wire fence. Frank had bought him as a rescue, and he'd instantly felt a bond with the old guy. Chance placed his head at the center of his chest and rested it there as Mike whispered mindless affirmations to the animal.

~

Tatyana approached the massive doorway. She'd never been this close to large animals in her life. The men who met the plane and read the envelope she'd been directed to give them recognized her immediately, and she recognized them. The pilots that accompanied David... No. The man standing three hundred feet from her was not David Xavier. His name was Mike White Cloud. At least that is what Gabriel had told her. Her handlers at MI6 had been there when she'd awakened after surgery. She was flown from the Maldives to London while heavily sedated. But that portion of her life was over as of three days ago.

Her arm hung almost lifeless against her side. The doctors promised more mobility, and eventually, with physical therapy, she would be able to use it to write and feed herself. Until then, she had been getting by using her left hand and arm.

She leaned against the wall in the shadows and looked at the man she loved. Mike, Chief or David, the name didn't matter. Mike didn't know she was MI6. Gabriel had given her the opportunity to tell Mike herself. Tatyana held onto a thread of hope that what they'd shared wasn't a dictate of his mission. There were so many things not said, so many lies told, and there was every reason to believe she meant nothing to him. Except for the flight to the Maldives. The way he made love to her, the connection she felt, bound her to this man. She risked everything by coming here. Her sanity, her tenuous justification to herself about the vile acts she'd been accessory to in order to bring down the Bratva, her shallow hope that maybe the man standing there would love her even after everything she'd done. What she'd done had stained her in ways she'd never be able to clean. For the thousandth time, she debated why this seemed like a good idea when Gabriel presented it to her. The answer that kept surfacing was simple. She'd lose everything if she didn't try. Because that man, no matter his name, made her broken life whole.

His low chuckle as he talked to the horse brought her out of her jetlagged stupor. London to South Dakota in… she lifted her left arm and checked the face of the watch. She did the math then blinked and shook her head. Twenty-two hours, maybe? No, twenty because of the American time zones. She fixed her addled brain on the reason she was here. Tatyana walked forward quietly. A huge animal stuck its head over the half door and blew out a huff of air. Taty jumped and squeaked at the sudden appearance of the massive animal. Her good hand clutched her chest in surprise. Two dogs sprang from the straw and barked.

"Tatyana?" His voice carried shocked disbelief. She cast a terrified wayward look at the big animal before she stepped closer to the reason she'd flown halfway around the world. He looked so damn good. His biceps strained the long sleeve t-shirt he wore. The boot-cut jeans formed to his powerful thighs. Brown cowboy boots and a wide leather belt with a huge silver buckle sold the cowboy look.

"See, you lied to me. You *are* a cowboy." She emphasized her accent. Mike dropped the hand that had been stroking the horse and put both hands in his pockets. His body stiffened, no longer relaxed like he'd been when petting the large brown horse behind him. "How are you here, Taty, and what's wrong with your arm?"

Taty stopped walking about three feet from him. She reached down and pulled her arm up and cradled it against her waist. She should have worn the sling, but the doctors wanted her to use it as much as she could to strengthen the damaged muscles. "The bullet damaged the joint and muscle. It will get stronger, but it may never be the same." She bit her lip and looked up at him through her lashes. She drew a long deep breath in before she answered his other question. "Your boss, Mr. Gabriel, came to see me."

His mouth opened and then closed several times. The doubt she saw play across his face turned into suspicion. "Why?" He stepped back and pulled his hands out of his pockets and placed them on his hips in a defensive posture.

Taty shrugged. "I do not know his motivation."

"Why are you here?"

"I was asking myself the same question just now. Do you want to know what the answer was?"

Mike's eyes narrowed and his jaw set as if he were grinding his teeth together. This wasn't the hearts and flowers reunion she'd hoped for.

"I'm here because I care about you."

"You don't know me. You only know my cover."

"And you don't know me. You've only met *my* cover. But there is truth to my statement. You can't deny it."

"Your cover?" he whispered.

"Until three days ago I was an undercover agent with MI6. I worked for eight years to get to the top of the Bratva to take down the organization, rung by rung."

"Eight years?" His voice broke.

Her eyes filled with tears, and Taty nodded.

Mike stepped forward and she looked up into his eyes. His hand palmed her cheek. "I'm so sorry. I wanted to tell you, but I…"

"You couldn't. And I couldn't. We were pawns in a bloody awful game. We couldn't stop what we'd started, even if it cost us each other."

He lifted her injured arm and carefully held her hand as his other arm reached around her and cradled her into his massive body. She'd forgotten how broad and tall he was, and now in cowboy boots, he towered at least a full foot over her, but she felt safer than she had in years.

"I thought I'd lost you." His admission echoed her

own thoughts. He lowered his lips to hers. She trembled at the soft sweep of his lips against her mouth.

"I didn't mean to fall in love with you." She breathed the most honest words she'd ever spoken against his lips.

"I thought I'd lost you." He repeated his words and buried his face in her curls as he held her as if she would break. "I wanted to tell you, to let you know what you meant to me before—"

"No, I understand. I knew in here." She interrupted and lifted her good hand to his chest and covered his heart. "I knew. You told me on the plane, didn't you? That's when you told me you loved me."

"I couldn't lose you without letting you know... somehow." His lips found hers again, and this time the kiss wasn't tentative or sweet. It was possessive and demanding. Taty opened for him and fell into the bliss of his desire.

"Ummm...We'll tell Frank you aren't coming to dinner."

A man's voice behind them startled her, but he didn't stop. He didn't loosen the tender grip he had on her arm or the possessive hold he had on her hair, allowing him to angle her head for a deeper kiss. Taty sighed into the safety of Mike's embrace.

"You aren't coming to dinner, are you?"

Taty recognized the voices and groaned when Mike lifted away.

"Go away." He directed his words at the men in the barn with them, but his eyes remained on her.

Love and laughter filled his expression, and her heart warmed at the genuine feeling of unadulterated bliss that swept over her like a crashing wave.

"Man, talk about unappreciative."

Mike finally broke eye contact and gathered her into him. His chest rumbled against her ear. "Go away. Now."

"See, right there. Yep, I agree, unappreciative and rude. He should really introduce us. I mean proper like."

"I agree! You know if that were our woman, she'd be treated better. Be introduced to everyone, but you know how these guys are. Neanderthals."

Tatyana turned in Mike's embrace. The twin on the right was staring at his brother, his mouth opened like a gaping fish before he snapped it shut. "Neanderthals? Ne-fucking-anderthals? Really? So now you are making generalizations about an entire career field? That is like saying all blonde women are ditzy! That shit will get you in trouble faster than a baseball bat hitting a beehive. Hell, who the hell are you and what have you done with my brother?"

He grabbed her good hand and pulled her toward the side of the building and closer to a smaller door she hadn't noticed before.

"What? No! You are purposefully misunderstanding me."

"Oh… I understand you! Hey, Chief, back me up here... Now where in the hell did he go?"

"You chased him away."

"I did nothing of the sort."

Tatyana laughed as behind them, the two continued to argue. Mike led her across the vast area between the massive barn and the log cabin mansion she'd skirted to get to him.

"Where are we going?" She hurriedly tried to keep up with his longer strides but had to jog every now and then to keep from being dragged.

"Somewhere private." He stopped and swooped her into his arms. She shrieked at the surprise move.

"Was I too slow?"

"Unless you want to make love here and now, yes, you were going too slow."

Mike's long legs ate up the distance toward a smaller house. Tatyana would have had to run to keep up with him. Instead, she spent the time kissing Mike's ear, down the side of his neck and running her good hand over his hard pecs.

"Woman, I'm not going to be able to wait."

Taty waited until he kicked the door shut behind him. She didn't care if they were in another barn, she wanted him, and she needed him. Now. "I like it when you get that way."

"I don't want to hurt your shoulder." He put her down and dropped to his knees in front of her and kissed her stomach as he unbuttoned her shirt. Taty ran her hand through his thick black hair and damn near yanked a handful out when he mouthed her breast through the lace of her bra. She knew on some level he was stripping her of her clothes, but there was no way she could focus on that minor detail when the man's mouth and hands caressed every inch of her body. She tugged at his shirt, desperate to feel his hot skin next to hers. He had it off in mere seconds.

"Mike, please. I need you to make love to me." Taty bent down and captured his lips. The lost, feral look of desire on his face sent a shiver of pure lust through her. He stood and kissed her, backing her up until the back of her thighs hit a bed. He supported her back and lowered her onto the mattress. He stood and motioned toward the middle of the bed. She pushed herself up and over with her good hand while she watched him take off his boots and lose his blue jeans, big silver buckle and all. His cock stood out from his body, hard and swollen, obviously ready for her. She licked her lips. God, she loved going down on him.

Mike stroked his shaft and smiled at her gesture. "As much as I want to feel your mouth on me, we won't be doing that. Not tonight. Tonight I'm making love to you." He hit the bed and crawled up to her.

"No. Tonight we are making love to each other." Taty smiled shyly when he stopped short.

Mike's gaze roamed over her before he spoke, "I never believed I'd find my soul mate." He lowered his body over hers after ensuring her arm was positioned in a way she wouldn't be injured. He kissed the dark red scars from the bullet wound and the surgeries before his lips traveled across her collarbone and lower. Taty felt the tears building, but there was nothing she could do to prevent them from spilling. She had been given the most precious gift in the world. A chance at love with a remarkable, caring man.

Mike hovered over her, his face displaying concern… and a little sadness.

She answered his unasked question, "I'm fine, just overwhelmed. I love you. I can't believe this. If it is a dream, please don't wake me."

He moved his hips, bringing his shaft to her heat. "This is real." His lips lowered to just above hers, his eyes still holding hers. Their breaths hitched at the same time as he entered her. His eyes closed as if against his will. His heat and size stole her ability to think of anything but him. She wrapped her legs around him and abandoned herself to the sensations he released from the depths of her soul. He was the center of her universe and had been since the day she'd walked into that chalet. It seemed eons ago, but it was only a few short months. The anxiety, fear, separation, and time away from each other melted into an amalgamation of emotion that built and swirled, taking her higher than she'd ever allowed herself to fly before. But in his arms, she was safe, and for the first time in as long as she could remember, she could show the emotion she felt. His touch, his lips and his whispered words of adoration filled voids that had only held darkness. With him, she was safe. He was her home. Her body pitched into a shattering orgasm. She barely registered Mike chasing his own release until his hips stuttered and he made a deep growling noise in the back of his throat before he found bliss.

Taty played with the damp hair at the back of his neck while he recovered. She couldn't recall a time where she'd been so... at peace. Yes, that was the word.

"You are thinking too hard." Mike still lay between her legs, his chest on her stomach and his head resting just above her breasts.

She chuckled, "I am."

"Tell me."

"I was afraid to come. Afraid that there was someone else, that there was no room in your life for me. I've done horrible things in the name of justice."

He lifted onto his forearms and locked his gaze with hers. "I can say the same. One day we will know each other's darkest hours, but whatever you tell me, it will not alter what I feel about you. I love you."

Taty lifted her good arm and traced his strong jaw with her fingers. "You understand I come with luggage?"

Mike's face split in a wide smile. "Baggage. You come with baggage is the saying."

Taty rolled her eyes. "It is the same thing, yes?"

"Technically, yes, it is the same thing." He lowered and kissed her thoroughly. She drew a much-needed lungful of air when he finally ended the kiss. "Whatever luggage you have, we'll handle it."

"So you want me to stay?" She smiled at him and batted her eyes.

"I want you, Taty. If you can't be happy here, we'll go wherever you need to live." His eyes reflected the sincerity of his words.

"I am happy wherever you are, my cowboy."

He laughed again and rolled to her side. "Seriously woman, I'm going to have to teach you American history."

Taty lifted onto her elbow and ran her hand down his washboard abs to his faint happy trail. She cupped his shaft that plumped in her hand. "I would prefer you teach me another subject."

"Which one is that?"

"Sex education, yes?"

"Oh, hell yes. But maybe we should concentrate on linguistics first?"

"Oh? What language are we learning?" Taty allowed him to move her back down to the mattress and position himself on top of her again.

He ran his cheek across hers and whispered in her ear. "Love."

Zane Reynolds walked down the hallway leading to the nerve center of Guardian's Cyber unit. Although he was currently between missions, he wouldn't have come back to this unit, not without cause. But, being called back by the Archangel himself was more than enough cause. When Jason King called, you dropped whatever the fuck you were doing, and you appeared. Even if it was… zero dark thirty in the morning. Still, it was familiar striding down the halls even after a two-month hiatus. Once Guardian had eliminated the threat to the Kings by taking down the Bratva, his reason to stay on as a personal security officer for Jewell King ended.

Although he wasn't directly involved in the clean-up operations, keeping something like Ski's defection to the dark side quiet wasn't going to happen, even in an enterprise as disciplined as Guardian. He'd heard Ski was the way in for the uber hacker Jewell had been tracing. The computer genius had used Ski's knowledge of the organization to find a way into the network, and while he was inside Guardian's mainframe, he had found out information about the Kings and even Gabriel.

Zane bet that little computer geek had those holes identified, plugged and cemented. He chuckled to himself as he punched his code into a cipher lock and laid his finger on the scanner. Hell, the woman probably built a cyber moat around her system too. She was that fucking good at what she did. Unfortunately, she was also absentminded, ate crap, if and when she did eat, had a foul temper and a mouth so filthy she could make a Marine blush. He knew that for a fact because she'd made him blush a time or two. Damn good thing the lighting in her office sucked.

He'd never admit that he missed the little hellcat. She was all claws and hiss, but damned if he didn't want to hold and pet her. He rolled his eyes at the thought. The woman didn't even know he was alive. The fact that he'd been reassigned probably hadn't registered for a week or two... if at all. She'd be glad to be rid of him, and that was the major reason he left without so much as a good-bye. She'd never wanted him around anyway, and he wasn't going to try for something that would never develop. He'd get over his infatuation with the spitfire. Someday.

Zane glanced at his watch. Three-thirty in the morning. It had taken him an hour to make the drive from his apartment. What the fuck was going on that Jason needed him here at this ungodly hour?

He opened the beehive's door and noted the night shift techies hard at work. Several looked up and smiled or waved at him. He waved back and headed up the stadium levels to the office at the top of the theater. Jason opened the door and put his finger to his lips, silencing the greeting that was on Zane's lips. Zane nodded and followed Jason into Jewell's office. The place was a fucking zoo. Papers everywhere, junk food wrappers and energy drink cans stacked on top of at least twenty pizza boxes. The chair she'd ordered for him sat in the same position, and it was the only surface that didn't have litter strewn over it.

He glanced at the workstation and sighed. Jewell was asleep at her computer. He followed Jason to the far monitor. The words on the screen at once filled him with anger and explained the disaster he found himself standing in. It was the chatroom she'd set up to taunt the hacker. The message was clear. Zane's blood boiled. He straightened and locked down his emotional response before he looked at one of the most powerful men in the world. Jason pointed at his sister and whispered, "She's been keeping this from us. We are going to need you again."

Zane turned from the computer screen to the woman half laying on the workstation beside him. Shit just got difficult again.

To Read Jewell's story, click here!

The End

Maliki

John

Jeremiah

Guardian Security Shadow World

Anubis (Guardian Shadow World Book 1)

Asp (Guardian Shadow World Book 2)

Lycos (Guardian Shadow World Book 3)

Thanatos (Guardian Shadow World Book 4)

Tempest (Guardian Shadow World Book 5)

Smoke (Guardian Shadow World Book 6)

Reaper (Guardian Shadow World Book 7)

Hope City

Hope City - Brock

HOPE CITY - Brody- Book 3

Hope City - Ryker - Book 5

Hope City - Killian - Book 8

STAND ALONE NOVELS

SEAL Forever - Silver SEALs

A Heart's Desire - Stand Alone

Hot SEAL, Single Malt (SEALs in Paradise)

Hot SEAL, Savannah Nights (SEALs in Paradise)

ABOUT THE AUTHOR

USA Today and Amazon Bestselling Author, Kris Michaels is the alter ego of a happily married wife and mother. She writes romance, usually with characters from military and law enforcement backgrounds.

Printed in Great Britain
by Amazon